I Once DROWNED

LEANNA BRIGHT

I Once Drowned is published under Reverie, a sectionalized division
under Di Angelo Publications, Inc.

REVERIE

Reverie is an imprint of Di Angelo Publications.
Copyright @ 2022.
All rights reserved.
Printed in United States of America.

Di Angelo Publications
4265 San Felipe #1100
Houston, TX 77027

Library of Congress
I Once Drowned
First Edition
Paperback
ISBN: 9781942549611

Words: Leanna Bright
Cover Design: Savina Deinova
Interior Design: Kimberly James
Developmental Editor: Elizabeth Geeslin Zinn
Editors: Ashley Crantas, Cody Wootton

Downloadable via Kindle, NOOK and Google Play.

For educational, business, and bulk orders, contact
sales@diangelopublications.com.

1. Biography & Autobiography --- General
2. Biography & Autobiography --- Women
3. Biography & Autobiography --- Personal Memoirs

United States of America with int. distribution.

I Once
DROWNED

LEANNA BRIGHT

This is a story told to me by a girl I once knew.

A Note from the Protagonist:

I was faced with a major choice in deciding to share my story. Would I keep the story to myself or would I reveal what I had done and been through? Relating my story meant I would sacrifice my pride and my need for approval from people. I may lose friends and family members, and experience judgments that I have lived without due to my silence. But that will also mean not hiding who I am. Most who know me do not know these truths of my past. But I realized this was a selfish act. I have decided that if my narrative might help others, it would be worth telling.

As much of a screw-up as I was, I am proud of the hope I kept and the urge to want to share something bigger than myself. That was a piece of authenticity shining through suppression.

And for this it is worth the sacrifice.

-Holly

This book is dedicated to my little angel,
in hopes that it will make the world a better place
"even if just a little"
so that you can dance freely upon the edges of the sea.

Love,
Mom

and

For my deceased brother, Jeremy. I feed the pigeons in honor of you.

CONTENTS

CHAPTER ONE

THE LUCKY ONE

I once drowned, and it was quite peaceful. I was three years old.

My twin sister and I had crept through the backyard gate that was left ajar by the pool man. We were fighting over a bathing suit, and my sister pushed me into the pool. The icy water stung my skin as my arms floundered, trying to defy gravity. I breathed in deep, inhaling water and chlorine, and my panic lost the fight to my mortal limits. I surrendered to peace. I remember the silence of the water, the tiny air bubbles floating up, tickling the tip of my nose. I felt peaceful; all fear left me. Blotches of color filled my vision, and then there was nothing.

Apparently, the maid saw me in the pool and pulled my lifeless body out of the water. In a frenzy, she sprinted to my mother, who was asleep inside the house, and woke her. Mom frantically ran to my side. Screaming, she called for the maid to bring her the phone, its long spiral extension cord winding out the door, and she held my lifeless body upside down with one hand around both of my ankles, draining the water from me as best as she could. With the phone lodged between her thighs, she called an ambulance. She did her best. She had once worked alongside paramedics and all of her previous knowledge superseded her distress.

During the scuffle to save me, my fraternal twin, Heather, was hysterical in the corner, completely beside herself.

While the paramedics revived me, my mom prayed to her own deceased mother to save me.

"Please, Mom, if you are here, don't let me lose a baby. If you never do anything for me ever again but this one thing, don't let me lose her, don't let her go…"

I heard my mother's prayer in the far distance. As my mouth dropped wide for air, my eyelids peeled open, fixed towards the sky just in time to witness a gust of wind pass through a tree, swaying its branches.

Her prayer was answered. I am here to tell the tale. Not many people can say they died and then came back to life.

From this point in my young life, a pattern began to emerge. I've been resuscitated several times: either by the grace of God, my instincts, or a form of love. My life has occurred in a series of cycles—constant rebirths—pressing the reset button until I got it right.

It began in Los Angeles, on a street called Sapphire Place. It suited us, as sapphire is not only mine and my sister's birthstone, but our mother's, as well. We were almost born on my mother's birthday, but instead we arrived early the next day.

My father owned a highly successful clothing store, Brookvale Men's Clothing, situated in Beverly Hills, California. Dad was the first person to sell unisex blue jeans in Los Angeles. It was a massive hit in the '70s, and by 1980 he was a booming success—even celebrities shopped at my father's store in Beverly Hills.

He hired my mother as an employee. Shortly after, he was swept away by her beauty and Southern charm. It wasn't long before my mom was his wife, and boss of the newly created women's department of his business.

My parents were married at the Four Seasons Hotel in Santa Barbara, California, on Valentine's Day. White doves were released, and Dom Pérignon champagne was on every table. It was an elaborate wedding, appropriate for an elaborately successful man like my father. My parents owned seven motorcycles, a Ferrari, and a Rolls-Royce. Dad's Rolls-Royce also appeared in a movie starring Richard Gere.

I was told my mother went into labor in the middle of a sip of champagne, while she and my father were eating a divine meal at a lavish restaurant called Chasen's. They rushed into their burgundy Royce and my father, unable to think straight, struggled to get the car into the right gear. My mother, while in labor, put the car in the right gear herself, and off they sped to Cedars-Sinai Hospital, where my twin and I took our first breaths. Three days after we were born, my grandmother walked in to see my mother bent down on hands and knees cleaning the kitchen floor as if it was like any other day. This just about sums up my mother and her resilience.

My parents were, independently of each other, powerful. Aesthetically, they resembled a beautiful Hollywood couple. Mom, with her jet-black hair, hourglass dancer's figure, and high cheekbones from her Native American background, was stunning. Her pale skin beamed and was given to her from her Irish mother. Mom had almond-shaped eyes and a debutant's smile that melted you with its warmth. My mother's Southern accent was often embellished when she was excited or extremely angry; this added to her charm. My father was Mr. California, down to the bright blue eyes and tanned skin. He was polite and polished. He had a strong chin, thick curly light brown hair, and was lean figured. He was always seen with a perfectly shaven face. Dad was organized and logical: always flawlessly dressed, attentive to color, fabric, stitching, and texture. His closet was meticulously organized, and when you hugged him he smelled of fresh laundry detergent. My father was admired for his refined clothing expertise. We had casual friendships with leading Hollywood families.

There is a tale of a Grammy Award-winning entertainer going after my father quite aggressively, jet-setting across countries while he went on trips to source material and fabrics for his store. They went on a date. However, when she walked into the restaurant, she asked, "Why aren't you playing my music?" In that moment, my dad decided the woman had too big an ego, so she wasn't for him.

He married my mother and took on her three children from previous relationships, my half-brothers, as his own. Despite being constantly overwhelmed, he was there. He took on the father role with gusto and became the coach for baseball and football games, made lunches, chauffeured school drop-offs, and bought clothing, food, and more. But there were also many lavish parties and passionate fights, and, frequently, long nights of both that changed lives forever for all of us.

CHAPTER TWO
KISSING EMPTY ROOMS

The first time I walked into my very own jail cell, I felt like I was sleepwalking and that soon I would wake up.

I remember the feeling vividly. *Am I dreaming or is this really happening to me?*

I looked down at my shoes, the shoes they had given me after I undressed bits of my body in front of forty other girls. They were three sizes too big, and no one I told seemed to care. In that moment, at the age of fifteen, I realized I no longer had a voice. Earlier, we had all been made to strip down naked in front of the guards. I had squatted and coughed to show I wasn't physically hiding drugs.

"Your turn," the guard said.

I was half-naked, freezing and exposed.

"Squat."

I squatted.

"Cough."

I coughed.

The officer forced me into the shower and dumped a bottle of lice treatment over my head. A waft of what smelled like a combination of licorice and alcohol violated my nostrils; the offensive liquid was sanitizing my scalp. My heavy eyelids wanted to succumb to gravity but I used all my energy in an effort to keep them open. I ached to sleep, to dream I was somewhere else far away from this atomic nightmare, and yet at the same time, I shut down within to protect myself from this severe pain and the internal questions that would follow.

The humiliation of the strip search protocol, upon entering juvie, was another piece of my emotional death. The polarity of these concrete walls and shackles compared to only a few months earlier, when I was swimming in my father and stepmother's pool in Los Angeles, was stark. The guard pushed me along a concrete hallway; I stumbled, almost dropping my towel, bed sheets, and pajamas. I passed a long row of cells and noticed the eyes and voices of many female inmates as they knocked on their doors, whistling and calling me a tweaker. I was immediately labeled as a meth addict. The inmates laughed and the guard chuckled under her breath as I lowered my head and my eyes to the ground.

Is this actually real? I asked myself over and over on the way to my cell.

The officer detached her large key ring from her belt, which was fitted with at least twenty different keys, all jangling into each other. They looked heavy. She unlocked the large steel door, swung it open, and said, "Go on."

I took a few steps in, not knowing what to do with myself.

"Bitch, my name is Jones," my cellmate introduced herself as the door slammed behind me. Strands of hair jutted out from her disheveled box-braid design. Her bottom lip was discolored, marked with blotches of dark brown and purple, and I wondered if she had been hit. The physical reminder of violence combined with the guards' disregard for me, the inmates bull-baits from behind steel doors, and the depressing green walls etched with graffiti caused me to mumble to myself, "Where am I?"

I had posed this rhetorical question to myself, but Jones responded. "Bitch, you in jail!"

It hit me like a freight train. There I stood, frozen in front of my cellmate, still holding my bed sheets, my towel, and my pajamas.

The awkward quiet was broken by Jones as she asked, "What did you do?"

"I didn't do it," I said quietly.

She looked at me skeptically, almost with pity. "I didn't either, girl; neither did the girl next door; neither did the girl across the hall. Hell, the guards didn't either."

Quietly I realized my truth would fall on deaf ears. If I wanted to survive here, I had to play the part.

My mother raised six children in her household. She and my father split when I was six years old. It was only a few years after my mother had given birth to my little brother Dustin that the marriage ended. I was left feeling split in two myself. I have often reflected on the fact I wasn't the easiest child to raise; I'm inclined to believe my parents would agree.

After my parents divorced, frequently adapting to new homes, neighborhoods, and schools became a common theme in our household. I presume it was due to my mother's lack of money after the divorce, but each new house was always smaller than the last. I can remember my mom hauling all of us and our belongings to a series of new neighborhoods, new homes. No matter how familiar, the pain of leaving each home always stung. I had a ritual that I didn't dare tell anyone about.

As my mother's hands clenched the steering wheel, moments from departure, I blurted out: "One last thing! I forgot something in my room." Then I pushed the car door open and ran into the vacant home. I bolted up the stairs to my barren room. By then, the silence had taken on its own voice; it was startling. The house and its space, once filled with bustling life and noise, now was silenced with void space in what felt like its twilight years. I placed my hand on the hard wall and, with a little kiss, I said goodbye to the house as if it was alive. I stood in the middle of the empty room to let the walls speak to me. I wanted each house to know it meant something to me; that even though we only stayed there a short while, I wouldn't forget it. *You are not meaningless, house. You protected us and will forever be with us—well, me. Thank you, house, for holding my family. I see you. You are not overlooked. Look after the next family, and goodbye.*

I don't know where I came up with these words; all I knew was I had to be alone to say them. Living with so many people, at times it was a struggle to hear my own thoughts or when the house spoke to me. But I believe the house said thank you.

And then, we'd dash off to a new world, and I always held a jitter within me, fearing we would never settle. New schools often meant shifting personas. I was forced to transform and change, pieces of what I knew dying and being reborn again. I was being prepared for my future. If I had seen into a crystal ball, I would have trusted that these experiences were teaching me to readily accept change.

The golden days of my childhood beautifully prepared me to be adaptable to anything. At least, that's how I choose to see it.

CHAPTER THREE
CALIFORNIA DREAMING

The yellow elementary school bus dropped my sister, my brother, and me off at a corner stop about a block away from our beachside home on Ocean View Lane. The three of us would have dramatic, competitive races to our house, starting the moment the soles of our shoes hit the black asphalt road. Our races were almost an angry thing, so full of youthful passion. It wasn't often that we diverted from our usual mad dash, but every now and again we would catch a glimpse of an older, retired-looking lady outside of her cottage-style townhouse; the roof was thatched with layers upon layers of ashy wood, like something out of Hansel and Gretel. I often wondered about this woman. At night, just as I would drift off to sleep, she would enter my mind. I thought of her as she pulled weeds from her garden and snipped at her roses; I would take note of her long hands with spindle-like fingers. She always wore her hair loose, letting the long white strands cascade down the sides of her thin, tall frame. I found her fascinating, and it seemed as though she noticed.

One afternoon, she caught our gaze. She invited us into her cottage for cheese and crackers.

We were always hungry right after school, so we happily accepted her invitation. We followed her up the stairs to her front door, slowly pausing behind her because she took each of her steps as though she were walking in molasses. We tried not to snicker at her pace, squeezing our lips tightly while looking at each other; we wanted our snack and couldn't have one of us ruining it for the rest.

As soon as we stepped into her home, it was as if she had been waiting a very long time to show us around. She took a few steps over to a box in the corner adjacent to us.

"Look at my pet," she beckoned in a friendly tone, her voice crackling.

What pet? I thought.

We looked at each other and wondered what she was talking about. Her house was cluttered, but she kept everything in neat little stacks; tiny ornaments were perched upon her various shelves and piles of books. She silently reached down into a plexiglass box and pulled out a large tarantula. My face flushed hot and my heart pounded as she introduced her wooly friend to us. I was petrified and kept back, surveying my fearless little brother and sister as they introduced themselves to the little fellow. She stroked the spider and gestured for us to touch him as well, but I couldn't bring myself to do it.

"He cannot bite you; that part has been removed," she calmly explained.

When she looked at me, I felt I was the only child in the room. She seemed to look into me. It was as if I was observing myself, watching the whole scene unfold before me.

The old woman told us we could call her Whinnie. Compared to my mother, who was take-charge, forever in a state of emergency, and simply didn't have the time to be curious, Whinnie felt utterly different and alluring. She held a calm, confident demeanor, like a point someone would reach when they have paid their dues. Beyond introducing us to her exotic pet, she unlocked a gateway within me, a mysterious way of living. Her entire way of being was like a visual riddle, and it woke something in me that day; enlightened me. She showed me that there are original people in the world that bestow curiosity and are in possession of something beyond what the eye can see, the creation of a sort of *magic*. Funny how it can be the most inconspicuous people that penetrate and shape the brain of a young child. She intrigued me, and ever since the first time she invited us into her home, I held a piece of her mystery within myself.

It was a lively and quick-paced life at my mom's. All of us children ran wild everywhere. We would come home, quickly change into our bathing suits, and take off to the beach, which was footsteps from our door. We would spend hours bodysurfing in the waves, making shapes out of wet sand, flirting with the white frothing dance of the ocean, and return home with salty lips and sun-kissed skin. Our family clan tread everywhere with dirty bare feet. We were unrestrained and free. My mother embraced this way of living.

There was only one rule: when the sun started going down, we were to come home.

I can recall that when we left our first home on Sapphire Lane, my mom headed north. The opposing headlights beat against my worried mother's face as we sped far down the 101 N freeway. It was as though the faster she drove, the further she was from her life of wealth and a committed marriage to my dad; it signified her goodbye. Previously with Dad, in our home on Sapphire Lane, we had been close to where Michael Jackson's family lived. Back then my brothers played sports with the children of the Jackson Five, and O.J. Simpson used to toss a football in the front yard with them. When you grow up in L.A., these types of relationships just happen among the wealthy. And then one day, after too much partying, and too many lavish long nights—maybe too much gin over too many years—you find it's all gone, and you have no idea how that happened.

My family had relationships with stars, big and small, most of which were made through my father's business. But my mom made sure to try and maintain the ones that were important. My godparents were Momma Mae and James Wade. James was an executive at Warner Brothers Records. We were often invited to Momma Mae's home in the valley. We loved going to her house, even after my parents separated. Momma Mae cooked us homemade salty collard greens and would give us goose grease if we had a sore throat.

Once, we were invited to a birthday party for a family member of the Jackson Five. It was like walking into a carnival. There was a large circus-sized popcorn stand at the entryway, an In-N-Out burger truck parked on a tennis court, and acres for days. A huge pool had brand new, high-tech speakers so swimmers could hear music underwater. There was a floating bar in the center of the pool, and glamorous people were scattered along the edge, wearing large sunglasses and sun hats.

I was playing in the pool, and I needed the restroom, quickly. I darted to my mother to ask where I could use the bathroom. Mom pointed me in the right direction towards the inside of the house. When I came out, there was Michael Jackson, standing in front of me, wearing dark glasses. He was a steeple before me, and I had to tilt my head back to meet his sunglass-shielded eyes. He must have been in his mid-thirties. I wondered why he was wearing such dark sunglasses while inside the house. He held my hand to greet me and I noticed how wafer-thin his skin felt. Everything about him was weightless and fragile, and his movements were achingly slow.

"Hello, what is your name?" he asked. He spoke in a high, soft whisper that I thought sounded more like a girl's than a boy's.

"Holly," I bashfully replied. Noticing the interaction, my mom quickly rushed over.

Michael continued, "Hello, Holly, are you having fun today?"

"Yes."

He giggled slightly when he saw my mom. He politely

greeted her and turned back to me, then pointed behind him to the stairs. "There are more toys you could play with up those stairs."

I politely declined, shaking my head, all while my mother gently pushed my back, saying, "Go upstairs, honey! See what is up there to play with!"

I felt shy, and my mom noticed. I could tell she wanted me to oblige to such a powerful star. But when he spoke to me, I continued looking down, staring awkwardly at the ground. It was eerie. Maybe because I was cold, wet, and no one seemed to notice the vast amount of water dripping onto the floor... but the idea of going upstairs didn't feel welcoming. My refusal to his invitation confused him, and I turned away, leaving my mother there, and trotted back to the pool.

Mom was left with what she called "absolutely nothing" after she and my dad separated. I don't remember the details around Dad losing his clothing store, but one day it vanished along with all the assets and money. We were now forty minutes north from that home near the Jackson's, and there was no O.J. Simpson playing catch out front with my brothers. My parents lost the business. My father came back for a short while to make things work. I now saw him return home from long days of cleaning carpets, with sweat beaded upon his forehead and dark circles around his tired eyes. My older brother Caleb helped, getting paid a dollar and seventy-five cents an hour.

In our new neighborhood, as one big bunch, my siblings and I would hop on our bikes and ride to the corner shop called The Bottle Shop. I was sent with a signed permission note to buy cigarettes. We bought copious amounts of candy after scrounging for coins and change in my mother's various hiding places. We squealed in delight as we stuffed our faces with cherry-flavored gum and Kit Kat bars. We loved these moments.

As beach kids, our lives had been splendidly simple, loose, and unchained, but the heaviness of the real world caught up. Our mother's stress, from trying desperately to keep it all together, was an undertone we tried to ignore but couldn't escape. Caleb carried the weight alongside Mom, his sense of duty superseding his youth. Being merely twelve years old and looking after children when he himself was a child speaks more to his nature than any descriptions ever could. He would babysit without complaint while Mom went to meetings, or hair appointments, which became a rare activity for Mom after Dad left. Dustin, the youngest brother, always had energy to burn, and as the years went on he seemed to gain even more. Some thought he was out of control, but to Heather and me, this was just his demeanor. He was a bouncing ball, hitting all of the walls at once. His curly, disheveled hair lightly bounced as he tirelessly galloped around the house. His mouth was constantly smeared with remnants of food as his ravenous metabolism churned through calories. We joked he was the Energizer Bunny. He was hard to keep up with; Caleb did all he could to help reign him in. Caleb's heart, all gold and light, sought to please my mom. I think making her proud and helping her feel secure was all he wanted. He would gently instruct us to clean our rooms, walking from one room to the next to make sure it was done properly. He scrubbed bathrooms while playing U2, UB40, Led Zeppelin, Van Halen, and Bon Jovi; he taught me so much about music. He would get up early on Sundays to make his famous waffles or pancakes. When I woke to the smell of sweet batter, I would leap out of bed and race downstairs to be the first served. When it was pancakes, he would patiently wait and watch for the batter to simmer before flipping the cake.

He waved for me to come and watch. "Come here, let me show you how this is done."

I stood next to him. Mom watched while having her morning coffee. She was the first one to wake and the last to sleep.

"Don't touch this because it will burn you," he said, motioning to the pan, "But see, when there are enough tiny little bubbles coming to the surface, this means it's ready to flip. Check this out!" He flipped the pancake, hollering, "Now that's how it's done, baby!" while wiggling his hips. He did a little dance before making a new one.

"Go wake up our brothers and sister. Let them know breakfast is ready," he said.

I dashed upstairs and woke all but my eldest brother, who was missing from his bed. I told Caleb and he sighed. Then my mother walked in, noticed his face, and mirrored his worried expression.

"Jeremy didn't come home, again," he informed her.

"Okay, let me call a few people and try to find him," Mom replied. "Goddammit, where is he?"

I watched her nervously talk into the phone, tapping her long nails against her desk. Sometimes the police brought Jeremy back home to us. Once, the red lights flashing through our front window disturbed our pre-bed movie time and we heard a big, bossy knock at the door...

"Shit," Mom said in a panic. She paused for a moment, forced a smile as if she was rehearsing for a movie scene, and with a brave face, she opened the door. We children ran and stood behind her legs, waiting to see what Jeremy had done. I knew he was spending time with a gang; but I still didn't know what all he did. I always knew when he came home, during the middle of the night, by the sound of his wallet chain rattling as he walked.

By now, Mom knew the sheriff on a first-name basis. He would apologize to her on behalf of Jeremy as if he sympathized with Mom. The moment the door closed she would pop Jeremy on the side of his head, bitterly reprimanding him. "What the fuck were you thinking?"

My heart broke for Jeremy because I saw that he couldn't physically defend himself; he would look defeated when Mom would do this. He never raised his hand to her. We kids would run to our wicker toy box, which we could only fit inside after dumping out its contents to the floor, and hide as the screaming went on and on and on.

It must have been overwhelming for my mother, with no husband to carry the brunt work, who would have all the right answers on how to deal with the teenage boy rebellion. My mother was from the southern United States, and in the South, from the way she told it, smacking your kids every now and again was necessary. They did this as a way to discipline and with the expectation that you wouldn't take it too personally, but that didn't make it any easier to watch or experience.

Not long after that incident, my sister's and my birthday arrived.

"Okay, girls, are you ready to pick out some TOYS?!" Mom asked with sheer delight for us.

We shouted back at the tops of our lungs, "Yes, MOM!"

Mom laughed. We piled into the car donated to us by my aunt and uncle, and Mom drove us to Toys"R"Us. Walking up and down the aisles, we couldn't stop our eyes from bouncing from one colorful doll to the next.

"I'll take this one, Mom!"

"Ok, honey, put it in the basket," she replied.

"Mom, may I have these jelly shoes?"

"Of course, put them in the basket."

We were in disbelief at the amount of yeses we got every

single time we asked for something.

Our basket was filled to the brim with makeup kits, dolls, paint sets, costumes...you name it, it was in our basket. My sister and I squealed at each other with bulging eyes.

We landed at the cashier. Mom smiled at us and handed him a check. I couldn't quite understand what happened but he said, "It didn't clear."

"There must be a mistake," she replied, waiting patiently while he called the manager.

"What's the problem?" asked the manager with furrowed brows.

"This man says my check won't clear, but my father just sent this to us for the girls' birthday and I know the money is in there," said Mom.

The manager tried again while the lady behind us sighed impatiently. Heather and I stood awkwardly looking at the ground, not knowing what to do.

"I am sorry, ma'am, we cannot accept this check," said the manager.

Mom started to fast-talk and asked if she could use the phone. We stepped aside while she called her dad, whom we only had seen a few times in our lives. No answer.

We quietly walked back to the car empty-handed.

"I am so sorry, girls. I thought the money was there. We will go back, I promise," my mom vowed.

Heather and I both were speechless. We knew we weren't going back—and we never did.

Afternoons at the beach and freedom aside, life at my mom's wasn't always easy. Fortunately, living near the beach wasn't a fleeting experience of the past, as Mom found our next rental within close proximity to our first beach house. These homes were forty miles north of where I was born. She had the pressure of both parental roles—weekday stress, six children in school who needed clothing, homework, meals, lunches, and to be up on time every day. Mom was wound up by cold calls, trying to sell her homemade chili, and this would cause her to lash out. She did a lot, more than what I knew about, to make ends meet. Caleb would comfort her merely by his presence as he stood beside her, saying nothing at times, just to show his loyalty. On one late evening, I tiptoed downstairs and tripped over our black dog, alerting Caleb, who was a dark shadow on the sofa. He cradled something glowing in his hands...

He whispered, "Hey, come here."

I sat down close beside him and whispered back, "What are you doing?"

He replied, "Energizing my crystals."

Stunned, I whispered, "How is it glowing green?" Caleb grew crystals in his closet. He would hide them from us. We were scavenger kids who were always wildly scrounging the house for things—a sense of personal space did not exist with so many children.

He said, "Here, hold it." I cupped the crystal and the color instantaneously dimmed. "See, we have different kinds of energy. You have to *feel* yourself and put yourself into the crystal."

"What do you mean?" I eagerly inquired.

"Think of you without your skin around you; think of your *energy*—we all have it and it's different from anyone else's in the whole world," he replied as he kissed my forehead and then instructed me to go back to bed.

I could never forget that night. Were there others that could do this? This was the first time I saw that people had the ability to be more than just a physical body. Undeniably, this moment opened a portal for me. It ignited a wonder that we are not a fleshly body but merely hosting one.

For a fleeting moment, I wondered if Whinnie had any crystals in her house.

CHAPTER FOUR

CLOUDED MILK ON THE ASSEMBLY LINE

I was eight years old, and it was the end of summer. On an early evening while the sun was setting, orchestrating pink and orange stripes in the sky, I sat beside my mother. Both of us perched on the front doorstep to our home. We watched God's light dim as the sun tucked herself in. I heard my mom blow out the smoke from the final drag of her cigarette. The distinct sound of ashes being crushed into an ashtray resonates with me to this day. Our neighbor's car drove up and parked next door. Exiting the vehicle was a blonde, well-groomed lady. I watched my mom target her, like a cat. *What is Mom thinking?* I wondered. The blonde opened her trunk and, with both hands, carried a load of bags into her house, leaving her trunk open.

My mom said, "Look at all those groceries." The lady came back for another load, leaving three or four bags outside her trunk. Mom didn't hesitate.

"Holly, make a noise if she comes back out."

Then she bolted towards the remaining groceries, snatched two bags, and raced back into the house. I knew my job; though my heart was thumping like a mad rabbit, I scurried in behind her, hoping not to be seen.

"Mom!" I said, "She's gonna know she is missing groceries!"

"Aren't you tired of having gray milk?" It was then and there she actually admitted to the milk being discolored. We had always wondered why the milk was a funny color, and she adamantly denied that anything was strange. We knew she had been pouring water in it to make it last. Now, she pulled out a gallon of fresh milk and winked at me.

"Here baby, have a bowl of cereal," she said with a smile. By hook or crook, Mom made sure to do what was necessary to survive.

As a young girl, I would wake up in the middle of the night quite often. We had a huge dog, a standard poodle named Cash, and we simply could not control the fleas on him. We would bathe him, but sand fleas would find their way back onto him, and no treatment seemed to stave them off. I could feel the fleas jumping on and off of my skin—especially at night. Cash loved to sleep with me, and the price I paid for his nightly companionship was a midnight flea reckoning.

While flicking off fleas, I heard my mom crying. The sound of sobbing was unmistakable. I didn't know *why* she was crying. I just knew she wasn't well, and even at eight years old I found myself wishing we would all be okay. Sometimes on those nights I would wake my sister, and we would argue back and forth in hushed whispers about who would go in.

"No, you go see if she's okay!"

"No, you go!"

I was afraid to disturb my mom's sadness. We would listen until we heard the sobs cease, and then we would go back to sleep. In the morning, we would watch our mom closely.

My mother had this unfailing ability to soldier on each day, regardless of whatever ailed her at night. Each morning, no matter what the turmoil from the night before, she would put on her game face and it was go time. Like a complex assembly line, she had six lunches, six kids getting ready, and one older kid, usually Caleb, to help.

There was a fragility to the happiness and free nature of the household. If any of us gave Mom an attitude, a domino effect would happen, crumbling the intricate structure of her flow. We would all be late, thus igniting screaming fights. In one way or another, we all learned how to pretend that everything was okay even when it was not.

I heard my mom's conversations on the phone, asking friends for extra money. Mom made friends with the minister at a church, and the church sometimes donated canned food. She sometimes didn't have a babysitter, and the youngest kids would have to go with her to her appointments. I take my hat off to my mom now, as an adult, but as a kid everything felt uncertain. One day my mom was in such a rush that she got into a fender bender on the way to a job interview, making her late. She put her hands over her face, and she started to cry; she turned on the radio so we wouldn't hear her sobs, even though we were in the back seat.

CHAPTER FIVE
RIVER DEEP, MOUNTAIN HIGH

I was a girl with an imaginary audience. I would skip into our garage, surrounded by the junk collected by my siblings, and live inside my own dream state. Because we were a large family, and the house certainly didn't have enough space to accommodate us all, the garage was part bedroom for my two eldest brothers and part playroom for me—or at least that's how I saw it.

In my mind, that garage had people in it, thousands of souls in a large audience. I could visualize them in my head, their faces a sea of excited eyes and eager smiles as I stood on a stage before them. I had a microphone—the stem of a vacuum cleaner—and I was Tina Turner. I had seen the dynamism of Tina Turner on TV one day, shaking her gold dress and tapping her feet robustly on stage. She performed like no one was in the room but her. I was just five years old the first time I saw her energy, and I was empowered by her force and command of the stage. I wanted what she had. Tina was instantly my idol. She became my imaginary triumph and my concealed success. I never told anyone else about her because what she had—what she meant to me—was so special that I had to keep it private. Maybe I knew that amount of joy was something that only came from knowing severe pain, but her spirit became a goal for me—what she exuded was somehow reachable to me.

Mom entered the garage to switch the clothes from the washer to the dryer and giggled at me, standing amongst my invisible crowd. She said, "The neighbors are gonna think you've lost your mind."

I thought, *One day they will remember that I was here doing this and that it all started in this garage.*

Mentality and mindset were powerful for my mother. We never locked the doors to our house, and when I would ask my mom why we didn't, her response was, "You attract what you fear, so we don't fear someone breaking in, and it won't happen." Funnily enough, we were never robbed.

She also had taped a check to her mirror, which was payable to her from the universe with "love" written within the dollar amount bracket, and from "the universe " in return. It was her way of manifesting her desires, constantly reminding herself as a daily goal that love was the supreme payback from life. These little things shaped me.

Ultimately, I didn't learn by what my parents preached. I learned by what they did when they thought no one was looking.

My gaze was drawn to my mom's ballet slippers that hung from the ceiling in her bathroom. She had been a dancer, once. I would inspect the dirt on the toes, fantasizing where she had danced and if she would ever dance again. I would break open my mother's makeup to smell her lipsticks, and I wore her blue eyeshadow when she went away for work meetings. Lancôme lipsticks have a distinct smell that brings me back to that bathroom and to her.

I thought my mom was the most beautiful woman in the whole world. My mother believed in the reinvention of oneself, and to me, she was the phoenix.

My mother's solution to anything was "get busy," and so she was always preoccupied. She was so busy her fingers twitched while she slept. I would watch them move to a silent tempo. My mom wasn't always patient, or even kind. You didn't run to her to have someone to cry to. She was, by example, a force of power; she maneuvered problems with whatever she had at hand, creating solutions by trickery or deceit at times. I knew at times what mom did was wrong, and it made me nervous, but I also knew there were reasons for it beyond my understanding. She made life happen for her through cat-like instincts and street smarts, and they were as valuable as the oxygen she inhaled to survive.

After the separation, my dad came back to see if he could make things work; this was the night he left and never returned. They got into a huge fight, and my siblings and I cringed as their screams and shouts echoed throughout the house. I could feel the electricity sizzling in the air like an encroaching storm. My older brother retreated to the garage as it escalated to decorations and household objects colliding with walls and slamming to the ground. My twin sister, little brother, and I ran to the white wicker box.

I lifted the lid and watched through the tiny gap. My dad picked up a lamp and was about to throw it. But he suddenly stopped, as if he was wondering what he was doing. My dad was a quiet man by nature. He only raised his voice when deeply provoked. He held his power in his silence—in my opinion, sometimes to the detriment of his relationships.

"I've had it. I'm going," he said.

I vividly remember the gravity in his voice. I knew it was all getting very serious because he grabbed not one work shirt, but the whole pile of them. I climbed out of my wicker tomb and followed one step behind him as he frantically rushed around, grabbing only what was necessary to escape. I pleaded with him not to leave, or to at least take me with him. I could see I was annoying him, possibly hurting him, but I was beside myself. My father was my guy. If he was leaving, I had to go with him.

Our beach house at the time was situated in a small alleyway, and I followed him out, almost stepping on the backs of his heels. He climbed into his white Acura sedan. He turned on the headlights, which shone in my eyes, making me squint through my tears. He ordered me to get back inside the house, but I protested defiantly and stood in the center of the driveway, blocking him. He couldn't go just yet, because if he was supposed to leave surely he would bring me with him. But he left. He reversed the car and went the opposite way. I watched the headlights backing up until they disappeared from sight. I waited for him to come back, because I knew he would, up until Mom gently asked me to go in the house.

My mother and father fought constantly. I feel that my father had lost himself deeply amid the demise of his business and the pressure of all us children, that he had to go in order to save himself.

Quite suddenly, in the late '80s, they lost it all. This is the story of many wealthy people in the '80s who fell victim to the use and abuse of alcohol and cocaine. Gone were the assets, the booming clothes business, the expansive home, the cars, and now, the marriage. My dad's current life was filled with long days of cleaning carpets, and the weight of it was too much to bear.

From that point on, the chaos and disorder heightened. It was a time for rebuilding, but it was overshadowed by crushing sadness. The pressure was felt throughout the entire home. At one point the washer broke, as it often had, and dirty laundry was piled beyond the height of the washer itself. I was forced to wear the same socks again and again. I smelled, and often my mornings would begin wet from a puddle of my own urine. During class one day, the teacher said, "Someone in here smells like nachos," while looking directly at me, as if I could somehow do anything about it.

But regardless of what was going on in Mom's personal life, beyond our knowledge, we kids were always busy fighting or playing with each other. My little brother Dustin always tagged along to anything Heather and I did, and Mom loved company, so she would often take in any friends, cats, and anything that needed a home, even though we did not have a lot to give. At one point, we had nine kittens living in our garage. Mom would hand-feed them milk, no matter how chaotic her day was.

CHAPTER SIX

FRACTURE

Anxiety is a funny thing. It comes from nowhere and everywhere all at once. It comes from long ago, prior to the existence of our bodies and, if left unhandled, it is experienced in the present with even further drama. I believe we come from long ago, prior to the bodies we have now, and we carry those past experiences with us in our souls. I see it as something similar to what people refer to as a blueprint, except it goes much further back. I must not be the only one who feels this way.

Before my judgment had become clouded, I had always innately known when danger was near. This talent was acutely attuned prior to losing my way. I could sense it in voices, feel it crackle through the air. I think I first became attuned to this through my brothers. I always knew when a fight was brewing between them. Most of the time it was just a simple miscommunication.

"I told you not to touch anything in my room."

"I didn't, bro."

"*I didn't bro.*' Yeah, you fucking did. Where are my weights?"

Sean did not like anyone touching his belongings. It was as though he was irked by being part of a large family. Being neither the oldest nor the youngest brother must have been a strange place to be among the pecking order. At times I believed he secretly wished to have been an only child.

It would escalate. Next there would be things thrown at each other, Mom screaming, a dish broken or a fork flung at someone's head, and my brothers darting after one another down the stairs to fight outside.

Mom would always run after them, screaming, "Goddammit, stop it! Stop it! You're going to kill one another! You, Holly, get in the fucking house!"

She would throw her lit cigarette to the side and reach for the hose, turning it on as fast as she could. I would hide, watching from behind the corner as she started hosing them down. What would astonish me is an hour later they would be sharing a meal, bloodied and bruised but laughing together. Mom dissolved her unease with another cigarette and I'd feel like I should move past what happened just as quickly, but I never did. This scene played out weekly, and somehow I never got used to it.

Even during times of relative calm, our home was filled with testosterone. Rap music would blast through the garage when my brothers were in there, especially when Sean installed subwoofers in their cars. I think they were a gift from his dad, although Sean may have gotten the money from somewhere. I heard the clinking of car tools and watched their faces turn red as they carried large black speakers in and out of the old, beat-up VW Bug. After they were installed, they would cruise the neighborhood, blasting late '80s rap with a leash stretched out the passenger window as they exercised our pit bulls, Bud and Weiser. Cash was left to lounge around; being a standard poodle, he offered the teenage boys no sense of masculinity. The boys had weights attached to the pit bulls' ankles to beef them up. This broke my heart. Their food was our leftovers. This worked in my favor when Mom made her famous meatloaf, in which case I would scoop clumps of my meat with my hand and reach behind myself to stick it to the wall. Cash would wait for me to give him the nod and he indiscreetly walked to the wall to eat his dinner.

I felt sorry for the pit bulls, and I pleaded to my brother, "Please don't do this!"

He just tapped on the side of my head, saying, "Don't worry about the dogs, Squirt."

One evening, Mom called us down for supper, our names ringing out one after the other.

"Holly, Heather, Caleb, Jeremy, Dustin, and Sean, get downstairs for dinner!" Mom shouted, and our dogtrot scuffles drummed a choppy beat as we piled into the kitchen.

The smoky-sweet aroma of hot dogs and beans for the third night in a row offended my nostrils, but I held this in secrecy.

Dustin, only five years old and just two years younger than me, said, "This again? Oh man, why?"

Caleb gently responded, "Watch your mouth, Dustin."

Mom scolded Dustin with piercing eyes. "Yeah, watch your mouth." Poor Dustin; being the youngest, he was constantly bossed around not only by my mom, but all of us.

But Dustin didn't listen. "I don't want to eat this gross food again, Mom. I'm going to have a bowl of cereal for dinner." He waltzed over to the pantry without a care. Not a second later, Mom snatched his arm and yanked him into the other room. I could see his head jerk and neck stiffen. A memory flashed to my mind, that very hand of my mother's cradling the fragile body of a kitten, dropping milk into its mouth with a tiny syringe.

My overwhelmed mother pointed into his face, sternly gritting her teeth, "You be grateful and you sit down. You eat your dinner." We knew how hard it was for her to keep enough food stocked in the house. Fear for my little brother's well-being crawled up my spine.

Dustin started to cry, Mom lost her patience and shouted

at him, and in a domino effect, the night dissolved into rage.

Later on that evening, a neighbor knocked at the door, asking Mom for money. His window was broken and he blamed us "wild kids in the neighborhood," saying a ball was thrown through it.

He was right. It was our ball, but Mom questioned him, defending us. "How do you know it was one of my kids?"

He replied, "I saw them."

She directed the question at me. "Holly, did you or your brother break his window?"

I sheepishly said, "Yes." Her eyes squinted and I knew I had hell to face later.

"I am so sorry. I will find a replacement window or I will cover the cost," she said to the huffing neighbor.

"I prefer to be paid in cash, and I will find quotes for the cost and repair," he said haughtily.

My mother, with a nod, closed the door.

A second later, her hand smacked the side of my head. "How dare you not come home and tell me right away!" she said through gritted teeth. "That man caught me off-guard. Go to your room right now." Even as a child I knew that she had no idea where she was going to get the money to fix that man's window.

I heard Mom on phone calls, one after the other, looking for jobs, or trying to sell her homemade chili. She would nervously pace from the kitchen to the front of the house, squat on the porch step to smoke near an ashtray full of dead soldiers, go back to the kitchen to fill her mug of black coffee and sugar, and again return to the porch step.

As a young girl, I had no concept of what to do with the

emotions I felt. No child does. We are at the mercy of our environment and the people in it. There was an unspoken understanding between my siblings and myself that we knew things were tumultuous, but we weren't to speak on them. Mom made it a rule that we were to keep family matters private. I didn't even have the words to articulate all I felt, but fight or flight chemicals constantly percolated underneath the surface. I felt the stream of adrenaline biting through my skin whenever panic was on the horizon.

In elementary school, I would plot my escape as part of my daily daydreaming in class. My mind was academically blank at school. When it came to history or math, I was totally lost. My admiration for my sister grew; her ability to focus was astounding to me.

Now, I wish my teacher had known the indicators of my struggle; that so many words that I had failed to grasp were accumulating. As simple and fundamental as word comprehension may seem, it was the catalyst for my desire to escape school. I didn't know how to tell anyone that I didn't understand, that I was failing to learn. But unfortunately, I now assume that most of my teachers weren't taught the signs of a student struggling to absorb any education in the way that I had.

I sat at my desk and waited until the moment the clock's hands hit ten, and then I stood, walked to the teacher, and said, "I feel sick. I need to see the nurse."

"Again, Holly? This is the third day in a row."

I shrugged, "I dunno, I just feel sick; I can't breathe."

"Okay, here is your hall pass. I will let the nurse know you are coming."

I knew my sister would be fine while I went home. After all, she was actually accomplishing something.

I walked slowly down the school hall, looking at the sea of bored faces through classroom-door windows.

I arrived at the nurse's station. "Hello Holly, I hear you are having breathing problems again."

"Yes," I said, "I can't breathe."

In our standard ritual, she checked my chest with her stethoscope, and I tried my hardest to breathe laboriously.

"Your lungs sound okay," she said. "Let me check your temperature."

I sheepishly abided and I tried to place the thermometer in what I suspected to be the hottest part of my mouth, under my tongue towards my throat. The nurse left the room for a moment, and I held the silver-tipped glass wand close to the nearby medical light, hoping this would make it hotter. The moment the nurse turned to come back, I pushed the thermometer back into my mouth. The nurse checked the thermometer and told me I may have a slight fever. She asked if I was well enough to go to class, and, as always, I said no. She called Mom to pick me up.

This scenario repeated almost every day, for I don't know how long. I would hear my mother's car screech into the parking lot of the school, and my heart would pound, knowing I'd be in trouble.

"Goddammit, Holly, I don't have time for this shit," she hissed as soon as I got into the car. "I have a meeting and you will have to sit in the car and wait for me. How long are you going to pull this sick card for?"

I sat in silence in the passenger seat, my whole body stiff, and watched her light her next cigarette while nervously tapping her fingers on her dashboard. In all honesty, I didn't need a medical condition to feel like I couldn't breathe. It wasn't physical; it was emotional.

There were so many words and concepts that I didn't

understand, yet was expected to, that I would get singled out for not knowing as if it was all my fault. Every day, I left school feeling like there was something wrong with me, when in actuality, no one taught me how to learn. It was like hiding in a cave from a storm raging outside, when in reality, there was no storm; I just didn't understand the wind.

Not understanding the basic elements of language is something you carry wherever you go. It falsely reflects incompetence to the outside world, when in fact, it's such a fundamental issue that it is painfully easy to overlook. If you don't fully understand words, how does one properly communicate? Communication is the most important factor of life, including how one communicates with themselves. I wish someone had shown me how to use a dictionary, and told me to never pass over a word I didn't fully understand.

One evening, Heather and I sat at the kitchen table, a book opened in front of us. I chewed my pencil eraser as I glanced down at the labyrinth of words mangled together on the page. I turned to see Heather intently reading.

"How do you know how to do it?" I asked.

"Do what?" she replied, annoyed at the interruption.

"Study."

"I dunno, I just do." She shrugged her shoulders.

"But how do you know how to? Do you read certain parts over and over again?"

"I just read what I'm supposed to. I don't know, Holly, just read the book and answer the questions." She bowed her head to her work and returned to studying.

I felt embarrassed for not understanding, even with the supplemental help from my teachers. It was as if I had gone too far into my confusion to find a way back. There was lack of context, lack of examples, and I didn't understand why I had to learn the lessons other than because I had to. I didn't see how most of my subjects related to my life, and so my interest dimmed. Memorizing is dogmatic and not truly knowing. It's a setup for failure. Lack of education leads to delinquency.

CHAPTER SEVEN
MY HIDDEN WONDERLAND

As time went on our conditions worsened, living as we were, but I had my happiness. Life through my innocent eyes was still bright and fun. I lived inside my imagination and I held it close.

We had a visitation with my father every other weekend. My older brothers stayed behind with my mom. She was very touchy about him picking us up, especially with his new girlfriend. In my mom's words, he was a "Disneyland Dad," and he gave us things my mom couldn't afford.

Eventually my father wanted custody of my twin sister, my younger brother, and me. There was a gradual, insipid notion that we weren't being cared for like we should have been.

Oftentimes when visiting with Dad, my meticulous and elegant future stepmom would notice the dirt under our toenails, or the unwashed, ill-fitted clothes I would pack for myself. The fact I constantly wet the bed concerned them as well. Plus, the scratches and scabs present on my delicate skin were a testament to how truly wild and free I was for a child. The freedom that fed my limitless imagination was a detriment to my body at times, as I would often forget I had one. Susan became highly concerned for our well-being; she would often openly comment that we were *unkempt*.

"Why are you scratching your head? Come here," Susan said one weekend. She was a hairdresser and always had a keen eye on our scalps; she had an inkling of what might be wrong. And her nightmare had come true. We had lice. That, paired with me wetting the bed, prompted my dad and Susan to begin the process of getting custody of us.

My sister pleaded and begged to live with my father. I hated feeling fought over; it created so much pressure. *Was I in trouble? Was my mom in trouble?* Someone had to be; that was my reasoning. *Stay quiet, Holly—whatever Heather does, just make sure you stay with her.* I would repeat that to myself, over and over again.

At ten years old, my twin and I embarked on a new life with my father and Susan. Shame washed over me as I stuffed my bag. *Do I pack everything? Are we coming back?* I gently tucked my loved and worn doll into a safe corner and zipped the bag closed. Dad and Susan asked if my brother wanted to come. He declined. Dustin refused to leave our mother. When our bags were full, Heather and I hugged my brothers tight.

Mom felt powerless in the custody battles, which would become a topic she'd often bring up afterward; how she would have battled like a gladiator if she only had the money. But things being as they were, the process was swift. My mom was cornered into signing the custody papers on the hood of her car.

"How dare you take my babies when you know I can't afford to fight for them!" she said in scorn. But then she handed him our clothes, stuffed in suitcases, and we piled into my father's car. And that was that.

As we drove south on the 101, towards West L.A., I realized I never got to say goodbye to the house.

The new silence at my dad's house—which some might call peace—was cutting. The fighting at Mom's, with shouts like thunderclaps and words bolting through the air, churned my stomach with each strike and ignited that primal urge to flee from danger. Yet the silence in my new home made me feel just as fundamentally uncomfortable. An eerie quiet, like a forest without birdsong. Everything was different and contradicting.

Even our eager, noisy, large dog was now replaced with silent, aloof cats—which I was highly allergic to.

Susan's discipline felt extreme, but it was an act of love. She had large, fiery red hair with eyes as green as sea moss. She embodied a glamorous woman with ladylike manners from the 1950s. She was fun and witty, and she kept everyone around her intrigued and happy; when she wanted to, she could find humor in almost anything. Her love was tangible. She taught us about food, cleaning, and how to revel in the joys of being female. She gave me earrings and makeup and pink nail polish. We played dress up, and being a hairstylist, she gave us gorgeous braids and updos, giggling alongside us the whole time. She wanted us to have the best—but her best for me included an entirely new understanding of what family, morals, and integrity meant. If my room wasn't spotless every day, then I wasn't resembling a lady, and a lecture would likely follow. It was wholesome, yet oftentimes it made me want to live without the attention to detail and the pressure of perfection.

Speaking with my mom became rare. I thought about her every day, and every night I prayed she would forgive me for leaving her. The guilt weighed on me, heavily and silently. Occasionally, Mom would phone, but my father and stepmother would always listen in. The calls were never private. We spoke over speakerphone, or with one of them on the other line from a different bedroom.

The home telephone rang and Susan answered. "It's her," she mumbled to my father, handing him the telephone.

There was a pause. "Yes," Dad said. "I will put them on, one moment."

He put a single finger up to his mouth and put the phone on speaker. Heather and I stood beside each other, waiting to be told what to do.

"Heather, Holly?" my mother's voice rang out.

"Hi, Mom!" we said simultaneously.

Relief seeped through me. "Hi," I said again, gulping to keep myself from choking up.

"How are you, baby?" she said in her fake-happy voice.

I knew that false tone well. She didn't know she was being listened in on.

"I miss you girls."

"We miss you too, Mom."

"Are you okay? I mean, is everything there okay?" she asked.

Heather and I looked up at Dad and Susan, and they nodded their heads for us to respond.

"Yes, we are okay, Mom. How are you?" I asked.

"Well, honey, I miss you very much. Everyone is okay over here. Have you started school yet?"

"Yes, we are going to a new school nearby."

"Oh, no one told me. What is the name of the school?"

My stepmom interrupted. "Hi there... It's Susan. Just a moment, their dad will pick up the phone and give you all the details. Say goodbye, girls, it's time for your homework."

"Bye, Mom," I said.

"Bye, Mom," echoed Heather.

Susan ushered us to our rooms and shut the door.

As a child, feeling like you need to be protected from your mother feels sad and unnatural. My father and stepmother's behaviors were far beyond my comprehension at the time. It was hard to trust anyone when you are taught you cannot trust your own mother.

All I knew was that I felt tortured by the fact that my mother was upset. I felt she was upset because my sister and I had chosen to live with our father, and not with her. The truth of the matter was that I just followed along with my sister's decision to live with our father. Separating from Heather was never even a flicker of a thought in my mind. I continued to hold my mom on a pedestal, so as not to abandon her fully. Whatever Susan did for us, I'd say that my mom did it better—but as I look back, Susan did her very best. In many ways, I could say she went above and beyond to look after us. For this, I am so grateful.

Dinner could be a maddening exercise in restraint for me. What had once been an individualized assembly line, often including me fighting Dustin off from eating all my food, was now a group event. I'd watch Susan talk to my dad, then watch my sister talk to Susan, all the while wondering if my napkin was folded properly.

For the first time in my life, I ate meals as a small, close family, all together at the same time, and we talked and listened about each other's days. But there was so much analyzing of my sister's and my psyches that I couldn't settle down and learn to enjoy their way of being a family. Looking back, it was the chance for a familial foundation, but it was uncomfortable, almost like teething. We had to learn how to sit with good posture, how to hold a fork, and how to chew and behave like a lady. "Holly, sit up when you are at the table. Hold the fork like this; there you go. You look beautiful. It comes so naturally to you."

Susan watched us like a hawk, like the way we wiped ourselves after going to the bathroom. She would say before going, "Remember, it's front-to-back. And remember, pish then stop, pish then stop to build up those muscles I told you about. You will thank me later!" Thank you, Susan, because it did help me. The wonder of Kegels.

She taught us how to put on our first bra, tucking the breast properly into the cup. She would show us and, as uncomfortable as it was, she was right to do this. I truly cherished my first

Victoria's Secret lotion that Susan bought me. She said it was so that, "No matter what, you'll always smell like ladies." I would stare at the intricate detail in the floral illustrations on the label of my new vanilla lotion.

On the weekends, we would play a game by visiting different luxury hotels and having brunch. I loved this. We strolled into grand marble-entranced hotels. Susan would point out the way people dressed, held their fork, sipped their coffee, how the napkin was placed in their lap. She would order sweet foods from the menu and we would *oooh* and *ahhh* at the flavors. She would say, "Now, this is the good stuff, kids." She was trying to show us the finer things in life. She was trying her best. But even when Susan thought she was inconspicuous, I heard every word she told my dad about my shortcomings by the day's end. I felt helpless and as though I should hide.

Becoming a stepmother of two ten-year-old girls at the age of fifty must have been a huge transition. I wonder what it was like for her, really. I mean, one day her whole world changed and it was suddenly filled with school runs, clothes shopping, medical care, implementing rules, food, mealtimes, and psychological responsibilities. I mean, my God, to try and fit in with the other moms at a later age was awkward. But Susan always said, "I did things my way in life. I didn't want to be married with kids at nineteen, and I didn't want to be a housewife. I waited until I wanted to do what I wanted to do and I'm better off for it. I want you girls to do the same."

I didn't know the source of any of the problems I had been told, or frequently overheard, that I had; but therapy was the natural solution to my issues at the time and, in my dad and Susan's eyes, I was the perfect candidate. I had been acting out. I would fight my sister the way I used to see my brothers fight. How could I be expected to cease doing something that was the norm for the first several years of my life? Heather always hid within a book.

Heather harbored her resentments, taking it out on you slowly if you crossed her, sometimes for months. I was more apt to openly and quite overtly let someone know if I was upset.

On top of the fighting, I also continued to wet the bed. I used and pronounced words incorrectly. I felt all this pressure, intensified by being constantly observed and analyzed. I incessantly competed for my dad's positive attention. I was looking for him to validate that I was, in fact, normal, and I would act overly cheerful to compensate. These were concerning factors that were openly discussed. Talking about it made me feel displaced, and I grew introverted. My inner voice became an echo of parental concern, rather than my own stream of praise and introspection for myself. It took away my internal optimistic gauge and replaced it with a narrative of being damaged goods. As innocently helpful as my parents were trying to be, they missed how they transformed how I spoke to myself.

In therapy, I would just let my therapist talk and make up responses so the hour would go by. After an uncomfortable session, she would say, "Go in the waiting room while I speak to your stepmother." I would cheerfully comply, but I felt exposed with the knowledge they were talking about everything I said. My trust in the process was broken at that point. I was analyzed at home by them constantly, and if that wasn't enough, they were sending me to be analyzed by a professional. I began to resent that I had to go to therapy, and that my sister didn't. Instead, Heather went to study the Torah. She got religion, and I got the psychoanalyst.

My nonconformity thrived within the social parts of school. Like a foxhole underground, I would hide within my music class and immerse myself, quieting the rest of the world around me. School was the merry-go-round of shared smiles and laughter-filled conversations. It fueled me. It was my own happy carnival and I didn't want to go home. When final grades rolled around, shame inevitably followed.

"Heather, please don't give them your report card," I pleaded.

"They will know if I don't."

"No, no, no, they really, really won't! They only know if one of us gives it to them," I begged.

"I am giving them my report card, Holly. I'm not hiding mine," she replied with an air of pride.

Having a twin is a double-edged sword indeed.

I was an unexceptional academic. I saw no point in doing well in subjects I had absolutely no interest in, and my sister's straight A's posed a lingering threat for me. If I wasn't matching her accomplishments, anything less was unspeakably noticed. No amount of music or art concealed my lackluster academics. They were my dark, rainy, dreadful shadow.

Little by little, I felt what would now be called depression set in, but it was difficult for anyone to identify because of how cheerful I could appear on the outside. Every night while doing our nightly chore—drying the dishes—I would merrily sing a tune from *The Little Mermaid*, fantasizing that at any moment my father would come and tell me how beautiful my singing was.

It was quickly determined how different my sister and I were. I was the social one and my sister was the scholastic one. I guess this was an attempt to give us our own identities and strengths. And it did, but in a larger way, it further separated us. I heard Susan say many times, "Holly knows how to naturally entertain friends when they come over and Heather is extremely good at school."

I was singled out for needing extra attention and challenging authority. My free-for-all lifestyle had halted so abruptly that I didn't have any time to adjust to, or comprehend, these new household standards. Heather settled right in.

One afternoon, after much contemplation, I nervously walked down the hall to my father. I did my best to conceal my nervousness. I decided it was time to openly tell him I wanted to be a singer one day. After keeping this desire hidden for ages, I finally wanted to openly state it in hopes it would prompt my father and stepmother to assist me.

"Is that your dream or your mother's dream?" he asked. He knew my mother had also wanted to be a famous singer. Bearing so many children halted this, and she forever held a space of sorrow for it.

"It's mine. I want to be the best singer in the world!" I exclaimed.

He looked at me without much expression and said, "Holly, I am going to tell you something that may not be what you want to hear, but is what you need to hear. If there is anything that I can tell you in life, it's to know what's real. I might hurt your feelings, but you will always know that I told you the truth..."

"Okay, Dad. What?"

"Singers that are the best singers in the world know when they are five or six years old. Singers like Mariah Carey, Barbara Streisand, and Whitney Houston... They have what they call 'star quality.' It's a natural talent they are born with."

"Yes, Dad. I know. I am going to sing like them!"

"Honey," my dad said, "No, you are not star quality."

I balked. I could hardly hold back my tears, but I somehow choked out the words, "Why not?"

"You're either born with it or you're not."

As my precious but secret dream, that I had finally had the courage to openly talk about, was being smothered by the thousand pounds of his pessimism, I quietly asked, "Well, what should I do?"

"Well, what else do you like? Pick something that you like."

I shrugged and thought for a moment. "Maybe a therapist?"

I knew this would be approved.

He nodded. "Well, I'm glad you found something else you can think of to do."

I walked away, my chest hurting from the air I was pushing down to try and not cry. I was able to shut the door and I belted into my pillow.

He thought he was doing the right thing. What he didn't know was that I kept this dream alive, and even though I later went on to perform, in my mind there was always his voice saying I wasn't good enough, that I wasn't star quality. I wonder now, with a better awareness, if someone had once told him that he wasn't star quality at something he loved very much.

My hidden depression translated poetically through pen and paper. I would often sit in my room at my desk with my *Alice in Wonderland* candle lit beside me, pouring my emotions out. My stepmom would sometimes read the poems and give me acclaim. I think she still has some of them, even after all these years.

Eventually, we got private lines in our rooms. Every time mine would ring, I would cheerfully bounce to the phone, even if a note of irritation colored my "hello's" because it never seemed to stop ringing. I had become very popular. Having so many friends was the highlight of my life. Heather and I were now more comfortable, but there was still a void I simply could not explain, nor wanted to, as this would further solidify my identity as the problem child.

Susan was strict, and my father and her were a unit. Discipline from him always felt humiliating to me, as opposed to humbling, or however else discipline from a parent is supposed to feel. If I had not completed my chores at the house before going to visit at a friend's house, my father would phone the parents of my friend and describe what I had failed to do. I would get punished for answering my private line one minute after the 8 p.m. curfew. As brutal as it sounds in retrospect, I believe it's hard for parents because they have to wait for age to catch up to us children before we can understand them. Without rules, there is chaos, but teaching that to teenagers only seems to create more chaos.

But life at my dad's house wasn't all bad; I clearly recall a lot of nurturing and fun. Sometimes Susan turned on Mexican music, grabbing my hand unexpectedly to dance together; I would look up and watch her soak in the notes, lifting her bell-sleeved arms high in the air, her colorful Asian-print silk robe flowing. My father would join in sometimes, as would Heather if she was in the mood.

I adored my father regardless of his strict rules. To me, he was a love that I couldn't get enough of. We spoke without speaking; a look would suffice any communication as we carried out our daily tasks with each other. I begged and pleaded for my father to take me everywhere, and anywhere, with him. I memorized his favorite songs to please him. I watched him play baseball on Sundays, and I was proud to be his personal cheerleader. I felt calm and relaxed in my father's company, unlike anyone else's.

My dad would cuddle me and whisper in my ear, "I love my little girl," and I didn't know how to react. I felt uncomfortable at first, even though I cherished hearing it. That kind of softness wasn't a part of Mom's way... Poor Mom was always in emergency mode. I have very real memories as a baby of the calmness I would feel only in my father's arms. My father and I shared many traits, and maybe this is what led him and my stepmom to do what they did. Maybe my father feared the day Heather and I were born that anything we enjoyed too much could potentially become a compulsion.

When Heather and I were living at my dad's house, there was a long stretch of time where she and I would meet at night in the middle of the hallway. We both would walk to each other without warning; it must have been the twin telepathy.

"Do you want to sleep in my bed or your bed tonight?" she'd ask.

We did this for quite some time, until Heather got tired of waking in my puddle of urine. I wet the bed until I was close to eleven years old. I'd wake in embarrassment and apologize to my sister nightly. Heather was gentle towards me, always careful to not hurt my feelings.

Susan began sitting at my bedside almost every night, lulling me into sleep by saying, "Okay Holly, I want you to close your eyes."

I would, and then she would say, "Imagine being in the most beautiful place you could dream of. What does it look like?"

I would describe different scenes, but one always returned: running with a child on the seashore, wearing white and giggling, and in our hands, we carried wands with ribbons attached to them. They would twirl in the wind. And I would then scoop the child up and kiss him.

Another night she asked me, "What does your future life look like?"

I replied, "I have a home, with a husband."

She asked me what he looked like, and I described, "He has dark hair and light eyes, and he has an accent."

This calmed me, seeing a future, being in a position of protection of a child, and in love within a sacred space of my own, a home.

Susan would kiss my closed eyelids and say goodnight. She was trying to ease something inside me before bed. I would hear her go to my father and whisper. I overheard the word "she" quite often, and I always assumed it was about me. I wondered if I had imagined the wrong things, and that if tomorrow I would get a lecture of my visuals being incorrect; that somehow this was a psychological sign that I was dysfunctional.

Later in the night, Susan would wake me to go to the bathroom in an effort to create a routine.

"Come on, Holly, bathroom time." She would wait, sleepy-eyed and leaning against the doorway until I went to the bathroom, her eyes closed, exhaustion on her face. Sometimes I couldn't go, so she would turn on the tap so that I could hear a stream of running water. I would relieve myself and sleepily walk back to her. She would hold my hand as I did a twirl under her arm, we would hug, then she would say, "I love you," and I'd make my way back to bed. We did this every single night until, within some time, I stopped wetting the bed.

My sister didn't need any of this extra attention, and I knew that. My anxiety over feeling like the screwed-up one became a chronic condition. It became how I spoke to myself. It was the jacket I now wore and couldn't seem to remove despite how uncomfortable it was on my skin. It was too tight. I even felt awkward in school, as if someone was going to find out what I truly was... Broken.

I went from feeling on edge to endlessly jittery. I couldn't get a hold on it. When I did succeed, it felt awkwardly triumphant.

CHAPTER EIGHT
A CRADLED FACE

Middle school, especially in West Los Angeles, was filled with creative types: the offspring of film producers and scriptwriters.

Holly, sit up taller so the teacher will notice you, I thought as I waited to be called on. My turn to perform would be soon. No amount of suppression I felt internally seemed to dim the urge to create, whether it be running for the optimist club,, performing, writing, or singing. This audition was for singing "The Star-Spangled Banner" at The First Annual Charity Celebrity Basketball Game. I didn't know which celebrities would attend, but I didn't care because this was my shot regardless. I considered if I could make the president of the school Optimist Club, which I had, then I could definitely win this.

"Holly, it's your turn," the choir teacher called to me.

I rose up, stood tall, and gave the teacher a nod as my cue before she played the backing tune for the eleventh time in a row on her piano. I took in a big deep breath just as I had practiced, opened my mouth, and pushed the sound out of me. As a child, when I would practice being Tina, in the garage, my mother would advise I push the voice out with the same muscles as going "poo poo." So I did this. I felt the stare from a schoolgirl sitting at her desk watching me with furrowed eyebrows. I felt self-conscious, but I kept pushing through my fear. I finished and sat back down. The nerves and adrenaline left my body as the next performer sang.

After school, I rushed down the busy corridor to the hall bulletin board where various announcements were showcased. My eyes scanned all the documents. I saw my name printed in bold as the official singer of "The Star-Spangled Banner." Gasping with excitement, I could hardly contain myself. I ran to my sister and twirled like a ballerina, professing my achievement. She rolled her eyes at me.

For the next seven days, the house echoed with the sound of my voice belting the notes of the national anthem. I wanted to call and share the news with my mom so she could come watch, but I knew it would have been too awkward, considering the conflicts she and my father carried between each other. I couldn't imagine them in the same room. Instead, I tried to concentrate on my performance.

On the evening of the show, my nerves gave me strange sensations, such as numb feet. I started feeling self-conscious when I was made to wear a black lace gossamer dress; to me, it looked like I was cloaked in cobwebs. Susan had bought it and dressed me, so I didn't protest as she braided my hair and painted my lips and cheeks with rouge.

As she delicately patted makeup onto my face, she said, "Remember, Holly, makeup is fun, but being a good person is truly what makes someone beautiful. And if you are not, no amount of makeup could cover up the ugliness of that."

My father drove me so he could stay and watch. To me, this was also my shot to prove to him I was star quality.

I entered the court, and there stood a handful of celebrities, all in a single line. I recognized some faces from soap operas, but I had no idea who the rest were. One man stood out to me. He was shirtless, holding a basketball. His hair nearly reached the small of his back, and he had a long face. He stood on a slant with the weight of his body leaning into his left foot, slouched.

The bleachers of the middle school gym were speckled with faces, a good portion made up of parents and teachers. I noticed a few students way up top. My cousin had arrived, and he'd brought a video camera. I could hear the echoes of conversations bouncing off of the gymnasium walls. I was beyond nervous; I felt terror. I felt like a fake. My feet were ice cubes and my breathing was shallow. I felt as though I was shaking, but my hands were still.

"Holly Cohen," was called from the loudspeaker. I looked at my father and he winked at me. I saw the record light flashing red from my cousin's camera. I was handed a microphone with a long cord and was instructed to walk to the middle of the gym floor. I looked for the duct-taped X and stopped there. It was go-time. I tried to embody my mother's fearlessness.

I stood up tall, pushed in my stomach muscles, and let my voice flow. I scanned the looks of approval from the celebrities' expressions as I sang to them. The microphone amplified me, which was jarring. It was so crisp. In a peculiar way, it was like an out-of-body experience; I could see the room at a 360-degree view—with sight which did not come from my physical body. The national anthem isn't the easiest song to sing, and has a particularly high note that requires precision. I definitely hit the note, but I was one octave too high, way above the key I was singing in. I froze and a voice in my head narrated, *Oh no, Holly.* I caved internally. My hopes to do my dream justice came crashing down. I lowered my head, pausing, wondering if I should apologize to the crowd.

During the brief silence, I heard the echoes of laughter. The sound came from high in the bleachers. My eyes darted in that direction, and there she was: the same disgruntled, furrow-browed girl from class. It was as if, that day of my audition, she had already known I was a fake. I sank further into defeat.

I finished the song, though with not nearly the same amount of gusto or pride. I heard scattered applause from the obliging crowd. As any professional would do, I thanked them. I looked down at the floor and started to make my way back towards the bleachers. I looked over my shoulder, toward the celebrities, and the shirtless man broke away from the group, tossing the basketball to another player. He walked towards me.

"You did a really good job tonight," he said, his voice soft and encouraging.

"Thanks," I replied, embarrassed.

"What do you want to be when you grow up?"

I looked down at the ground, ashamed of my own dream after such a debacle. "A singer," I whispered, my eyes slowly meeting his again.

He smiled. He raised his hands to my face and cupped my cheeks. I didn't know what to do. He looked into my eyes and said, "You keep that dream and don't you ever let anyone take it away from you, okay? Not even mean girls in bleachers, okay?"

I was in disbelief, but his words invigorated me. My hope was pieced back together.

"Okay," I said back.

"Promise?"

"Promise," I replied. We made a little deal. He high-fived me and ran back to his team.

I stood there for a moment, dazed, and I walked back to where my father and cousin stood.

Dad asked, "What was that all about?"

"He said I did a good job and to keep singing," I replied.

"Did he really?"

"Yes," I said.

"How beautiful, kiddo," my father replied.

With one sentence, the man had resurrected me. Later in my life, his encouraging words persisted to cut through my scathing inner narrative and kept me going through my darkest times. His gift was the gift that kept on giving. To this very day, it still does.

That man was Anthony Kiedis, the lead singer of The Red Hot Chili Peppers, and one day I intend to thank him personally.

I felt like a caged lion in my dad's home. I think I would have felt caged with any authority figure I didn't understand or agree with. Later, as I transitioned into high school, my desperation grew, as did the comments differentiating my sister and I. My father and stepmother's rules were the snaps from a training whip.

I saw myself as something pure and good—a girl connected to something bigger than herself, something intangible. But somehow, on the outside, I appeared so careless. The dichotomy of my human experience, against my inner understanding of my own soul and its connection to a mystical world, bewildered me at times, and certainly those around me. Maybe this is what being a teenager is.

I said prayers to God every night and made sure I put in a prayer for everyone I knew. It took me about six to seven minutes to complete my nightly ritual. *Please, God, make sure my mom is happy. Make sure all my brothers are safe. Oh, and don't forget the dog, Cash. Please, God, if you could help him with his fleas, he would be so happy. Please, God, protect my grandpa and grandma. God, please, please, don't forget about the teacher who broke his finger. Yes, that's the one. I know you can hear me.* I always fell asleep beautifully after praying.

CHAPTER NINE
THE DEPARTURE

I took the idea of getting married in a white dress very seriously, even at fourteen, because white represents purity.

After being begged by a friend of my sister's, Robyn, to accompany her to a boy's house—she eventually convinced me to tag along. This was a boy she had a crush on. Heather didn't join because she had homework. I had been grounded recently, but Susan allowed me to go out with Robyn for an hour. I was happy to escape the house as I was finishing yet my second stint of conjunctivitis. My stepmom kindly offered me a pair of rose-colored sunglasses to wear, suggesting to me that if I wore them, no one would ever know. I waved goodbye and told my family that I would see them soon.

I cheerily walked down the street to where my friend's car was parked: one of the perks of hanging out with a girl a few years older than me. I inhaled the fresh, clean, midday air. When I peered through the shield of my glasses, the balmy sunlight slightly burned my infected eyes. I quickly ignored that.

My friend, Robyn, said, "Let's head to my boyfriend's house. He lives right up the street. We can't go far anyway since you only have one hour. Oh, and he has a brother for you, so you're not left out."

I knew she did things that older girls did, but I didn't think she expected me to be that way, too. I felt special that she wanted me to come with her. She introduced me to her boyfriend's brother. Being there as her friend created the assumption that I, too, was promiscuous. This was one of the first times I realized that people do, in fact, judge you by the company you keep.

Without much talking or any indication of what was going on, the older brother, Travis, took my hand without permission and led me to his room. Even though I had not actually wanted to go with him, I was caught off guard by his confidence. I felt an incredible pressure, being caged in a room alone with him while my friend was doing things next door. Curiously, I studied his face as he nervously tidied his room, tripping over his baseball bat lying on the floor. As he tidied up, he quickly spat out questions for me to answer about myself. I believed he came from a good family, from what I could gather by the family portraits that hung above the staircase on the way to his room, but my eyes could not get past his enormously far-reaching nose. Plus, there was a bump. Superficial as it may have been, fourteen-year-old me honed in on this feature, and I couldn't make myself focus on much else.

His towering, lengthy body loomed over my tiny frame, adding to the illusion of him being in charge. But he had benevolent eyes, and they begged for me.

"What do you want to do?" he asked, seemingly unaware of my anxiety in the moment.

I replied with only a gesture, shrugging and bashfully looking at the ground.

"Do you want to sit next to me? You're so beautiful," he replied and patted the bed for me to come closer to him.

I obeyed. It felt nice to be called beautiful. I wanted to be wanted; I gave my authority away, even if the circumstances weren't ideal. He wasted no time and leaped for my lips before I could think any further about what I might have really wanted. It was the first time I had ever been kissed this passionately. His face smashed into mine, along with my rose-colored glasses, the nosepiece digging fiercely into my skin. His hand, lacking finesse, instantly met my breast along with the inside of my thigh. My invisible boundary being violated felt like a glass full of nerves being ferociously shaken within my belly.

His opposing hand swiftly moved to my core in between my thighs.

"Take off your shirt," he commanded breathlessly. He reached to take my sunglasses off and I stopped him, grabbing his hand as his fingers hooked the rim. I didn't dare show him what my eyes really looked like, and had I known my friend had such a plan that I was now fully involved in, I would not have come with her. But there I was, and if he saw my eyes, he would have been disgusted with me. As uncomfortable as I was with the pace he was going, I still didn't want to ruin this feeling of being lusted over.

He reached again for the sunglasses and I stopped him. "Please wait. I have to wear these."

He narrowed his eyes at me with a confused look, "No, you don't. Take them off, please. I want to see your beautiful eyes."

Bubbling over with guilt and shame, I admitted what I was hiding, but he ignored me and proceeded to pull me closer to him. I knew what was next.

Slowly pulling them off my face, I managed to mutter one simple request, "Can we at least light a candle?"

My fantasy of losing my virginity involved a sense of spirituality. To me, a candle represented spirituality. It represented light. I would often stare into the flame as I wrote my poetry; it took me somewhere far away. I saw candles in romantic music videos, movies, churches, the lit menorah. I wanted it to be above this experience—as if it meant not only bodies, but also spiritual expression. I knew he was very frustrated, going around the house, having to search for a match or lighter. He had a candle in the room, probably his mother's, but I could sense his irritation with me as my request had paused the entire moment—right in the heat of it. I wanted some otherworldliness in that moment of attempted generic I-saw-this-on-TV-style teen romance. I knew it would be pushing it too far to ask for music too.

In an effort to stop what was happening and backtrack a little, I asked to get my friend. He told me not to bother, that they were very busy and we shouldn't disturb them. I brought up my conjunctivitis again in hopes he would be more understanding. Instead, he looked at me and said, "It's ok, don't worry. I don't need to look at your face. I can turn you around." There was an awkward silence, piercing the moment further. As he put on the condom, flashbacks of sex-ed class interrupted the visual. He put it on correctly, just like we had learned with the banana at school. With my rose-colored sunglasses still covering my eyes, I was smashed into a pillow from behind. It smelled like a boy, identifiable to my nose by hints of oily hair and sweat on black sheets that needed washing. I could feel pain from the glasses pushing into the soft skin on the bridge of my nose, but I didn't stop or try to move. I just let him continue.

I felt pressured to submit to the expectation. I submitted to him. I inherently wanted to please him. He wasn't anything to me, I had no reason to feel beholden to his emotions, but I did anyway, and I gave in to what he asked me to do. There was nothing romantic at all about the situation; not one thing. Even with my insistence of having a lit candle, all I could really feel was the tension in the air—from having asked him to stop what he wanted to do, and search for a lighter just to appease me.

He couldn't finish. I was so upset and angry with myself for allowing someone to take something that was so special to me. When I was with him in that moment, I tried to take in more, but I simply couldn't. The rubber from his condom hurt me. So I stopped him and apologized. I wondered, *Wasn't something supposed to break?* I rushed to the bathroom after getting dressed and checked my panties. There was just a little blood; not what I expected. Then I realized that something had been taken from me that I'd never get back. The guy had been horrible enough to squash my face into a pillow; he used me, a stranger, for his own satisfaction—someone who also had an eye infection. He didn't care about anything other than himself, and I felt like I couldn't say no.

When I lost my virginity, I actually felt a part of me had died. The shame I felt was not only for me, but for my family. There was a feeling of undisclosed disapproval. Losing my virginity was quite influential in my attitude towards sex and men. It took something that I could never get back, but it didn't take all of me. The next morning, I stared in the mirror to see if I looked different; it was the same face as the day before, yet I was no longer a virgin. Did Travis take advantage? Yes, he did, but truth be told, I allowed him to.

I recalled all the moments I had practiced saying no with my friends, with my family, and at school. My cherished romantic ideas about what my first time should be like were now gone. The drive in me was strange; a need to please. Believing my friend was doing the same thing next door was an immature judgment on my part. As we headed home, I openly admitted to Robyn what I had done; I assumed we would bond over it. However, I was met with humiliation as I found out that I was the only one having sex that day.

I couldn't tell my dad or stepmom. There was absolutely no way I could envision talking it through with them. I couldn't handle the psychoanalysis from my stepmom, nor the harsh discipline from my dad. Plus, it was blatantly humiliating, and what would my sister say? I would have added several brownie points to her perfection list in comparison to me. Many years later, I found out how upset my sister was that she wasn't there to protect me from her fast friend. It was nice that she wanted to look out for me, even though the time had long since passed.

Travis must have felt quite guilty in retrospect, because a few days later he delivered a dozen roses to me at my dad's house. I was shocked he knew where I lived. The roses were just a shameful reminder of how terrible I felt about myself, and Travis kept bringing me roses and wanting to be with me. That was the last thing I wanted. Whenever I saw the flowers, my body would flush with the disgrace of what I'd done.

A few weeks later, while we were eating dinner, there was a knock at the door.

"Holly, get the door!" Susan said.

She normally never had us greet a visitor. Discouraged, I opened it about two inches, just enough to see who it was. There Travis stood, his sheepish body language probing me for a hello. His mouth curved up as he offered a red rose. I cringed. My whole body flamed with anxious dread at seeing him. *Doesn't he have any self-respect? Why does he keep coming here?* When I thought of him, I could only see the red stain on my teenage panties.

I sank into a slump of shame.

I went to shut the door, but he caught the doorknob with his hand and pulled it back.

"Why don't you like me? I try and try. Please, tell me what is wrong with me," he pleaded, furrowing his brows in protest of my cold stare.

I wanted only to say the cruelest thing possible to him. I wanted my words to penetrate through any self-confidence he may still have had to stop his incessant courting.

"Because your nose is way too big, and I can't see past it!" I shut the door.

I heard him shout, "I will fix it!" Then there was silence.

I shrugged off his reply because it didn't make sense to me. No one could change a thing like that, and I felt confident and pleased with myself—that he would forever leave me alone once his mind reconciled how cruel I could be. How could he ever want someone so cold? I ripped him to shreds with one sentence. I got rid of him for good.

A few weeks later, the phone rang at the house.

It was Travis. "I got a nose job, Holly. I look much better," he said, point-blank. "You should come and see me. I look much better," he repeated. *He cut into his face for me? Was this real?*

But how could I have been surprised? After all, it was LA, and he went to Beverly Hills High.

My stepmother said visiting him was the least I could do. She said I should go to his bedside and just say hello. My objection to him and my lost virginity was now completely upstaged by his holier-than-thou act to please me.

I gathered myself as best as I could. His house wasn't far from ours in the well-manicured parts of Beverlywood. But it felt like revisiting a crime scene. Everything was different. My hair had lost its bounce, and I didn't notice any pleasantries of the day. This time, I was met at the door by his mother.

"Hello, Holly. Travis knows you are coming. Please go straight upstairs. He is in his room. Can I get you anything? Water, juice? Anything at all, please let me know."

"Thank you, I am fine. I'll just head upstairs," I replied, avoiding any further contact with her.

Great. They all seem to know; they all want us together... Is she thinking I am going to marry him?

The hanging family portraits led me to think they were such a "normal" family. *Must be nice*, I thought. Parents married, just the four of them—it looked so customary.

I entered his room again. The smell of musty boy stung my nostrils. There he was before me, on that same cursed bed with a thick white bandage over his nose and a single purple eye.

"Hello, Travis," I said, forcing a tone of kindness to pass

through my lips.

He replied in a cracked, weakened tone; it sounded like he was exaggerating his wounded state. "Holly, please sit," and he patted the bed next to him, mirroring himself from before. "Look, I got my nose done. It should heal within a few weeks," he assured, trying to smile.

"Travis, how could you do this to yourself?" I asked him, searching his eyes.

"This is what you wanted," he retorted.

"Travis, I said that to hurt you so you would leave me alone. I didn't ask you to get a nose job."

"So this doesn't change the way you see me? The answer is still no?"

"You make me feel like we *have* to be together because of what happened. I just don't feel it. I don't know; I'm sorry."

I did not know what else to say. Silence crept between us and I glanced over at the small jar candle I'd made him light.

"Get out," he snapped, turning his gaze away.

I was astonished. He took something from me in such a vulgar way, and now that he had voluntarily cut into his face, I was expected to nurture him? It made no sense to me.

I stood up from his bed and left without another word, and I never heard from him again. I lit my *Alice in Wonderland* candle and poured my heart out, pen to paper, all the mixed emotions that had been stirred up from what I had done.

I hope he is out there somewhere, being loved and told how handsome he is.

CHAPTER TEN
A CLOUD TO COPE

Because my stepmom was so involved in my life in many ways, I believe she was able to find out I'd had sex with him in full certainty. I assumed she probed my sister's friend until it was admitted. I also considered the idea that my stepmother had asked him to bring flowers so that I felt pursued and nurtured. I could be wrong.

It wasn't too long after the whole ordeal that I got my period. My twin sister got hers too, and we both tried tampons for the first time. My sister attempted it but said she would prefer to use a pad. I went to the bathroom and found I could do it.

I went to report to my stepmom. "I managed to use the tampon. I could do it!"

"I bet you could!" she replied, her voice dripping with derision.

All of the shame I had previously felt washed back over me, and I never discussed it with anybody.

I felt anxious walking in the hallway at school. I found relief in realizing Travis went to a different school, but my nerves revved up again in knowing Robyn didn't. I wondered who she'd told. The stares and nods of either approval or disgust from my fellow classmates led me to believe everyone must have known what happened. The only relief I had was a compliment on my Puma sneakers' laces, which I had tie-dyed. In class, I went to sit at my cage of a desk for the hour, legs twitching anxiously.

As the teacher was trying to control the morning chatter,

the speaker crackled with an announcement.

"Holly, Holly Cohen—please make your way to the principal's office."

I wanted to sink into my chair. All eyes were on me as I walked out of the class. I sheepishly and slowly walked to the principal's office. *What have I done?* I thought to myself, scanning my memory bank for any obvious offenses. I couldn't think of one. *Does he know I had sex?*

Our principal welcomed me sympathetically into his office and motioned for me to sit down. *Has someone died?* I thought to myself.

"Holly, are you doing okay?" asked the principal.

"Yeah, I'm fine."

"Has anything happened at school that we need to talk about?"

"No! I love school."

"Your stepmother has called me saying she found a very sad letter. It was what she called a suicide letter that you wrote."

"What?" I almost shouted, flabbergasted that she knew, and now he did too. I had written my deepest personal emotions; no one was supposed to find out. Instead of writing my feelings in my diary, I had opted for a letter this time, tucking it safely away in my underwear drawer where no one would ever think to look.

"Yes, she and your father are very worried. Are you thinking of harming yourself?" he gently asked me.

"No! Never! I wouldn't even know what to do. It was just a note I wrote about something inside me dying, not me... Just a situation I was dealing with. But it's over and completely handled now. I was upset, but it wasn't a big deal."

"We have a school counselor here that is always available to you if you ever need it."

I thanked him and calmed his concerns, and he

apprehensively excused me back to class after making a phone call to my stepmom.

I was fuming. She had invaded my privacy. I had written that note and placed it in my color-coordinated underwear drawer, which had been a mandatory rule from her. She must have searched through my personal space. I couldn't even write a letter to myself about how sad I was at losing my virginity. I had no respected space, not even in my own mind. Yet I also knew I would have no right to say any of this or defend myself. I knew I would be analyzed and sent to a therapist that very day. By that point, it had been years since I had seen a professional therapist. My stepmother had taken on that role.

In high school, the portal to escapism cracked open. I didn't seek out drugs, but being included in any social circle meant a great deal. It distracted me from thinking about my mishaps at home. With large, curly, untamed hair, a nose that my face hadn't grown into yet, and unbalanced body parts, I felt like an ugly duckling, so being popular assuaged my concerns.

A classmate had a supply of marijuana. He sold it to make extra money. He was round and pudgy and not my usual type, but I liked him; he was soft, smart, kind, and generous. I would accept his free nickel bags because I didn't want to be seen as uncool. I took the bags and placed them in an Altoids mint box. He thought I was using the drugs, but I had simply collected them.

Word spread like wildfire that Holly was a pothead, along with who my crush was: Joshua Fieldman. Joshua was tall, two years above me, popular, confident, and had ashy blue eyes, wavy dark brown hair, and a keen mind. He would break away from his uber-popular crowd and walk to me during lunch. I felt special, and all my girlfriends would nudge me, giggling, after he waltzed back to his group. Naturally, whatever he was into, I was more inclined to act interested in. Joshua asked me if I wanted to go for a ride and offered pot, and suddenly it all became serious. I could no longer playact at using weed. Strangely, the pot did not affect me in the slightest that first time. I was relieved that I didn't have to feel guilty when I returned to my parents.

Joshua said it would take a couple times before I would feel anything. This was okay with me, because it meant we would hang out more.

The first time I was consciously aware that I was high, was when a couple of friends and I drove to Santa Monica beach after school one day. I will never forget when I finally got high. We laughed so much my stomach muscles ached. I felt nothing but joy and a sense of carelessness. The world in my mind went quiet and I was elated with the idea that peace had been attained, even if just for a few hours. I felt safe smoking with Joshua, who knew what he was doing. It couldn't have been more of a stereotypical, Southern California moment if it had been scripted for a teenage film. We were in a classic 1965 Mustang, watching the sky turn shades of pink, orange, and purple. Wind in my hair and Led Zeppelin playing on the Classic Rock 93.1 station, we glided down the coast without the slightest worry. The driver was a boy Joshua's age.

As we shared a joint, that first wave of relaxation poured over me, and I melted from head to toe. I put my head on Joshua's shoulder and he kissed my forehead. Life was complete. I planned our wedding in my mind. When it was my turn to hit it again, I held my breath as long as I could and released it slowly, watching the wafts billow out in front of my face. Smiling, I stared into Joshua's eyes as the smoke exhaled from my mouth, and behind the cloud I could see him smile back. We nodded our heads to the music. Everything was going to be okay in that moment, and I felt it to be true, truer than anything else I knew.

I couldn't hear my mother or my stepmother. I couldn't hear my father or my sister. I didn't know I could stifle those voices like putting a muzzle on a vicious dog's snout. Slowing down was nice.

Underneath the smoke screen, I began to silently question my safety as I got higher. *Am I okay? It should wear off in a few hours. You'll feel better when it does, Holly... Wow, I'm really spinning.* A blanket of quiet had quelled my inner voice, but at some point, the blanket had to come off and each time it did I became depressed. I had a secret, and secrets make souls heavy. Each time I came down it would make me anxious and irritated, and the cycle would repeat. Get under the blanket again and again.

I walked into the house, looking down at the ground.

My father asked, "Holly, what's wrong?" I had to meet his eyes, and he noticed how bloodshot mine were. They barraged me: "Why are your eyes red? Where have you been? Holly, be honest, you will not get in trouble." They already knew. Without much more probing, I admitted that I had smoked weed. I told him and Susan because I knew that if I didn't tell them, I would not outlive the severe investigation. At first, I never admitted it was with Joshua, because I feared they wouldn't allow us to be together again.

I was also sneezing profusely. The two of them informed me that I obviously had an allergy to weed, which wasn't all that surprising, as I had reactions to many common allergens.

I showed them the tiny little baggies of weed I had collected in my Altoids box. I emptied them in the toilet in front of them in an effort to show I had learned my lesson.

I sat on the couch with them, my head in my hands, hair tickling my thighs. There I was again: Holly, the problematic child. My stepmom took me by the hand and looked into my crimson eyes. "Holly, if you want to experiment with marijuana, please do it at home." Heather walked past, rolling her eyes at me.

I was baffled. Was Susan serious? Why would I smoke weed at home? That took all the fun out of it. What was I supposed to do, tell them the next time the mood struck? Although the gesture came from a place of good parenting, it was completely unrealistic. I hadn't really wanted to tell them I'd smoked in the first place and, like most teens, I didn't intend on sharing any future dabbling with them. They knew far too much about my personal life already and it contributed greatly to my constant state of unease.

Pot helped to dull the anxiety. But as soon as it wore off, I was hit with a catastrophic deluge of all the issues from which I had temporarily found reprieve: from struggling to tread water, to being swept away in hurricane waves, to drifting in a weightless current, then back to frenzied thrashing, over and over again.

A seemingly never-ending cycle.

I couldn't grasp onto healthier coping mechanisms. I watched my sister escape into books. She had a natural ability to read for pleasure, and it saved her. I couldn't make myself sit still long enough to read a book. My mind would wander off and I would end up worrying, and then I'd worry about having to reread a passage, then I'd re-read again and frustration would kick in. My own solution—putting on the mask of carefree entertainer—was more fun. Most psychologists would probably say I had ADD, or some comorbid anxiety disorder, or something even more intricate and problematic. As I look back now, my difficulty concentrating stemmed from never understanding the core principles and terminologies that were the foundation for all of my lessons. Sometimes the simplest answer is the truest one, a la Occam's razor. These days it seems easier to look for a disorder label, and we call this *professional.*

Chasing the drug-induced freedom became my hobby because it was also Joshua's hobby. As I stared out the window of his car, high, watching the buildings pass me, I felt as if I was tucked within clouds inside a plexiglass bubble, the world and I utterly separate. This became my great escape. Yet somehow, I could never again get back inside that bubble.

I daydreamed about my Joshua. We talked every day. I called him all the time, and to hear a voice that was happy to talk to me gave me much joy. To feel love was euphoric. I felt like an ever-blooming lotus flower, and celebration filled the air of my heavy world.

On a Friday night, just after I'd hung up with Joshua, there was a knock at the door. I opened it and it was him. I gasped; I had no idea he was coming over. We locked eyes, grinning, excited about what this Friday night would bring. Previously, we had talked about going to *The Rocky Horror Picture Show* one day.

He asked to speak to my dad, and officially asked for permission to take me out on a date. I admired his confidence and manners. That was my first official date. It was different than just driving around with him.

After agreeing to let Joshua take me out, my dad handed him an extra twenty dollars and said, "This is for you to treat her to something extra nice."

Surprisingly, Joshua turned to me, right in front of my dad, and whispered in my ear, "I love you." I softened, my heart utterly disarmed. The date went perfectly, although *The Rocky Horror Picture Show* wasn't my thing. We shared a milkshake using the same straw and held hands throughout the whole show. Just the touch of his hand jolted a shock of excitement through me I had never felt before. This started my enjoyment of love through men, because it came along with no strings attached. It was fresh and invigorating and without pain. My dad and stepmom stayed awake to hear how it all went.

CHAPTER ELEVEN
THE SILENT ORCHESTRA

Reality always set back in, and with every new disapproving look from my parents, I rebelled more. And as the favoritism increased towards my sister, I began to blame the insufficient attention from my father on his stress and his absence on his work. Susan entered severe menopause as my teenage hormones emerged in full force; the way she sought Heather, and how flagrantly they showed off their special relationship, reinforced the fact that my father wasn't home enough to offer such a bond to me. I started running away.

One night, I walked out the front door. It was cold, dark, and well beyond my curfew, but I didn't care. I called Joshua before leaving and told him to meet me under the large tree at the park, where we'd occasionally meet after school. We would cling to each other, tightly hugging, melting into each other.

That night we lay on the prickly grass, holding hands, talking, and gazing up at the stars through the large branched oak tree, utterly in love. Our kisses were sweet. My heart would sing, and I felt admired. I thought about him all day. I needed him; he was my light. Every elapsed minute on these nights with him ticked towards the next lecture, so I made sure to gulp up his approval before being met with dissatisfaction from my household.

I plodded home quickly and discreetly opened the door, which alerted my stepmother, who called my name with scorn. I sat at the edge of their bed, listening to the lecture, the TV light bouncing light off their faces in the dark, making them look scary. I sank further into contempt for them when they called Joshua's parents and told them they didn't approve of him meeting me at the park so late. I prayed I didn't get Joshua into trouble; he was the only thing that made me happy. I hoped he still would want to see me.

The following morning, I heard my name again.

"Holly, please come here so we can talk about last night." I sat for over an hour on the toilet seat while she blow-dried her hair and lectured me.

My stepmom's menopause made her hearing exceptionally sensitive. Every morning we had to tiptoe around because she couldn't stand the sound of normal footsteps on hardwood floors, and at times we would speak in near-whispers to her. In between her unbearable hot flashes, she would get mood swings and it was like living with a ticking time bomb.

That afternoon, she arrived home with groceries from Vons. She'd bought eggs, so, as usual, I placed them in a tray and then put them into the refrigerator. I presumed if I helped before being asked this would earn me some points. After she saw what I had done, she became furious that I had done it without asking her. She took the eggs out one by one, throwing each one angrily into the sink. She said I might have mixed the new eggs with old ones that had already been in the refrigerator.

That moment was such a pivotal experience for me. As uneventful as it may sound, it is something I can never forget, because then I knew it didn't matter whether it was something big or something as innocent as putting away groceries—I was going to be in the wrong. I couldn't win; I was constantly defeated, and I couldn't take the pressure anymore.

While smashing all the eggs into the sink, she yelled at me, "Holly does what Holly wants! Heather would have asked first, but no, not Holly! She just does whatever she wishes without thinking about anyone else."

I left the house that night and called Joshua. I ran as fast as I could, my eyelids stung by the unforgiving cold air. I whizzed past houses of people I knew, hoping they wouldn't come out and recognize me. All I thought about was being with Joshua, my safe haven; the person who still saw the good in me. While I ran, I cried. I wasn't quite fifteen years old at the time, and even though all I did was go to the park, my dad deemed me as a runaway on that night.

After three more months of avoiding the house at any cost (and tiptoeing on the hardwood floors while I was there), I told my dad I did not want to live with him anymore. I wanted to go back to my mom. We all sat on the couch together. My father slipped off the edge of his seat, fell to his knees, and began to weep. I had never seen him cry like this. I froze in my immaturity. He, my sister, and my stepmom hugged. My stepmom told him maybe it was best, and that I would come back once I knew what it would be like living with my mom and brothers.

She looked at me and said, "Look at how you are hurting him! I have never seen him cry like this. Please, Holly, go! Go wait outside for your mom." This statement summed up how I felt living with the three of them; look at how I was always hurting them.

I packed and then sat on the porch with my suitcases until my mother arrived. I felt as though my dad was crying in some sort of defeat, as if my mom had won the unspoken battle between the two of them. But I had to leave for my own sake. That was the first time I ever saw my father sob.

For the first few months back at my mother's house, it was uncomfortable and unsettling. I had expected that my older brothers would be excited for us to be together again. Both she and my siblings carried an undercurrent of disapproval in their tone towards me. I had to earn my way back into the group from being a traitor. They were hurt I had left in the first place.

Once again, I had to change schools—and this time without my sister. I didn't even consider school when I had planned on leaving. Then I'd come home, harshly greeted by my brothers' teasing. "This ain't Daddy's house anymore," they all would laugh.

My old school, where I had been so popular, was far from me now. Back then, I couldn't wave my hand quickly enough to keep up with the morning greetings in the hallway. My sister would call and complain, saying, "Your friends walk up to me and only ask where you are; they don't even say hello to me!" I had always prevented my sister from having lunch with my friends and I, so they hardly knew her. To me, that domain was unapologetically mine. I could be me without feeling the guilt of socially overshadowing my twin. If she took over the social scene, what would I have left? That was all I had.

I found myself friendless and ate lunch for the first weeks with non-English-speaking classmates. I missed Joshua, but I knew I was far from him now. He had promised he would drive to my mom's on the weekends. The non-English-speaking students were quiet, and sitting with them meant I didn't interrupt any conversations. I plopped myself down upon half-dead grass near the bleachers.

I would earnestly study my peers in groups, laughing and eating together, sharing inside jokes I wished I could be a part of. I would gaze at their perfectly straight blonde hair with tanned skin and white teeth, with blue-and-white-striped shirts and coral dresses; beachwear that I had long ago abandoned. I was an outcast and sheepish. I looked down at my shiny steel-toe leather Doc Martens I had begged my mother to buy me, and my floor-length maroon velvet skirt I had bought from a goth store called Hot Topic. I wondered where I'd fit in. My hair was wide, kinky, and uncontrollable; my mother often would touch it and say, "I love your hair. I couldn't count how many hairs you have on your head." To me, it was the kind of hair only a mother could love. I flattered myself with thinking that anyone even noticed. I chewed my lunch with the ESL class in silence, and I missed my sister, but not the silent comparison to her. My twin had never socially thrived, and now neither did I.

Two weeks had passed. At any moment, the likelihood of the teacher publicly calling on me to answer questions I didn't understand drew closer. *Be invisible... Don't make eye contact with the teacher or she will call your name.* I wanted to be unnoticeable in class. How come I never retained scholastic information like my sister did? My hand met my stomach in a comforting reflex, trying to quell my internal roller coaster. Then, the blessed lunch bell. Walking among the high-pitched laughter of girls and their inside jokes again spurred my desire to belong.

I sat on the quad, opened my lunch, and turned to the girl to my right. *Just go for it, Holly!*

"*Hola, ¿cómo estás?*" I asked.

She smiled and replied, "*Muy bien! ¿Hablas Español?*"

Knowing I didn't have much more vocabulary to spend, I replied, "*Poquito.*"

She met my grin with a warm smile and we simultaneously returned to eating our sandwiches. At least it was a small connection.

A sudden shadow blocking the warm sunlight interrupted my thoughts. A hand extended straight towards my face. I squinted my eyes as I glanced up at a girl about my age.

"Hi. My name is Chelsea. What's your name?"

I quickly sat taller. "Hello, I'm Holly," I said, one eye still squinting.

"Why don't you come over here," she pointed to the large group of straight-white-teethed girls wearing coral dresses, "and have lunch with us?" Her voice dropped to a whisper, "These kids don't speak English."

Her deep blue eyes oddly cooled my anxiety. I responded as if I never knew they didn't speak English, "Oh... Wow, okay cool, yeah, for sure."

She reached for my backpack and picked it up for me. She continued, "I think we have English together?"

"Yeah, we do."

"I haven't seen you at our school before. Are you new?" she asked, but before I could reply she introduced me to her group.

Her group included a curly-haired girl named Lisa. Chelsea then pointed to a girl who stood behind a blonde surfer boy with shoulder-length hair, whose pants sat stylishly low on his hips, and she said, "You can't see her because she's always swarmed by boys, but that is my sister."

I peeked at her and her sea green eyes caught me off guard. She hopped over to say hello. It was like the world was moving in slow motion. She was the kind of girl all the boys wanted: flirty, not coy. Her long blonde hair contrasted her summer tan. She was petite with a bum that looked like two perfect round balloon bubbles had been joined together. Her belly button showed below her khaki mesh spaghetti-strapped top. She wore an array of colorful bangles and a bell anklet that chimed as she walked. She had tiny hands, wrists, and feet, and there was not a blemish in sight. She smelled of vanilla mixed with ganja; it swirled around me when she breezed up. Her name was Bethany.

I was introduced to a few other girls and finished my lunch with my new group. The lunch bell rang, alerting us to say our goodbyes before we scuffled to class. Chelsea chimed in, "Hey, Holly, wanna hang out after school tomorrow?"

"Sure," I replied. If she only knew the fireworks that sent off inside my body.

"Meet me at the front of the school after sixth period." I

nodded and hurried to my next class.

That same day after school I bumped into another familiar face: Lisa. She offered to walk me home.

"So, we have musical theatre together. I recognize you from class. Where are you from?"

"LA. I used to be in theatre there, too," I replied.

We chatted a little and it wasn't considered inappropriate to welcome her into our home to meet my siblings. How contrary to adult life. As kids, we make friends so easily until we are weathered by wariness and trepidation. We would be wise to try and learn from our time as youths, before we are jaded by adulthood rather than the other way around.

I asked my mom for permission to go to Chelsea and Bethany's house the following day after school. I never feared my mom overthinking these things too much. She quickly said yes.

I waited out front after sixth period, and then heard voices.

"Come on, Holly," said Chelsea. "My sister will meet us at home. She takes too long saying goodbye to everyone after school. Follow me this way."

I bounced between bodies, chatting and laughing. We wove through the crowd as if at a busy train station and, when we broke free, there was an instant hush. Suddenly we were walking side by side in silence.

"Where's your house?" she asked.

"We live across the street from the school. I just moved in with my mom," I replied. I quickly changed the subject and asked, "Are you and your sister close?"

Chelsea replied, "Yes, we are super close. She's my best friend." I wished I had that with my sister. We were doomed to be separated by our opposing personalities, which was dramatized by our parents in an effort to make us our own people. I'm not sure it was ever in our best interest. I always felt guilty for being me; somehow being outgoing and social came with a curse. My sister herself never intended for this.

We arrived at her home. From the outside it looked semi-manicured. It was a townhouse in a lower income area where the lawns were left to die and there were plenty of electrical poles in sight.

It was dark inside. There was foil on some of the windows and I thought maybe they couldn't afford curtains. Full ashtrays were everywhere. There was a naked mannequin in the living room draped by what looked like Mardi Gras beads, and clothes in stacks were scattered throughout the small, unkempt space. I thought maybe someone worked in the clothing business. A cat leapt wildly from one stained sofa to another. Moments later, I recoiled when met with the scent of a dirty litter box.

A minute later, Bethany burst through the front door, "I am so high! I have the munchieeeees!" Her bells jingled as she pirouetted in, entertaining us. Her almond-shaped eyes were tiny red glassy slivers accompanied with a Cheshire cat grin. We followed her a few steps to the kitchen. It was furnished with dated yellow-brown wood cupboards, and there were stains in the tile grout on the counter. My eye always caught dirt since my stepmom had taught me how to clean and be aware of unkempt areas.

Dirty dishes filled the sink, to which Chelsea said, "Oh no, Mom is going to be pissed. Dad didn't do the dishes." Then she turned to me, "Do you want a bowl of cereal?"

"Sure," I replied.

Chelsea placed a chair in front of the fridge in an effort to reach the Cocoa Puffs cereal.

"Oh no," said Chelsea. She continued, "Mom left Dad a surprise..."

"Great..." Bethany sarcastically said, "Now they will be fighting all night long." She left the kitchen and headed to the bathroom.

"What surprise?" I asked.

"You don't wanna know," said Chelsea.

"Two lines of energy," Bethany shouted while going to pee with the door open.

I climbed on top of the chair to look on top of the fridge and saw two lines, one beside the other, of white-pinkish powder. "What is that?" I asked.

Chelsea said, "Powdered energy."

Oh no, I thought. *That's the stuff that makes my brother so mean.* I swore to myself many times I would never ever touch that stuff, though something within me shifted viewpoints, knowing parents did meth.

Chelsea and Bethany glorified the effects of smoking bowls. I admitted my own affinity for it too. We agreed one day we would all smoke together. That day came sooner than I had expected. The following weekend, we were stoned.

Even though there was a clear lack of boundaries at my mom's house, I was pleased to be able to say goodbye to my nebulizer breathing machine. Carrying it to school when I had severe flare-ups was a real downer. I suffered from severe allergies, and now that I wasn't living with Susan's cats, I didn't need it anymore. My mom swore the breathing solution was a drug and she put me in swim class to strengthen my lungs. My lungs did strengthen, but soon after, Mary Jane became my inhaler.

Bethany said, "Weed naturally opens your lungs."

Bethany invited me to join her in her morning ritual. We would meet to smoke a bowl at 6:45 a.m. It eased the anxiety of going to school by putting a foggy mask over everything I felt. I was constantly waiting for the other shoe to drop, and I didn't know when it would happen. The marijuana masked my concern with not grasping my education. The day before I asked the teacher for help and instantly regretted it. Being cross-examined publicly deterred me from asking any more questions. I couldn't figure out why my classmates understood lessons and I didn't.

I fell further and further behind, and soon high school became unimportant; honor roll, or even straight C's, were a lofty achievement I had no hope of reaching, so I didn't bother. The carelessness from being high meant no more worrying about getting good grades, but in the same way it scattered my attention, so I couldn't concentrate if I wanted to. My eyes would slowly scan the room and I'd realize time was moving slower than it should be. I constantly yearned to be lost in a haze, yet at the same time I felt further exposed because I couldn't function normally—sober or high. I was at a loss of control. Sometimes the weed made me feel sick, or I'd fall asleep in class, but I couldn't say no anymore; I was chasing that first carefree time I got high.

I found it ironic how Bethany and Chelsea's parents could tell us not to do something they themselves were doing. They openly allowed marijuana. Susan and my dad may have offered to let me experiment at home, but it was a desperate cry to keep me safe, and never would they have smoked it themselves. This impressed upon me there was some type of ethical boundary.

My boundaries became blurred. I smoked myself into oblivion. For me, weed was the gateway drug. The carelessness was addictive. I lost my gauge and limits. I lost sight of my dream to sing. I was as distant to that aspiration as my father's conviction was. I withdrew further from reality and from my role model, Tina. As the distance grew, it hurt less and less. Hushing my father and stepmother's voices of disapproval became easier; my bad grades left no impact.

Heather mentioned life had become easier since I had left. And as for her and Susan's untouchably close relationship, well, the higher I got, the less that hurt, too. I watched from the outside now, fully numb.

CHAPTER TWELVE
A FADED DOLLAR TO A LOST WORLD

I stole Mom's ATM card and withdrew from her bank account. I needed the money to become numb. All of a sudden, I started having lots of secrets, and the secrets took hold of me, and they took hold of my decisions.

I was losing my grip. I was at Lisa's house the day it slipped completely from my grasp. Lisa's dad, whom she lived with, would ritually get high every night. Knowing this, we would scrounge around his room to find his leftover roaches. If we looked hard enough, we got lucky, and it didn't take much to feel the effects.

Lisa had a crush on James, a boy who had started smoking meth. He came over to join us. He said meth was no big deal, that, "It's great because we can stay up all night talking."

Lisa's dad would come home late from the bar and, in his relaxed state, he allowed sleepovers. Lisa was friends with Vivien, James' sister, and oftentimes I would meet with her at Lisa's house and we all smoked pot together. The four of us were thick as thieves on that unforgettable night; Lisa, James, Vivian, and me. Bethany wasn't able to make it; she was with her boyfriend that night.

We girls had nicknames. Lisa was Fire to match her fire engine-red mane, Vivien was Pubes to match her extra curly hair, and they both agreed to name me "Lady," mainly because I always crossed my legs, chewed with my mouth closed, and tried to speak intelligently, as my stepmom had taught me.

We agreed upon the date of our big night. James left to bike to the dealer's house. In the meantime, we smoked one of Lisa's dad's joints, giggling about how Lisa could do foreign accents when she was high. We played with hair and makeup and made funny faces with Lisa's sunglasses collection. We listened to Bob Marley and Sublime, a local band out of Long Beach. James arrived back with a tiny bag. It contained pinkish rocks. He emptied the rocks onto a school notebook and asked for one of our school IDs. He wasted no time. I watched him— we all did, quietly, intently—as he crunched the pink, pebble-sized rocks into a soft powder, and he then urgently asked for a dollar bill to roll in the shape of a straw. My heart felt like it was pounding into the next room. When he handed me the bill and said, "Your turn," the thumping dropped into my stomach.

Lisa turned to me and, like any good friend, said, "You don't have to do this." She grabbed the dollar bill from my hand, but I somehow didn't believe her.

"Are you going to do it?" I asked.

Both Lisa and Vivien simultaneously answered, "Yes."

Vivien added that if I didn't want to I should go home, because they had been planning this night.

I was fighting two minds. I didn't want to be left out. My mind went straight to school and imagined how they would have inside jokes and bonding from this night, and I would know nothing about it. It felt unbearable. I couldn't go back to being an outsider. The force behind wanting to belong is powerful. It can take you either straight to success or straight to your destruction.

"No, no, no. I'll stay. I'll go after you," I said.

I watched both Lisa and Vivien jolt and grab at their faces in shock and pain. Their faces were twisted up in a wince.

Lisa passed me the faded, rolled dollar bill and giggled, "The pain is already gone and I'm like, whoa! This feeling is fucking amazing."

Vivien joined in, smiled, and said, "Oh my God, whoa. What do we do now? We need a project!" she said, looking elated.

They stared at each other's eyes, watching pupils dilate. Vivien grabbed Lisa's art pen and notebook and delved instantly into her own creative world.

I took the dollar bill. I had my school ID, which I used to take only a quarter of what everyone else took. I made a joke out of it and said bashfully, "I'm just leaving more for you guys, because I will have to go home soon anyway."

Radiohead was playing in the background, and I deliberately waited a few moments for the chorus of "Creep" to snort my line. It had to be the moment within music for me. I imagined myself as the angel that the singer was referencing as I jumped deep into the den of peer pressure. In a sense we all were the lost angels in a lost world.

As my body absorbed the chemicals, my eyes seemed to instantly grow wider; I could feel my skin stretching. I felt an urge to draw but my movement impulse was paralyzed. To merely think was matched with blackness. I was a carcass, absent of a mind, and all I could do was sit, suspended. I felt wide open and like absolutely anything was possible. It was like liquid courage—a persona that I snorted that covered up my own, which I saw as broken. I never made it home that night; not because I was running away, but because I couldn't let my mom see me like the zombie I had become.

A few days passed without much sleep, and the world was gray. I felt exhausted, yet the chemical wouldn't allow my brain to shut off. My stomach knotted in hunger pangs, but my dry throat closed with the thought of food. I was unable to chew. Natural healing responses from my body shut down and were replaced with a wired, nervous energy. My thoughts raced and I was unable to stop them; sleepless and without food, I became like the walking dead. All I had were beverages to keep me from total collapse. This went on for days and started a pattern; there were many times I didn't make it home, I couldn't face my mom in that state, or my old, heavy reality any longer.

Teachers called, wondering why I wasn't showing up to class. Voicemails piled up onto our home answering machine. I stopped taking Joshua's calls because I didn't care anymore. I started to think my parents might have been discussing my aggressive rebellion. I never really knew because the thought of my mom and dad properly talking never seemed to be a rational option for either of them.

Due to my absences, and falling far behind my peers, my mother thought homeschooling would be a better option. She disenrolled me from school and I was placed in a homeschooling program. I attended a local office once a week to turn in and collect my schoolwork. My backpack weighed my shoulders down, as did the work, which I never understood. My mom trusted and expected me to handle the work and I simply felt relieved that I didn't have to sit through six-hour school days. My homeschool teachers were aware that my grades were never above a D-, but every Monday there was a blame game as to who was at fault—me or the teachers who never set aside one-on-one time. Empty promises were made that I could never fulfill. I couldn't do work I didn't understand, even though I earnestly wanted to, but eventually I felt careless about it. Every week it was a letdown, which further drove me to not show up. I was now more concerned with perfectly drawn black eyeliner and well-moussed hair.

I would visit my father on occasion, caught in a tug-of-war between my parents. I felt like a tolerated guest in his home. I had been homeschooling for a month now back at my mom's house.

He and Susan were full of fear for me. I had morphed into an uncontrollable, moody druggy. My runaway escapades, lost virginity, suicide letter, forbidden sleepovers, theft of what little money my mother had—all of this was compounded by worried teachers and lies upon lies from my own cover-ups. My rebellion utterly bewildered them.

One weekend, while at my dad's house, slumped on the couch, I could tell he was stewing on another speech.

"Dad and Susan, I'll be in my room studying if you need me," Heather said.

"Of course you will," I sarcastically replied.

Dad launched into his speech. "Holly, you have a problem; you have to know this. Your mom isn't doing the right thing. We've told her many times how worried we are. We knew she wouldn't be able to parent properly. Look at how you're turning out."

I stared at the ground. *Here it comes again. I'm damaged goods.* It was always a speculation as to when all my problems had started, exactly—at my dad's or at my mom's? Both parents had reflected on this.

"We know you are doing drugs," he said.

"She's not really listening to you, honey; you can see it in her face," Susan said.

"How do you know?" I snapped.

"Don't talk back to her, Holly," my father warned. Susan appeared to gloat when he chose her over me. "You're very good at what you do, Holly," Dad continued. "You don't get caught."

"What do you mean?"

"It's a compliment; you are very clever, like your mom." I knew it wasn't actually a compliment. When my father called my mother clever, he meant manipulative and sneaky. Dad openly discussed my mother's negative traits, and it hurt when he did. I wondered if I was enough like my mom that he would refer to me, and dislike me, in the same way, too.

I gave him a glare of teenage disdain, enhanced by my black-lined eyes.

"You know how to get your way and get away with it," he said.

My stepmom chimed in, "Holly, what your father is trying to say is that we are afraid we are going to find you dead in an alley. We've tried to help you and you don't want that; you don't listen to anyone. Holly doesn't like rules, so we think we need to find someone's rules you will listen to."

"You have a problem, and you don't seem to care," Dad said. "There are no boundaries that you follow, no matter whether you are here or at your mom's, and she's letting you get away with illegal drug-taking. I can't let you kill yourself. We've tried everything to help you, and you can't keep doing this—Holly doing what Holly wants."

My stare was held to the wooden floorboards. I was caving in, but no one would ever know.

Susan turned to Dad. "There's that place around the corner; maybe we could look at that."

"What place?" I asked.

"It's like living at a dorm with a bunch of other girls; it could be fun. We won't tell you what to do and your mom won't tell you what to do. Someone else can tell you what to do."

"You mean that weird place your friend's daughter went to? The one for retarded kids? I'm not going there!"

Susan said, "If you were to get caught, this would be easier because you would have consequences for your actions; but Holly, you're good; you're *really* good."

She turned to my dad to say, "Honey, she needs control." And then she looked back to me. "You've given us no other option, Holly, than to get some control over you. You don't want to abide by our rules in this house; you don't want to abide by whatever rules your mom has over there. We don't know what you need, but there seems to be no rules when it comes to *Holly*."

I just continued to stare at the ground. Apparently, Dad thought I wasn't taking him seriously because of it.

"Don't you see yourself? What are you doing with your life? You're going to end up like those loser kids. Come on, Holly, don't bullshit yourself. Tell me while looking me in the eye that you don't have a problem; be honest with yourself."

"I have a problem. Can I go now?"

He shook his head. "How do you do that?"

"What?"

"Respond like this. How are you so fucking selfish?"

"I don't know." I looked back towards the ground.

"Get outta here, I'm done with you. I wash my hands of you. You are so fucked up in your thinking. You can go back to your mom's and fuck yourself up some more, if that's what you want. Go live with her and your crazy brothers."

Dad kept shaking his head. He looked at me in disbelief, let his gaze drift, and then glanced back at me once more before walking away.

"Honey, don't work yourself up," Susan called after him. She waved her hand up at me to go. I walked to the adjacent room to see what my sister was doing.

I asked her if she had heard what they said. "I don't know, I'm doing my homework," she muttered.

I left her room and went to mine. As I was walking, I overheard Susan talking to my dad.

"I know that judge," she was whispering. "I am going to talk to him about what we can do and what our options are. He's coming tomorrow for a haircut."

The next day, Heather and I went to work with Susan. She

had a chair at her own salon inside my dad's clothing store. A man arrived for his appointment and I knew he was the judge. Susan asked if we could go into my dad's office and shut the door.

"I know she's talking about me to him," I said to Heather. Through the narrow window, I watched my stepmother and her client speak. She looked directly at me and then whispered in his ear.

I nervously mumbled to myself, "What is she telling him?"

I left the office and walked to the bathroom, and instantly their conversation stopped. I felt on display, and my stomach was churning.

"Come over here, Holly," said Susan, "He wants to talk to you."

He looked in my eyes and said, "She's not lost; she still has a spark in her eye."

What?

"The kids I deal with have no spark left," he explained.

Despite his reassuring tone, I felt destroyed. I knew she had told him how screwed up I was. I knew she was seeking advice for her lost troubled child. That afternoon, Susan took us back to the house, and asked for me to stay in the car. As Heather was getting out, she reminded her to feed the cats.

"I know what to do," Heather said. They shared a type of smile that I hadn't seen directed towards me in years.

This moment cemented a concept in my head that I could only put words to as an adult. Whichever aspect of someone you bring to light and focus on is that which will grow; the grass will grow where you water it. This is in no way relinquishing my own responsibility, but it sheds a beam of light on an unacknowledged dark shadow: we continuously pigeonhole those around us, often without even realizing it.

"Holly," said Susan. "We are going to go and have a look at

this place around the corner. I've already called them and they know we are coming," she said.

I stayed quiet. Maybe going somewhere else was the right option for me. None of us seemed to have the answers.

"See, look how close this is," she said just a few minutes later. "It's just down the street."

"Oh, wow! Yeah, I will be so close," I replied with genuine enthusiasm. I had hope something new would help, although, I simultaneously felt confused and angry that I was considered unsolvable when my family had a part to play.

I was misunderstood. I remembered back when she would lovingly look at me and say things like, "Oh, Holly, wait there while I mix some color; I just saw where we need to highlight your hair with gold in the front." Now I received scowls like she was protecting my father and sister from me.

We drove past a black, wrought-iron gate, which opened for us after we called in from a security monitor. The grounds looked clean; the grass was lush, and the landscaping was well manicured. The building reminded me of an upscale dental practice. It looked rather new, and welcoming. We parked and Susan complimented anything positive that she could see.

We were greeted by a nice-looking lady with short, shiny red hair who introduced herself as Emily. She was tall, with freckles sprinkled across her pale skin, and green eyes that glowed like emeralds.

We walked inside and looked around. I saw a living area and a hallway with lots of rooms, co-ed style. It smelled slightly sterile with wafts of freshly vacuumed floors. We walked to a circular room that joined the hallways, and further down were all the therapists' offices. We got a tour of the classrooms and the nurse's station. Across the grassy quad was where the younger kids lived, she explained.

I asked, "What kind of kids?"

"Kids that are readjusting to a home setting or are up for adoption," she answered.

Susan was very impressed. I felt like a ghost in my own life, as if I was watching everything unfold from the outside. My control weakened as I slipped beneath the surface of the water, flailing in the depths of a churning undertow.

Susan asked for her card, and said, "I will be in touch."

We got back into the car and she asked me, "Could you see yourself living there?"

"I guess so." What would have really happened had I said no? Did it really matter?

She replied, "Don't worry, kiddo, we will work it all out. See, we knew it wasn't for retarded girls."

Later that night more whispers echoed through the hallway between my dad and Susan. I heard my dad's voice raise, saying, "Why should I have to pay for her fucking mistakes as she ruins her own life? Oh yeah, and you think her mother is going to pay for half that rehab? Come on, Susan, get real."

I wondered if I should go, and where I would go. *Mom is probably mad that I'm still here*, I thought. My weekend visit had extended beyond what was expected. *But will she stay mad after I come back?*

I fell asleep heavy-hearted, the kind of heavy that now, as an adult, I would compare to someone being interrogated in a public court hearing. Although I felt such deep pressure, I woke up every morning as an actress in my own life, as if my worries were nonexistent. I found myself in search of ways to run from them as I would cheerfully greet whomever I passed in the house.

The following day, I said good morning to my dad, but he shunned me in stoic, cold silence. He did this when he was really angry at my sister or me. He wouldn't speak to us for three days, sometimes. Everyone got ready for the day quietly and departed. I was left with no specific instruction, and I remained alone at Dad's house the entire day while Heather went to school and both Susan and Dad went to work. All the voices of my worried parents filled my mind, the decisions being made on behalf of me took over my own voice, and I started to convince myself that maybe rehab wasn't so bad after all. Maybe it was the best way out for me. Homeschooling at Mom's gave me too much time on my hands; plus, I was with my brothers at home during the day, who were getting high and sleeping with my high school girlfriends.

I heard Heather come home, so I left my room. In the kitchen, the pantry, fridge, and freezer had organized shelves for each of us. I went to the freezer and saw a frozen Snickers bar. I had just gotten my period; my mouth salivated as the thought of chocolate swirled in my mind. Heather saw me and said, "That's Dad's. We're not supposed to eat it."

I thought, *What's the big deal? It's just a candy bar.* "I'm going to anyway," I replied.

"Yeah, but it's not on our shelf," she said. After having lived at Mom's without these pedantic restrictions, I had come to realize how ridiculous they actually were. If it was food, it was offered to anyone at Mom's. To me, it was another way Susan and Dad enforced unneeded control in their environment and I resented it.

I didn't think twice as I grabbed it, defrosted it in the microwave, and ate it. My sister watched me like I was a courageous warrior, and I kind of liked that.

I saw my father's car pull up to the house and into the garage. When he came inside, he unlooped his perfectly knotted tie. He told me, "I have a plan to get you the help you need." Relief and appreciation washed over me; I could hardly believe he was speaking to me again. Usually it was a two- to three-day affair of silent punishment. Late in the evening, I heard Dad walk out the front door. I peeked through the custom-made wooden blinds, wondering where he was going. It wasn't typical for him to leave at night. I snuck to the window and watched him talk to what looked like one of his employees, and the man passed him something small. I questioned why his employee was wearing a puffy jacket, hat, and sunglasses on a summer night. *Couldn't they have talked at work tomorrow?*

The next morning, Susan asked me to come into her bathroom, her tone heavy. I thought *Oh my God, I'm in for another lecture.* My sister left the bathroom just before I walked in. I was pretty sure I knew what they had been talking about.

Susan said, "Come in" with a concerned tone. She left the door open, which she hadn't done with my sister.

She looked me in the eye and asked me very seriously, "Holly, did you take your father's candy bar from the shelf that isn't yours to touch?"

The word "No" exited my mouth without consideration.

"Holly, I am going to ask you one more time," she spoke extra slowly, "Did you take the candy bar from your father's shelf, when you knew it wasn't yours to take, and was in fact against the rules?"

I knew if I admitted it, I was in trouble, and if I denied it, I was in trouble, too. I decided to take my chances, opt for a way out, and I again said, "No."

She pointed her curling wand at my face. "You are unbelievable, Holly; how you can look me right in my eye and lie? Lie so easily? I know you took the candy bar, and I also saw the crumbs in the microwave. You fucking forgot to wipe those up."

I knew I was caught, but for some reason I hung onto my position. "What crumbs?" I said, with a look of disbelief.

"Holly, you're going to lie to me looking me right in the eye, right into my eye... Heather," she called out into the room. "Did

Holly take the candy bar?"

I knew I was screwed.

"Yes," said Heather, appearing in the doorway. "I was there," she added.

"See Holly, I already knew," said Susan.

Realizing this was plotted, derision flooded my tone. "Why did you even ask me, then?"

"To see if you would be honest. But you looked me in the eye and lied to me instead," she replied.

To me, that chocolate bar represented more than just a forbidden snack. It was a form of excessive control. I thought by going ahead and eating it, it would show them that it wasn't important enough to control.

"Well, I'm so sick of you testing me. What do you want me to look at when I lie to you?" I paused and pointed, "Your ear?"

She lunged at me with her curling brush. I ran into my room and she ran after me. I knew my stepmom was raging with hormones from menopause. I also knew she was overwhelmed with me, that she had no idea what to do with her other stepdaughter. We grappled, both falling to the floor, me on my back with my legs spinning like a bicycle. She was flailing her arms, attempting to hit me in the head with the curling brush. I placed both my feet on her chest and kicked back like a kangaroo. I felt sorry the moment I did it, as I realized how lightweight she was.

As Susan staggered back, I screamed, "You are not my mother! Get off of me!" And I meant it.

She said, "Good! You're right! Get out of here, go to her!" Her chest was heaving as she tried to catch her breath. "I wash my hands of you, Holly. I want you out of this house."

She then said that before she left for work, she would tell my father what had happened.

As her words poured salt into the open wounds, I decided

to escape.

I called my brother Caleb to pick me up and told him what had happened on the drive home. When we arrived, he advised me, "Go upstairs and do your homework or something so that you're not in trouble when Mom gets home."

I didn't wait for the opportunity. I went straight to Lisa's house.

I was desperate to be as high as a kite in the wide-open blue sky of numbness. I craved a single moment of freedom from the rush of thoughts impeding my brain like a herd of galloping horses.

My mother called Lisa's house phone to speak with me. I mustered up the courage to take the call. I knew she was already fuming at my extended stay at my dad's house.

"Get your fucking ass home, Holly. I never gave you permission to go to Lisa's, and I want you back here in ten minutes."

I was a no-show. There was no safe spot, except at Lisa's, high. Ten minutes turned into overnight, one night turned into another. Messages were left on Lisa's voicemail. Even though I knew I was in serious trouble, my days meshed into one another, and somehow every hour that passed made it even more impossible to consider going home.

There was pounding at the door.

Lisa scrambled up and looked out the peephole. "Fuck, Holly, it's your mom."

"I'll hide in the shower; don't tell her I'm here."

"Fuck, Holly!" said Lisa.

Hidden behind the curtain, I could hear Lisa answer the door. "Hi–"

My mom interrupted her. "Where's Holly, Lisa?"

Lisa said, "I don't know, she's not here."

"Then you won't have a problem with me coming and having

a look?" my mom replied.

"No," said Lisa, although it sounded like Mom didn't wait for her answer. I heard her come into the bathroom and pass by the shower door. I made sure to stay perfectly still in case the shower curtain moved.

Then, I listened to her footsteps stomp back to the door.

"If you hear from her, you call right away," my mom demanded. "You hear me, Lisa?"

"Of course I will," Lisa responded.

It was a gift to have had such a loyal friend. Until this day, she has always remained just as kind.

Later, I got texts from Bethany and Chelsea separately, both saying that my mom was on the hunt for me.

I got even higher than the night before and passed out at Lisa's.

In the morning, my dad and stepmom called. They said they were not angry at all and needed to speak to me. They explained they were on their way to Long Beach to take me out for breakfast. I was surprised due to the way things were left, and because they never came this way. I felt appreciative of the softness in their tones, and considered that they were going to apologize. They said I wasn't in any trouble and that they wanted to talk to me about the rehab. At this point, I needed it. I was fucked no matter which path I chose. It was as obvious as a dangerously red jellyfish in light blue waters.

CHAPTER THIRTEEN
THE SILENCED PLEA

"Get in the car."

My dad had a bristling way of talking to me when he was acting as an authority figure. The tone had dramatically changed from what I had heard over the phone. Was I now in trouble?

I was surprised to see that Susan was in the back seat. Once I got in beside her, she joked, "Honey, lock the doors in case she tries to escape; she's a cute criminal and someone will snatch her up."

Susan made a space between her and I as she moved herself towards the window, not losing grip of my hand. She bumped her head against the glass. This was unlike her.

My dad looked at me through the rearview mirror.

"Holly, you are to follow my rules," my father commanded. "I am going to stop you from hurting yourself."

My thoughts spun wildly. Susan stroked my hand to comfort me and said, "Holly, Holly, listen to me, you need to know I am on your side. And we spoke to the judge about Boarders, and he said in order for you to go to that nice place—you still like that place?" I paused, waiting to hear more but I realized she was doing the same.

"I guess so. I don't know, it seemed okay." I felt like I had to like this place, now that so much buildup and effort was put in.

"Okay, I know you liked it, I saw your face when we were there... You know you need to go there, right? I mean, Holly, if you don't you will wind up dead or at best, a drug addict for the rest of your life. We must get you the help you need. Daddy and I are doing just that." She continued on, and I listened. I felt like I was being lectured again.

"Okay, okay, Holly, this sounds more dramatic than what it really is, but you have to trust us. Okay?"

She waited for me to respond.

"Um...okay."

"What the judge said was that you have to get arrested. It is only for paperwork and we have already made sure you will go to Boarders. Okay?" Her green eyes searched mine.

I stayed quiet, grappling with what was being said to me.

My dad interrupted Susan, taking over the conversation, as if he was the final word in the matter. Susan always gave him that power.

At the red light, he turned around to directly address me. "Holly, I am taking over on making decisions for you, because you need to know you are not making the right ones for yourself. Listen to me; this is what we are going to do. I'm not allowing you to have the choice in this because I know, as your father, that this is the only way to save your life."

I nodded. It was so serious, so heavy. And there I was again, the girl who couldn't make a decision for herself, and definitely not about something she didn't fully understand. I was a passenger, not even close to being in charge of my own future. His words—his perspective—got to me and became my reality.

Hearing my father tell me my life was in danger and that he wanted to save me pierced me. I began to believe him.

He parked directly in front of a building with mirrored doors. There was no obvious signage, but I trusted that whatever we were making this stop for was short, and that we'd be off to our breakfast soon. He turned around from the front seat and asked for my wallet.

He said, "I am your father and your best friend right now."

I saw his eyes tear up and his Adam's apple move with a large gulp. "I am going to put this inside your wallet." He pulled out a bag of drugs, but it didn't look like the drugs I took. "Holly, you have to trust me. I am not steering you wrong."

"What is this?" I asked.

"It's cocaine."

I didn't do coke; it was expensive and the high was short, which is why it was called "the rich man's drug."

"This is your ticket to Boarders and we know that is where you need to be."

I truly and wholly believed that he was attempting to do the right thing. My father was a good man and I loved him dearly. I wanted his approval so badly it hurt, and in that moment, agreeing with him brought me closer to it.

He said, "This is the way to your rehab; you cannot trust yourself to make healthy choices. You need to come with me, Holly. Let's handle this problem you have once and for all. I love you; you are my little girl. I can't let you do this to yourself. You can't go back to your mom's, Holly."

"She's strong, honey, she will go with you, I know it in my gut," Susan said, turning to me. "Go on, Holly. If anyone is strong enough to do something like this, it would be you." She slowly and calmly spoke as though I was a three-year-old. "Your father will come on this side of the car and get you, and you just walk in. Trust him, Holly, he has your best interest at heart."

Dad came around, opened the car door, and wrapped his hand around my upper arm to escort me. I heard Susan warn him, "Don't let her run, honey."

With the car door still open, Susan continued, "*I'll be right here when you get out. Trust your father, Holly. He knows what he is doing. I am so proud of you. Look how courageous you are.*" It sounded like she was underwater.

He ushered me into the building, through sliding glass

doors. Before we approached the woman behind the plexiglass, he asked her, "Do these doors lock?"

"Yes, sir, they do," she replied.

Even if I thought about running, I couldn't anymore.

"This is the girl that I called you about. I am the man who called you," my father said matter-of-factly, not looking at me, even though I was staring at him. *He called ahead to warn her?*

"Yes, I remember," she replied, taking a quick look at me.

As she moved out from around the plexiglass, I could see she was a police officer, and I knew then things were bad. Really bad.

My father turned to me. "Don't you try to run," he said through clenched teeth. His eyes were hard, his face stoic.

I listened to him. I was scared of him. I was scared, period. It was paralyzing.

I watched as he handed her my wallet. She began rummaging through it. "Is this the wallet that it's in?"

"Yes," Dad replied. They held it up, inspecting it in front of me. My chest felt like it was collapsing in on itself; my heart raced so hard I felt it in my ears. She pulled out a tiny bag of white powder.

"This is the cocaine I found in her wallet," he said.

I was outside of my body, watching.

"So, this is yours, young lady?" she said to me.

My dad chimed in, "Tell her, Holly. Tell her it's yours; tell her the truth that I found that in your wallet."

Subserviently, I muttered, "It's mine."

He looked at me with a measure of approval in his eyes. "Good, Holly."

The officer's face bore an expression I couldn't quite describe. There was no sympathy in her eyes, but there wasn't hate, either. Numbed indifference would be the closest match.

"I'm gonna come around, and we can talk." She approached

me and began to read me my rights, and she put handcuffs on my wrists—just like they do in the movies. That was the first time I'd ever even seen real police handcuffs, and there she was, putting them on my teenage wrists.

"Hmm, you have really tiny wrists," she noted as the icy steel manacles closed over my limbs and my life. "You need to come back here," she instructed, leading me by the cuffs. She searched for a single key while I waited in silence. She unlocked a door and led me away. As I craned my neck around, I saw my father had vanished.

The officer pointed at an adjacent room. "Go in there and she will take your prints, g' yon," she said, not articulating herself. She watched me as I walked in.

There stood a chubby woman with dark-rimmed glasses that reflected computer light. She stared at a bulky screen, and from what I could see, as she never lifted her head to look directly at me, she had brown hair tied in a neat bun and dark eyes. She held her hand out, gesturing for my index finger.

Without looking at my face, she pressed my index finger into ink, slightly rolling it. "I am taking your fingerprints."

I knew why, because I had done a middle school science project about how every person has a unique set of fingerprints. What I didn't know was where my fingerprints were going, because I wasn't a criminal like I had studied about in middle school.

"Where are my fingerprints going?" I asked.

She replied sharply, "Your booking."

"Booking what?"

"Whatever you are being booked for."

I shook my head in denial. "Where are my fingerprints going?" I was in complete dismay, and I felt like every word I spoke was perceived as argumentative, regardless of how I said it.

"They go on your file. Don't worry, the ink washes off," she replied monotonously.

"What file?" I inquired, feeling wrong for even asking.

She slowed to a stop for just a moment, frustrated. "Listen here, until you go to court, there ain't nothin' to say. For right now, this is what we need to do. This is procedure."

The legal jargon reminded me of being back at school, compiling old anxiety with brand-new fear. I was drowning. My racing heart had slowed to a normal rhythm, but shock was setting in.

The officer from before strolled in.

"Is this your wallet?" she asked.

"Yes," I answered.

"Is this your purse that the wallet was in?"

"Yes," I repeated, but with a caveat. "It's my purse, but it's not my–"

"Your what?" she said.

I thought about what my dad had said and how screwed I was now. I replied, "Never mind."

She moved on. "Your fingerprints are taken. I'm going to let you go now, and you'll have a court day for sentencing."

I knew parents wanted what was best for their children—at least that's what we're told. For mine, that came in the form of having me arrested.

On the forty-five minute drive back to Beverly Wood, my dad said, "I am proud of you for taking this step." He explained that he and Susan had gone through a lot to find out what was needed to help me, and that he also put himself at risk to help me. But in that moment, I was deaf to his sacrifice.

Once inside the house, with my stepmother right by his

side, my father turned to me, his expression grave. "Listen, Holly. I've done you a favor here. I've asked them to allow you to come home with us, on the promise that we would get you to court for your court date. The judge can then assign you to the rehab facility near our house—which is what we've requested. That's what we'd like as your parents; it's what you need. And then you can at least be in our neighborhood and we can see you all the time."

I looked at my dad, shaking a little. My mind was all twisted up. I was grateful for having been allowed to go home. I felt appreciative. I felt that there must have been something really, terribly wrong with me. Maybe he was doing the right thing.

The policewoman had explained to me and my father that if I missed a court day, there would be a warrant out for my arrest, and it would go on my record as well. It was at the cost of my freedom that I not miss the date. I wasn't fully sure I understood what the word "warrant" meant, but I knew it was bad.

"You can never share how this went down with anyone," he said, his eyes fearful and loving. "I'm doing this for your own good, trust me."

From that point forward, the notion that I was powerless oppressed me. Dad and Susan were the pinnacle of hypocrisy to me, and yet I was supposed to live with these people and believe that I was back in a good home. I knew they loved me, but their love had driven me to be handcuffed and booked for drugs that I didn't even do. My voice was to be unheard; my beliefs and opinions were futile.

In thirty days' time, I was due in court.

For that entire month, I was terrified, in shock. In the first few days, waves of fight-or-flight sensations shocked my system day and night, even if I was just lying on my bed and staring at my ceiling. I went to bed every night making different types of deals with God as if it would mysteriously help relieve me.

"Holly, they will put a warrant out for your arrest and take you into custody." My dad would say this every day without fail, trying to embed in my mind that if I ran away, it was all over. But I couldn't grasp that concept, not as a teenager. To me, my life was already over. How much worse could it get?

The days became repetitive, lifeless. I was weighed down by my past failures in that house and how unhappy I had become as a child, and my misery affected everyone. Flashbacks flooded my mind like a broken dam. Lectures, bedtime talks, color-coordinated underwear drawer, tidying closets, stacking the dishwasher properly, facing my angelic sister. *You are unfixable, unresolvable*, they whispered.

One afternoon, Dad and Susan arrived home early from work. This was out of character.

"Holly, we have an errand to run—get in the car before we hit too much traffic," he said.

"Why, Dad? Where are we going?" I shouted from my room.

"We want to show you something," he said.

Susan and I piled in the car.

"I brought this for you, sweetheart." She handed me a Twinkie. I was reminded of when she would prepare our school lunches, making sure we had all five food groups, and also a sweet treat.

Dad drove for quite a while. Following directions from a printed-out sheet of paper, he exited the freeway. It led us to a rundown neighborhood. A dreary-looking building loomed in the distance.

"That must be it," Dad said.

He pulled into a nearby parking garage, and drove to the

rooftop.

"Okie dokie, we are here," he said, his cheerful mood at odds with the dull, concrete structure. We stepped out. I followed him and Susan over to the edge. They both stood on either side of me as we took in the view.

The large building had many windows that I couldn't see inside, plus a large grassy area and rows of concrete pathways, all exposed and empty.

"Holly, do you see that?" Susan asked.

I nodded.

"That is the juvenile hall."

I observed the building, noticing the spiraling metal that had razor spikes protruding out from it.

"What is that?" I asked, pointing to it.

"That, Holly, is barbwire," Susan replied.

"What is it for?"

"I guess it's so they don't escape."

"Because they will get cut?"

"Well, yes!" she replied.

I was horrified at the imagery of someone bleeding out after attempting to escape.

"We brought you here because we wanted to show you where you could end up," Dad said. "Holly, if you keep doing what you're doing, then this is where you're headed. We have done our best to make sure the judge will send you to Boarders, but you can't make one more mistake."

We've done our best? You mean it's not guaranteed?

I quietly inspected the building, wondering what went on inside. I never once seriously considered that I was a candidate for this kind of place. Even with my arrest, it seemed impossible to me I would end up here. Yet I felt the heavy weight of my uncertain future.

My dad and Susan wanted to know all the things I had

done while I lived with my mom. They wanted details. They wanted to know what my mother did, what my brothers did. I felt waves of overwhelming guilt. Whenever I was interrogated about my time at my mom's, I felt as though I was betraying her by answering them. Instability and doubt clouded my opinions of both parents and morphed into feeling unloved.

Part of their conditions for living with them was that I work, so my father called a friend and got me a job as a cashier at Lenny's Deli in Los Angeles. My grandfather ate there every Sunday night, and my dad got lunch there most days so he knew the owner and the waitresses. They knew my face too.

Each day that I worked, I tried to pull the veil over my own reality. I would consciously remind myself to act normal. Meanwhile, I knew in the back of my mind that I was facing court and the judge, and possibly jail. I was already in a lower echelon of society at that point. I had a record even though I didn't fully understand what a record did. I was a bottom feeder. No one could be sure that I wouldn't go to jail. It was the great gamble. There was no direct answer to anything in my life. To add to that, being back at my dad's house had me under their watchful, suspicious eyes. My stepmother's demeanor remained that of a person making mental notes on how she wanted to change me, and yet that she also saw me as unfixable. Heather avoided me as best she could. I frightened her more than anything.

Wave after wave crashed onto me as if my body had been bolted to the sand where the earth and the ocean meet.

I contacted a friend in Long Beach and scored a vice to escape from the silent hell I was living in. Never before had I chased being numbed like I was chasing it in that moment. It masked the pressure and the pain I felt. Crouched over the bathroom toilet at the deli, I crushed up a line and inhaled deeply, making sure to flush the toilet at the same time to

Leanna Bright

drown out my snorting. Exiting the bathroom stall, I presumed I might run into a customer. Instead, I found myself with my coworker. Her suspicious stare didn't escape me.

Making mistakes adding up people's checks didn't feel nearly as embarrassing this way, nor did the thought of my arrest interrupt any bits of carelessness I tried to chase; I could soar above, a bird riding the breeze, everything else inconsequential below. The knots in my neck melted and vanished.

The night before my shift, compulsive flashes of all the scenarios of how I continuously made mistakes played on repeat. As a cashier, I was expected to add and subtract the sums effortlessly, but I never understood math. The meth made the anxiety easier to not think about, yet the aftermath was a further descent into the spinning typhoon, lost at sea; that was my life.

Sometimes, sober or high, I would make up totals. Customers would get their receipt and every single person would tell me I was giving them the wrong change.

"Excuse me, young lady, this isn't right," they would say, trading exasperated looks with the person in line behind them. Their withering expressions said, *Do you not know how to add?*

"I am so sorry," I would say.

I would uncomfortably wait for the customer to tell me the correct total so that I didn't make the same mistake twice. This was its own, entirely unique level of shame. My heart would pound feverishly and I could feel my face flush all the way into my ears and down my neck. It was the same, ruthless embarrassment from my school days when I didn't have the faintest idea what was being taught in class.

I threw off the deli's accounting so much that they called my father to explain to him how terrible I was at my job. All that did was make me more reluctant to come in, not more inclined to do a better job.

All of my anxiety, my terror, piled up. I didn't have any space in my head for any more humiliation or fear, not with the hearing date looming. Flashes of barbed-wire fences crept into my mind. The image of a bloodied body scrambling to climb over the edge filled my brain. My own impending doom literally haunted me. So, one day I just didn't show up to work; I ran away from home.

It was about a week before the court date.

I went to Lisa's house but I was turned down; she couldn't keep me there any longer. Her father wouldn't allow it. I meandered down dark alleyways, seeking out people even Lisa didn't know. Before too long, I found the familiar front door of a dealer's house.

Instability filled the air there. Everyone coming in and out seemed to exist in a constant state of unease, or they hardly seemed to be there at all. The walls and floors were stale. There was graffiti sprayed on the living room wall, prompting me to wonder, *Won't the person renting this place get in trouble with the landlord for the writing on the walls?* I later realized how ridiculous wondering about that was, surrounded by anarchists and drug lords.

Every time I laid my head down, I would use my massive hair as a barrier between my face and the surface on which I slept, as there was a layer of grit from years of unclean people and unclean habits. But I was there now, and the place felt so absolutely abhorrent that I ended up furthering my descent into drugs in order to deaden myself to the environment, too. I had to numb myself to the horrors it cost to numb myself in the first place. The cycle ran deep, and I was fully entrenched.

On the day of court, I was trying to forget that I was going to be in a courtroom soon—in five hours—in three hours. Time was suspended and I felt like every move I made was in slow motion. The light from the watchtower had gone out and I needed air, I needed help...real, authentic help.

I had one bar of charge left on the cell phone that Caleb had given my sister on a home visit, and which I had taken. I called my mom. She picked up and upon hearing her voice, a knot filled the space in my throat, and my voice crackled through it. I was feeling both relief and impending doom.

"Mom, I have to come home. I have to tell you something."

Once through her front door, I started explaining as best as I could what all had transpired. "Dad put some drugs into my wallet and got me arrested, and I had to say they were my drugs even though I've never done or seen cocaine before."

I saw her eyes change from worry and dismay to rage.

"What do you mean? He had you arrested and you admitted it was yours?"

I recounted the entire incident to her and explained how I now had a felony charge on my record.

The reality of what I was telling her sunk into both of our minds almost simultaneously. Upon retelling everything, I realized truths I hadn't been able to clearly see as they were happening to me. He hadn't gone out and gotten any drug like marijuana. He had actually gone out and gotten a narcotic, which would ensure a felony charge.

My mom wasn't just pissed. She was Southern pissed. It all came roaring out of her.

After some time sitting with my words, she said, "There is nothing I can do now to help you. That's been taken from me." She asked me when I was due in court.

"In two hours."

"Oh my God, Holly!" She jerked herself out of the shock of my story. "Look at what you're wearing—look at your face! You look scary. Have you been up all night?"

"Yeah, I have, but I need to go to the court, because if I don't go, I'm going to get some type of warrant for me, searching for me. It's a horrible mess," I explained, trying my best to contain my own panic-stricken mind.

"Just–get—get in the shower! Now! You don't have much time," she demanded, rushing over to me and ushering me along to clean myself up. She wanted me to look as presentable as possible. She was aware that how I looked would have an effect on how I was perceived by a judge. I had been living like a squatter for the last several days, on drugs and without any self-care. I had lost so much weight that the waistband of my jeans had to be rolled a few times in order to remain on my hips. My pupils were severely dilated, and we had no time to dry my full mass of hair before the court appearance.

"Here, put this on for luck." Mom flashed me a turquoise necklace. She stood behind me and I could hear her heavy breathing as she clasped the chain. It had been her mother's necklace. I knew she was as nervous as I was, which made me more nervous since my mom could face almost anything with a straight face.

Mom was able to get me there on time and as clean as possible. My court-appointed attorney met me upon entering and began giving me instructions on how to act, what to say, and what to do.

He asked my mom if he could speak with me privately. He posed this as a question but it really wasn't.

She pointed over to where my dad and Susan were standing and said knowingly to my lawyer, "So they got here before us? And I bet they spoke to you already too, right?" That also wasn't really a question.

She excused herself, but before going she let me know that she was "going to be right there" and pointed to a wooden bench. She sat and then scooted closer to the lawyer and me to try and overhear what we were talking about.

"If the judge asks you how you plead," said the lawyer, "I

suggest that you plead guilty. At least this way, you will be sentenced to rehab. Then you can go and get the help you need. If you plead not guilty then you might just go to jail, and I can't really tell you what will happen."

"But they weren't my drugs," I said, squinting my eyes at him in search of some sort of logic. I wanted him to *want* to fight for me—for the truth.

He stopped for a moment and changed his demeanor to that of someone who was attempting to level with me.

"Listen, Holly, do you admit that you have a drug problem?"

"Yes," I confessed. "But I didn't do the specific thing that I'm here for." Even with the drugs I had done, I couldn't seem to bring myself to say the word "cocaine."

He shook his head. "I suggest, regardless, you go to rehab. You should plead guilty so you can go to that rehab around the corner from your dad's house. Wouldn't that be nice?"

"I guess so," I said, remembering my father's voice declaring that this was the only way to save my life.

He continued, "You don't want to live with your dad, right?"

How did he know that?

"No, I don't."

"And you don't want to go to your mom's, right?"

I suddenly thought about how nice the freedom at Mom's was, and I said, "I don't know—"

He interrupted me and said, "In the state you are in right now, are you high?"

"I was, but not anymore I don't think."

"You need rehab, and that will be provided for you, and your parents want that for you. This is what's best for you, Holly; I think we all can agree on that."

He looked away from me and toward the courtroom. "Trust me, it will be better than jail."

Even though I had two houses, I was a kid without a home. I needed a friend—in my parents, and in my siblings. I wanted warm arms thrown around me and to hear the words, "No matter what, no matter what you do, I love you and support you." I wanted to be reminded of my best qualities when I forgot...and boy did I forget. It wouldn't have mattered which parent said it—I just needed to hear it. I needed to trust it. I still had the programmed comparison-reflex to my silent, obedient twin.

The judge did not react to my plea. I think I had expected more from him. He looked over some papers and said, "You can go to the Boarders Center; it's on our list of rehab facilities."

I looked at him expectantly, hoping that he—the judge, the end-all-be-all, all-knowing master of the courtroom—would have something more insightful to say before dismissing me.

"I hope you get the help you need," he said, looking at me. He shifted his eyes to the bailiff. "She'll now be taken into custody." He unceremoniously thumped his gavel.

Everything became a question. I didn't know for certain yet where I would end up, but it was explained to me by the bailiffs that I had to remain in juvie until a place became available at rehab, at the Boarders Center.

A police officer came directly over to me. "Please, ma'am, put your hands directly behind your back."

My eyes watered and an unrelenting fountain of tears began to drip down my face. I realized there was no turning back. The officers tried to clamp the cuffs on tightly and it hurt. They were a size too big. I stared at my wrists as he struggled. He shouted for smaller cuffs.

The officer had instructed my family to remove all my jewelry, and my sister shook as she tried to take my necklace off. It had been a symbol of protection, which failed me, an attempt from my mother to save her daughter from drowning again.

I looked at my father's face but he avoided my eyes, looking down at the floor and shaking his head in disappointment the same way he did the day he washed his hands of me; disappointed that I hadn't shown up to court clean and sober, perhaps disappointed that it hadn't gone down the way he had planned. I was so scared. I don't know what he expected me to do with all the fear he had instilled in me, forcing me to change by threat.

My sister gave up trying to remove the necklace and my mom, in her take-charge manner, did it herself. The whole ordeal was all a big jumble, them trying to prepare me and the officers waiting expectantly, and amid all of it I was just trying to say goodbye to my family, not knowing when I would see them again.

As I was being taken away, I looked over towards my sister and mom to have one final moment of connection, even if it was just a glance. To my surprise, my mother raced towards the doors of the courtroom and shoved them open dramatically, walking away. Years later, when I asked her why she hadn't waited to say goodbye, she told me she was scared she'd attack my father and injure him severely if she didn't get out of there immediately.

The officer cupped my upper arm tightly. He led me into a steel elevator where several other girls stood shackled by the ankles. I looked at the cold metal; it represented what was to come...a cold, gray, lifeless, and stale existence. I tried to walk in cadence so we didn't trip. I cried in the elevator, the back of my head pressed against the icy wall, internally repeating *fuck, fuck, fuck*. I had slipped below the surface, outcasted from the world, and floated into the abyss, losing my last breath. I didn't feel I had the right to ask where we were going but I did anyway. There were only blank stares from the other girls, silence from the officer. This small avoidance pierced me profoundly, as it was now clear what I had become. Unheard.

After lining us up and chaining us by our ankles, securing us, we were shuffled onto a prison bus. No one talked. I stared out the window at the passing rooftops—at my last bits of freedom, not knowing if someone told my mom where I was going.

CHAPTER FOURTEEN
WISHING ON A STAR

"I don't belong here" was the one and only clear thought that reverberated through my mind, and oftentimes out of my mouth, once I arrived at juvie.

I felt lost. The concrete, dark gray floors stretched on endlessly. I found myself a blank canvas amongst a sea of poor tattoos. I was surrounded by orange-hued blonde hair. I knew from Susan that meant it was a bad dye job. The crooked teeth and tiny dots tattooed near the eye or thumb didn't strip the beauty of the girls around me, but rather let me know how uncared for my peers had been.

My passage into juvie wasn't anything like adapting to a new school—which was the only other passage I had experienced prior to this. I clearly remember the guard whose task it was to handle my admission to juvie. I remember her boyish haircut and the way her long acrylic fingernails looked, but I imagine she remembers nothing of me. I was just a number to her. She was spitting out questions at me, rushed and impersonal. When she was finished, she dismissed me cursorily, and I had to move on to the next officer in processing.

I retreated into myself, feeling all the guards' weighty stares. I was not viewed as a normal girl; none of us were. We were all questioned like liars and thieves, and seen only as a number.

"No one told you how you walk around here?" an officer barked at me.

"No," I responded, trying to sound polite.

"You walk around here looking at the ground. You don't look up. Your hands should be in a diamond shape behind your back!" he growled, seemingly enthusiastic to have the opportunity to explain this rule to me. "Is that a piercing on the side of your nose?"

I winced, "No." It was a scab from an old pimple and I didn't want to talk about it.

He continued, "You can look down at the ground now until your name is called."

"Oh my God, this is barbaric," I muttered out loud. No one reacted.

This withdrawn, minimizing, self-deprecating manner of carrying myself affected my demeanor for years to come. Even later in life, as an adult, I carried myself in this servile manner. I had boyfriends, long after my time in juvie, who would encourage me to stand up straight, to look up.

The sorrowful nature of my inner narrative fit too well into this new scene. The temporarily suppressed memory of my mother in court popped back into my mind. As I was being doomed to juvie, she thrust her hands up in shock and disbelief, saying, "There is nothing I can do for you now!" I suspected that Susan wanted me out of the picture so that she could have a peaceful life with my sister. I ruminated on the memory of my mother's arms flailing in the air and my father shaking his head in disappointment day in and day out. The click of the handcuffs was similar to keys jingling, taunting me with possible reprieve from my cell.

Gang initiation was one of the most common causes for girls to be in juvenile hall. I heard one girl had run up to a woman and stabbed her. Another had shot someone in a phone booth.

Most girls displayed loyalty to their gangs with tattoos on their faces and bodies. Gangs scared me. I couldn't fathom holding a knife to scare a stranger, or shooting a gun to take a life. It wasn't even in me to consider joining a gang.

Most of the girls I came across in juvenile hall had "a cousin" who had died by violence, and often, someone close to them was a gang member. A story I heard over and over again from the girls was that for initiation, you had to participate in a fight. You would get to a park at 2:00 a.m., and you'd get beaten by your own crew. The street term was "getting jumped in." It was spoken about with pride. "Yeah, I got jumped in when I was twelve. Got my ribs broken, but I fucked two of 'em up so bad they were twitching and shitting on the floor."

Their lives were often full of brutality and cruelty. Some of the girls had mothers on the street, and some had been raped by a family member; maybe even their own grandfathers.

But this didn't excuse their own ruthlessness. I wondered why I belonged locked up with young women who stabbed people. Hurting someone to that degree felt far from anything I was capable of doing. True, I had fought my sister, but I'd never left scars or wished to end her life. Yet I was treated as one and the same with the stabbers, the thieves, and the ones who had acted with a pure evil that I had not yet imagined was possible. In darkness, I'd cry myself to sleep with the frustration of two voices barraging me, one telling me why I deserved to be there, and another screaming about the injustice of it all.

The feeling of unfairness was like a shadow by my side. It had always been there but now it was prominently showing itself. I wasn't actually guilty of the crime for which I had been convicted. I truly didn't belong there. It was all a farce. And the most painful thing that I had to confront was that I had agreed to it. What a mindfuck.

My first couple of days were a fog. I woke up to a living nightmare each morning.

After my initial withdrawals, the minutes before bedtime

were a dreaded, painful time of silence. My thoughts would spiral out of control, and I began to cry myself to sleep each night. The pain of continuously swallowing the knot in my throat would finally release in those evening hours—but I had to do this silently. You didn't want your cellmate to hear you crying. There was an implication in juvie that you were not allowed to be vulnerable. Juvie was a type of calloused environment that I hadn't known before. You kept soft feelings suppressed. However, my spark of connection with the other girls never wavered. I didn't seem to be able to stop reaching for a bond; I just controlled it when I had to.

As I sat at the steel meal table, I thought, *This is the fastest I've ever chewed.* At every sixty-second interval, a guard would snarl a reminder that we had a minute less. Those five minutes to nourish our bodies were the most exciting minutes of the day, but I lost track of the days—was it the weekend?

Everything in juvie is routine: the time you wake up, the time you eat, the time you go to the bathroom, the time you get to watch TV—or a movie maybe once a week—the time of the study period they might allow, exercise time, shower time... and if you are not obedient, time outside your cell is at the minimum.

The only delicacy we were allowed at mealtime was small packets of jam. It became my favorite thing, unflavored instant oatmeal and jam. I started to play a game with myself, guessing the flavor of the jam I would get each day. I didn't like the milk; I gave away my carton of milk to other girls and made friends that way.

One girl was seven months pregnant when she landed in juvie. I didn't know what she could've possibly done to end up there while pregnant, but my heart went out to her, being sent to teen prison while carrying a life inside her. One day she wanted more milk, and I had given mine to another girl. An argument developed between the two of them over the milk. The pregnant girl grabbed a loose chair and started to beat the other girl ferociously over the head with it. A siren went off in the meal hall, and screaming commands were thrown at us— *Lie down, now! Facedown on the ground!* I reluctantly pressed my cheek to the cold, dusty, concrete floor and tried to see what was happening around me. My eyes darted around wildly, trying to trace where all the sounds were coming from. There was a hissing sound and then, all of a sudden, I couldn't breathe. I couldn't get enough air into my lungs. I thought I was having a severe allergic reaction. My nose, my eyes, my mouth, all of my orifices were singed with an invisible inferno. I was choking with each gasp of air that I took. Then I realized we all were. They had pepper-sprayed us—even the pregnant girl.

Blinded by blazing tears, I saw nothing as we were snatched up and herded like cattle to the showers, where they turned the water on us all, fully clothed. My mouth opened for air and I tasted milk. I could feel it dripping all over me. I recoiled; I detested the beverage. The guards screamed at me to drink. Drowning in milk, could this get any worse? I loathed milk as I loathed where I was at that moment. How I came into possession of the milk is still beyond me; I suppose the guards sprayed us with it.

Oftentimes, the guards would resort to pepper-spraying an entire room when it wasn't necessary. This lack of justice should have been against an ethical and moral code, yet that weapon was used irresponsibly. Did I do anything to deserve to be pepper-sprayed? Did I matter?

The cells had cracks in the walls, and these allowed me to talk with the girls next door. Or to quietly sing to them. Somehow all the Chola girls knew the oldies from K-EARTH 101. I had memorized these songs to please Dad. He liked them and would look at me adoringly in the car when I proudly recited all the words to his favorite songs. The girl in the cell right next to me loved the song "Wishing on a Star." I would sing it to her softly. It was a small delight in an otherwise desolate tomb.

Each day I lived in hopes that my review would occur and I would be sent to rehab. I was excited at the prospect of a change. And getting to go to court was exciting for another reason: despite being shackled hand and foot, I would be handed a paper bag containing a sandwich and a granola bar with chocolate chips. It was as if there was magic in those sack lunches, like reaching into my Christmas stocking.

The smallest things became so exciting. My mother was permitted to bring shampoo and conditioner for me. When she brought me a new scent, I was appreciative and delighted. If she told me a story—even the smallest bit of gossip—I would meditate on it for days. I imagined their lives. And I imagined my own, similar to the way Susan had taught me before bed. The distortion of time and energy in that place gave me incalculable time to think. I absorbed every bit of information around me, whether it be the text, brilliant colors, and glossy texture of a new magazine article, or the sterile, sanitized smell of our coarse, fresh-washed sheets.

The walls of our cells were mint green; the old, chipped paint was covered with graffiti from pencils or paperclip etchings. Anywhere there was a surface, there was graffiti. The bed was a thin mat, just an inch thick, and it was laid upon a concrete bed frame. The sides of the bed frame were made from iron and bolted to the floor. The floor was cold, grey concrete, a similar shade to that of steel. There wasn't a desk, and if you got a toilet, you were lucky. There were windows, but they were painted black so that you couldn't see out except for small chips. I would look to the sky; I wanted to be *in* the sky. The chipped window paint provided a doorway back to being six years old at the beach, staring up at the heavens, sun-kissed and carefree. I could almost taste the salt and hear the roar of ocean waves while feeling Mother Earth cradling me, nurturing me.

The room was designed to be stale, with fluorescent lighting above. My light flickered. No one cared enough to fix it. To me, the flicker was symbolic of us inmates; no one cared to fix us either. There was a tiny window on the cell door and between the two pieces of glass was crisscrossed wire, like a small, thin chain-link fence. We would try and look through our rectangular windows when we heard that someone new was coming, or if we heard guards' keys. The anticipation of jangling keys gave us a Pavlovian response, in hope that something new would occur. Nothing about your old life could be retained; personalities were shaped by the monotony. You just gave in to prison life because you weren't given a choice anymore.

There were stories of things I didn't even know people could do. I learned more about what it meant to be a criminal in juvie.

I was offended by the tattoos on the girls, and I never got used to seeing them—especially around their eyes and on their necks. I would wonder if it hurt to get the tattoos, but you don't ask that sort of question in juvie. Even if you did ask, no girl would ever admit that it actually hurt.

The attitudes of the girls in there were impossible. One sarcastic comment lead to another in response; almost every conversation included some type of put-down. It was a cycle of badass-fakery. No one would lift their façade of hardened tough-girl long enough to allow anyone to get to know them. No one would attempt a real conversation. Everything said was either a threat or meaningless scorn—there was no in-between.

And then there were the younger girls, who were just a little bit softer, who hadn't done as much. I felt I could relate to them a little bit more, because they were not as jaded. The demographics of juvie were a sad reflection of societal issues. There were mainly black and Latina girls in there with me. It seemed to me that there was a big problem with where they lived—lack of opportunities for their parents, and lack of education for themselves. It was like they were doomed to the system eventually. I was definitely the only white Jewish girl there. As a matter of fact, the entire time I was in juvenile hall and boot camp, there wasn't another Jewish girl that I ever met.

CHAPTER FIFTEEN
THE HIGHER POWER

It was Sunday, and so it was time to go to church. It didn't matter if we were religious or not. You could either go to the Protestant church service or the Catholic church service. For someone like me, who was being brought up by my dad and stepmom to understand Judaism, and my mom, who believed in the science of mind, nothing offered by juvie connected me to my roots. I can imagine that so many people there reached out to a higher power when they were at their lowest. Even where to seek answers was chosen for them.

Maybe that has changed since I was there. I hope so.

I didn't—and still don't—see how *forcing* a foreign religion onto inmates serves rehabilitation. Or how punishment does anything but create further descent into degradation.

In church, we'd be lined up in two rows, heads down, hands in a diamond shape behind our back. This was the moment that we were finally able to see boys. The exhilaration. The girls would look around to see if they might find one of their "gangster-homies" who just got put in. Just for a glimpse. The girls would stare, nod their heads, throw up gang signs, trying to communicate.

The one redeeming quality of church on Sunday was music. A defining moment for me was the first time I got up and sang a song in the church. I offered to sing because the girls in adjoining cells encouraged me. Those bedtime lullabies I sang through the cracked walls inspired me to sing something soothing for them all. I chose "One of Us" by Joan Osborne. It was quite a popular song in the '90s, replayed each hour on the radio. Before I went to juvie, I had seen the music video for the song when it came on MTV. Joan Osborne had hair a lot like mine—big and very curly—and that song, in that moment, in that place, had significance. But from the inmates' perspective it was hilarious; the little white girl got up to sing a song. It was my first solo performance in juvenile hall, and in church. The whole room was packed. I wanted to let them know that God was still in all of us—at least that's how I saw it; no matter what, you couldn't challenge my viewpoint.

I pondered the lyrics, "What if God was one of us, just a slob like one of us?" I chose this song knowing we, as a group, may have been seen as slobs, but we were never abandoned by God. I saw God everywhere. I saw God in a passing officer who would smile sometimes, or when someone would share the hair conditioner, or hearing someone utter, "Don't worry, you will get out of here soon," for support. Spirit was, in fact, everywhere, even in us slobs. At least that was still what I saw. I still saw beauty.

"What's this bitch gonna sing?" I heard in a loud whisper as I walked up to the podium.

I don't know what I expected when I began singing. Even though I knew better, I think I believed there would be some backing music to accompany my voice, and cues provided by an officer—like karaoke music. The usual Holly daydreaming fantasy. But there was none of that, of course; we were in juvenile hall.

As I stood there, my hands went cold, my feet became clammy, and my heart slammed in my chest. I almost decided not to do it. These people looked like they were awaiting their turn to be rewarded in Hell. They looked miserable.

As I began singing, I stared at etched graffiti on the podium in front of me—gang names, gang signs. It briefly occurred to me how industrious the kids in juvie were to be able to artistically carve into a podium with a forbidden, hidden object. The wooden podium was almost as tall as me. I could barely peer over it, and I don't think the crowd could see very much of me. Everyone looked so uninterested in the song. The one I had chosen for all its meaning. I learned something within that hollow moment; I realized that no one cared as much as I thought they would. It didn't matter if I was a good singer or not. The guards had no interest in anyone's talent. In juvenile hall, if you want to get up and sing, you get up and sing. That's all you get. Then you sit down and look at the ground.

I wanted to ignite something. I wanted to share a piece of myself, a part of my hope for all of us. But the energy of the room and guards alike was so low, like they were only bodies, vacant of a soul, and it wouldn't have mattered if I were the Dalai Lama. It was what it was. No divine manifestation, Jesus Christ, Buddha, Apollo, Ra, or Captain Crunch would have fazed them. An array of spiritual scripture wasn't even available anyway. How could I blame them? Could juvenile hall be fertile ground for growth and rehabilitation? From what I had seen there was never a chance for it.

CHAPTER SIXTEEN
PIGEONHOLED

At night, I would stare at the fluorescent-lit ceiling with its sterile lighting and replay moments of time over and over again in my head until I fell asleep. It held me captive, my mind submerged by the wrath and weight of those raging waters. I would justify my own actions and then justify my father's. An array of oddly juxtaposed emotions stretched my heart thin. I knew that even if my father hadn't gotten me arrested, maybe I would have ended up being caught anyway; but the idea that I could have lived a completely free life ate away at me.

If I could have told my younger self something, it would have been to speak up and tell people how scared I was. I would have found a way to express to them that I was dying on the inside—having my fingerprints taken and handcuffs put on my wrists was all a symptom of a much bigger problem with me, one that had begun long before I had tried any drugs. I was the type of child that needed a confidant within my parents. Instead, I was deemed culpable and my opinions seemed valid only if they aligned with theirs.

There was such a sense of loss in being so vulnerable, and in genuinely believing that my father knew what was best for me. I was too young to articulate the thought, "Dad, I trust you, but I don't believe you."

I loved my dad so much that I truly didn't want to perceive him as wrong or make him out to be the bad guy to anyone, even myself. I was willing to take the blame and remain silent, just as he had requested. I saw his point of view; he loved me, and I knew it. I didn't want to blame my father and diminish any belief that he loved me.

My young adult life was one big institution after another, constantly being told what to do, without any opportunity for self-determinism. The only freedom of choice that I had was rebellion. So, that's what I did. I was good at it. But there was a dualism to my rebelling. Besides rebelling against rules and structure, I also rebelled internally against the narrative from the system and even from my dad and stepmom. The narrative that my life was shit and I belonged there in a place like juvie. I knew my future would be clean, lively, and warm, no matter what anybody told me. I felt it as confidently as I could feel my left hand. It defied logic and was impossible for anyone's eyes to see. But I could see it. So fuck yeah, I rebelled. I rebelled against the future that they all thought I would have.

Through the small chips in the black paint of my juvenile hall cell, I would stare out that window for hours. It was much different than when I would daydream in school. I'd see a plane go by, and I'd imagine who I was going away with into my future life, the same way my mother and Susan taught me when I was a little girl. Little did I know then how powerful envisioning my future life would be.

There was a lesson that I had to learn. You can harness power from despair. A lotus flower blossoms and blooms in muddy water.

CHAPTER SEVENTEEN
A MOMENT IN TIME

"I never wanted to stab that girl," one inmate told me. She was thirteen, and her gang had pressured her into attacking an innocent person at a pay phone. Other girls glamorized their gang initiation, but I could see through it. They were fakes; they were good inside. They were like me.

And then there were girls like Rodriguez, who really were better off the street than on. Earlier that morning I woke to Jones' bed made and no Jones. She was gone and I never saw her again. After lunch, I walked into my cell and another girl was there. Even though she had mocha-colored skin, she still looked pale. I was sure she was still high, based on the way her large black eyes darted all over the room and then back to me. She carried an air of unpredictability; I felt jeopardized in her presence. Then the door closed and it locked.

It was the first time I had seen so many tattoos on a girl's neck and under her eyes. It was a double-digit number surrounded by circular shapes. I wondered what it meant; it looked like a gang symbol.

As I moved to sit on my bed, she asked, "What you here for?"

I quickly made up a crime to get her to believe I was badass enough to be in juvie. I thought this would help my image. "GTA."

"Yeah, I done one of those." She leapt at me, as if to sniff me like an animal does. With primal movements, she turned to me, her hand on my thigh... She started to move in towards my center in between my legs.

My heart thumped, my mind racing with what I should do next, but I was frozen. She seemed to slither all over me and I realized her eyes were still open, looking at mine.

"You can't never touch me the way my papi chulo touches me," she whispered. "You wouldn't know what the fuck he does to me, oh my god. He makes me quiver here..." and her hand met my core. I gasped, she quickly pulled away with no awareness of my response, and she began to laugh.

She then leapt to the middle of the room, pacing back and forth, reciting to herself as if I was invisible, "If he's fucking cheating on me, I will fucking kill him... He better not be fucking some other bitch, fuck, I'll fucking kill her too, oh my god, I know it... I know he's fucking some other girl... Fuck, why I have to get locked up?"

I listened and tried not to stare at her.

She then turned to me and asked, "What the fuck you wanna do?" Her hands opened towards her own vaginal area, showcasing it with her head cocked to the side, as if gesturing to the act of a sexual invitation.

"I dunno." I cautiously shrugged.

If I make her feel like I want her, does this help me?

We heard the guard shout, "Ladies, step outside your cell, hands behind your back. Face the wall." Rodriguez and I both stepped outside.

"Cohen, step beside her." I saw Rodriguez glare at me through a black strand of hair that had fallen in front of her face. It was the look of a predator. My blood turned cold.

I walked when I was given permission to, got my tray of food, sat down, and said nothing. I always checked every bite of spaghetti for maggots; I hoped this was a joke; it was commonly laughed about between the other girls, but nevertheless, I checked along with everyone else, suspiciously stabbing the sauce and sifting through the meat.

I couldn't speak to anyone or focus on anything—other than the possibility of getting strangled by this beast I was going to sleep next to. She seemed to know some of the inmates here, nodding to some girls at the table while she lazily smacked her food, as if she had all the time in the world. She ate as if she was being served her dinner at home. Comfortably. Maybe it was gang members from her own gang that she knew.

It was shower time after dinner. I knew it was safer, because we would be surrounded by other girls and officers. The joke to not drop the soap was still passed around from time to time, like an oldie but a goodie. The shower experience turned from shameful self-consciousness to something extraordinary. I started to see all of the different shapes and colors and forms of bodies as art; a sea of flesh-colored sculptures, perfectly designed as an expression of unique and beautiful art. To see beauty under such duress, even in such ugly places, became a game. This little game cultivated a precious gift that I held close; it serves me until this day.

After the showers, the girls would stroll back to their cells. I could hear the sluggish pace from the slippers slapping the floor lazily as they walked. I could smell the scent of freshly cleaned bodies in the air. The girls were relaxed, fed, cleaned, and it was leisure time in the cell until lights out. I was now a clean body trapped in a dusty cage with a tormented soul. I looked over at Rodriguez's bed in fear of my retribution.

She was brushing her long, dark hair repetitiously. I blinked, and then she was in front of me. Her fist came at me, flying straight beside my head. I could hear the wind of it passing my ears, and my chest felt a sharp stab from the fear. She laughed.

"Don't take much to scare you." She found this amusing, to watch me flinch like a scared child that had been beaten by a parent. "You think I would really hit you in here? Fuck no, I need to get out to see my papi." She let out a huge sigh and jumped beneath her sheets happily, as if mimicking sleeping at a new hotel. She tucked herself in. "Do you have any magazines?"

"No," I replied.

"Damn girl, you fucking boring," she said. I didn't know what to say.

"Lights out, ladies." The guard's voice echoed from the hallway. She closed one thick steel door at a time. I was on high alert as the melody of her keys came up to our cell and then clanged as they smacked against the door. She bolted us in. I vowed to not fall asleep. I knew Rodriguez would be wide-awake since she was probably still high on meth.

To my utter bewilderment, she passed out. I sighed with a vague sense of relief but I stayed awake. Until I didn't.

I felt something on my face and tried to wipe it away. It moved over me, and the scent of floral shampoo entered my airways. I peeled my eyes open to focus, and there were two black holes staring into mine. Rodriguez grabbed my hands whilst sitting on top of my pelvis. I jerked my head to one side. I innately felt her authority over my body.

I thoughtlessly blurted, "What are you doing?"

She sarcastically replied, "What the fuck it look like I'm doing?" I rapidly started to think of how to get out; I tried to not challenge her. Still I searched for a solution, my mind riffling through ideas, like a high-speed camera *snap-snap-snap-snapping* through ideas.

"We will get caught," I said.

She replied, "Nah, the guard just checked, they come past every fifteen minutes. "

"How do you know?" I asked.

"I timed it, bitch, now shut the fuck up, you're wasting time." There was nowhere to go. I was meat. That was it. I felt the weight of her meshy body on me. The dough-like composition of her form. One of her hands pushed my two wrists over my head, pressing them roughly into the coarse sheets, letting me know that's where they'd stay.

She said, "Don't move." The other hand was already inside my core plowing into me while she said, "You're tiny, you like two fingers?"

Will I get torn inside if she has nails? I thought. I tried to remember if I had seen her nails and how long they might be.

I whispered, "We will get caught, please stop."

"Maybe you like a whole fist, maybe I should fist fuck you."

I looked up at the low-lit fluorescent light above us; one bulb was out. I felt liquid drip from my eyes down into my ears. I was quiet; I did not cry out loud. Normally I could hold back tears, but they kept flowing out of my eyes. In this moment of extreme pain, my soul had exited my body, but snapped back in when, for a split moment, I thought I had to go to the bathroom. I saw her head turn to the side as if she heard a noise. She pulled out of me, leaped into her bed, leaving the covers off. She laid like a starfish as if she had been sleeping deeply for hours.

She whispered, "I fucking dare you."

The flashlight peeked into the small window and I closed my eyes. The guard was doing the routine window check with the flashlight. I heard the tap of it against the small square window; it skimmed over us before the probation officer walked away. I was waiting for Rodriguez to move but she fell asleep and started to snore. How could she sleep so deeply like this? After what she had done? I blamed myself. I should have done more to stop it. It was the second time I allowed my body to be taken over by someone else.

Eventually, I must have fallen asleep again, because I woke up in the morning. I quickly looked around to see if everything was okay around me. Rodriguez was sleeping. I'd heard if I was sick, I could complain and the guards would have to help me.

Our doors would open before breakfast. Girls would walk to and from the bathroom, brushing their teeth and getting ready for the day. I walked to the nearest guard and dramatically claimed, "I am really sick."

"Whatchu mean sick?" she said in a condemning tone.

"I am really sick in my stomach, and my chest feels like I can't breathe. I think I need to go to the infirmary." It was the same excuse I used to escape school as a child. Had I been better educated, would I have been here in the first place?

"If you that sick, then you don't need your breakfast, do you?" She thought I would reverse my claim like a child would.

"No," I said. "I can't eat; I'll throw up." I put my hands over my stomach and chest.

"Wait in your cell, Cohen, until someone can take you; we're all busy this morning." I dragged myself back to my cell. Rodriguez was awake in the room, waiting for breakfast to be called. Her leg bounced up and down as if she had a twitch in her foot. She was biting her nails and staring into blank space.

"Fuck, I'm hungry," she said. I realized her nails were short, which set me a fraction more at ease. "Fuck, I need to eat," she said again. She looked up at me. I could feel her stare as I sat on my bed.

A staff member called, "Ladies, be ready to step outside your cells with hands behind your backs, and face the wall. I will call your room, one by one, then you will step out about-face and wait." Our room was called, and I stayed on the bed.

"What you doing?" she asked.

"I am staying here; I'm not hungry."

"Pussy," she said as she stepped out.

The staff walked me to the infirmary. I sat down in a chair, waiting.

"Cohen, come in," a lady said, gesturing for me to enter the room.

I was glad it was a lady doctor. A woman about 5'6 stood before me. It was like there was a haze around her. She had blonde hair and calming green eyes.

She warmly said, "Tell me what's happening."

I said, "I feel really sick"

"In what way?" she replied. I looked down at the ground. I really wanted to tell someone what had happened. The knot in my throat grew, and there was pressure behind my eyes. She looked so soft. I was desperate to seek solace from softness, a trusted adult. But I had to hold back. If I ratted, I honestly didn't know what would happen to me.

"I just feel pressure on my chest."

"Okay," she said. "Let me listen." She gestured with her stethoscope. I couldn't hold them in any longer, the tears came out. I was lightly gasping for air in between the shuddering sighs of breath as the droplets ran down my face. Maybe I was triggered by the care she was giving me.

"I dunno, my stomach, and I can't breathe, please, I'm just sick, okay? Please believe me, I am really, really sick." When I heard my own desperation, it made me sadder.

She knelt down to meet me at eye level. "Okay," she said, "I believe you." She wrapped her arms around me. For a moment, I wondered if this was legal...then I collapsed, the way I needed to. She let me.

"Has someone hurt you?"

I stayed silent, embarrassed as I wiped snot from my nose. "No, I'm just really sick. I think I need to stay here."

She intuitively asked me if I wanted to stay for the entire night. I desperately replied, "Yes."

She didn't push any further. I stayed there, safe, under bed watch for the night. For all those hours, the memories of being violated flooded my mind. I didn't get the good night's rest that I thought I would.

The next morning, the doctor walked in, smiling.

"Shhhh," she said, and brought over a white box. It was filled with donuts. "Pick which one you want before the others get to them." For a short moment I was a little girl; I picked the pink donut with rainbow sprinkles. A circle of sugar, a slice of heaven. I ate it slowly and savored every small nibble to make it last longer.

The nurse said she couldn't hold me there for another night without a valid reason, so I had to go back. Before leaving, she said, "You need to tell someone if you are being hurt."

I nodded without saying a word. I thanked her. She looked at me and smiled, and before I left the room, she said, "Cohen?"

I turned around.

"This is just a short moment in time for you."

It felt like I was *seen*. "Okay," I replied.

A few years later, I saw Rodriguez on *America's Most Wanted*.

I was delivered back to Rodriguez for a period of twenty-four awful hours. I listened to her romanticize past murder, swapping stories with others. I tried to prove to her I was an ally by laughing at her jokes or asking her questions about her life, but it was useless. She was too far-gone. She would stare blankly at me as if I didn't have the right to laugh. If I agreed with what she said about someone, she would reply, "What the fuck do you know?" The truth is, I didn't have the demon in me to fight her demon. Another truth is that I'm proud of that.

That next night after showers, a guard ordered, "Cohen, pack up your stuff, you're moving." *Did the nurse help me out?* I wondered.

This was the guard who sat at the desk with a list at the end of the hallway. The list had who was housed in which cell.

"Did you tell them anything?" Rodriguez interrogated. "I bet you fucking did. I should kill you now," she repeated again and again.

"Please, I didn't say anything. No one knows anything," I pleaded, trying not to look her in the eye.

I was petitioning for my life. The way she was dominating me with her presence, staring me down, ready to fight, told me she was poised to attack. I had my stuff in my hand, my towel, my blankets. But I was still inside the cell, alone with Rodriguez.

She looked at me and she said, "You are fuckin' lying to me, because I saw the list. I saw the list, and I saw your name crossed out!"

What was crazy was that people like her are actually quite intelligent. The most predatory people are oftentimes the most keen. When she said that to me, I started to actually fear for my life. She had done her homework; I had, in her eyes, outed her.

By the grace of God, the guard returned, and she moved me to a new cell.

Juvenile hall was sectioned in three different codes of criminals. There were the criminals that were jailed for misdemeanors, merely passing through, with minor infringements on their records. The second section was for more serious crimes, like car theft, and the third was for those whose crimes had intent to kill.

Rodriguez belonged in Code Red. She belonged with the most dangerous girls in juvie. It was a careless mistake on the staff's behalf to pair someone as vicious as her with someone like me, with a non-aggressive, comparatively minor felony.

My new cellmate was utterly different. I could actually converse with her. Her name was Lopez, and she was fourteen years old. There was some normalcy. I told her I could sing and I knew all the "Oldies" songs from the '50s and '60s.

Lopez had also been caught stabbing someone as part of gang initiation. The gangs so often became one's family. They paid your bills, fed you, put a roof over your head. Many young people were forced into gang life because of poverty. They could no longer visualize a better life for themselves after being beaten down by years, generations, of suppression in one sad way or another.

No matter where I was, I was still just a teenage girl. In my new cell, I had a toilet, and in the silver flush button on the wall, I saw my reflection. Overgrown, bushy eyebrows were the main feature of my face. I heard myself referred to as Jesus a few times; I thought perhaps it was the song I chose, or maybe my middle-parted hair, but now I realized maybe it was my eyebrows. Lopez politely asked if I wanted her to take care of it for me.

Since there were no tweezers in that place, the girls got resourceful. She would manipulate an elastic rubber band between her fingers to create a pincer.

After she had finished my first elastic band tweeze, I eagerly checked myself out in the flusher-button; I was relieved to find that I looked somewhat like myself again.

"Don't get too excited; you just look a little bit less like Jesus," she joked. To me, with her flawless porcelain skin, black hair, and dark, warm eyes, she resembled the Virgin Mary. And there we both were, not exactly the Pietà, but close enough.

My father's first visit to me took a few weeks to happen.

I couldn't tell him what had happened with Rodriguez, in case he spoke to a guard. That would have made things more dangerous for me. But I insinuated to him that I was scared. He looked around and tried to make jokes about how the other girls looked, their eyebrows, their discolored hair, their tattoos.

Is this where you wanted me to be? I thought to myself. I couldn't bring myself to say it out loud.

He said, "Have you had any problems with the other girls?"

"Yes."

He said, "Jews are smart; they don't fight. And you have Jewish blood."

I feared for my safety, and there he was making jokes. He acted like he didn't care or didn't believe me. As if I was someone else's problem now. It filled me with so much sadness; he couldn't even admit to himself that I was in danger in here. I wanted him to say his plan went wrong. I wanted him to feel the fear with me, and I somehow yearned for him to admit it so it could bring us closer.

Dad didn't know that in that place, in prison, if you didn't fight, then your strength and courage were questioned by the other girls. And that you're picked on if you're weak. My father said, "Be smart," but there is no "smart" in juvie.

Later that week, I received a letter from my father, stepmother, and sister. They told me what a wonderful time they were having in Hawaii on a family vacation. I was gutted and angry that they were writing to me about holidaying in Hawaii while I was locked up. The letter sounded like it came from Susan but it was in my father's handwriting. How could they do this? How could they think it was a good idea to gloat about a vacation? I took my aggression with me into the cafeteria at dinnertime.

That evening, the pregnant girl took my milk without permission. I gave her an angry look, and she glared back at me.

The girl on my right saw our interaction, and she felt entitled to take my bread. But I wanted my bread, and I grabbed it back. Then she reached over and took all of my jam packets. So, I grabbed her whole plate and threw it across the room. I was so done with all the stupid looks and threats. I thought, *If I won't have my food, neither will you.*

The girl stood straight up to fight, and so did I. She put her hands against my shoulders and pushed me. The girls started shouting, "Fight, fight, fight!" With a pounding heart, I pushed her back. There was an emotion in me that said this was so against my nature, but fuck it; I was one of them!

Next thing I knew, a siren went off; a head guard came in and shouted, "Get your faces towards the ground, everybody!" Then, I was being pepper-sprayed. My face was on fire; my skin was on fire. They allowed us to feel the full torture of this for several long moments before the routine cleanup began.

And that was my first fight in Los Padrinos Juvenile Hall.

I was told to go back to my room and gather my belongings. I was being transferred to solitary confinement, where I spent the next forty-eight hours without human contact. That time was dark and lonely. The girl in the room next door continued to scream and kick the door. The guards kept warning her she would be put in a jacket. She didn't care. I kept thinking, *Please stop...for yourself and for me.* I wanted to sleep the forty-eight hours away. Food was eaten on the floor in my room. I had a bathroom, so there was no need to go out. I would shower and walk straight back to my cell. The bright light in the dark tunnel of solitary was my imagination, as it led me back to my dreamscape future that I used to mock up as a little girl before bed with Susan. And I visualized the midnight sky with big bright stars, just like my mom said to do: "Reach for the stars, Holly, make them big." They became so big I could touch them. Without the darkness, they would not have shone so brightly.

CHAPTER EIGHTEEN
FLAT CHAMPAGNE

Even in juvie, even with the guards on watch every hour of every day, even with the locks and cells, people found ways.

I was transferred to a room where the inmates shared a common sleeping area filled with bunk beds. There were sixteen girls sharing the open space.

A girl slept next to me. On her wrist, I read SPEEDY. I was intrigued and later asked her if that was her drug of choice: speed.

"No," she spoke in a low voice. "I like crystals. Like my name." Her real name was, in fact, Christina.

Chitchat was inevitable, and eventually our conversations led to what drugs we had done. She asked me what drugs I had used. I told her I had only ever tried one form of meth, called Pink Champagne.

She nodded, seemingly familiar with what I had described. "The stuff I do is completely clear."

"What do you mean?" I replied, intrigued by the difference.

"Yep, my dope is totally clear," she reiterated with pride. "It's Flat Champagne. Do you want to try some?" She looked around to see if anyone was watching and she pulled out a bag. Then she plucked out one tiny crystal that was just as she had described: perfectly clear and quartz-like.

I was both shocked and awed to see this crystal that was so clear and so perfectly cut, like a magnificent sparkling stone. My mind raced with what felt like a million thoughts. I wanted to know why it was so clear, and how she managed to smuggle it into juvie. I also worried about who might see us—I couldn't believe she pulled it out, in juvenile hall, when a guard was five bunk beds to the right. It was quite the brave move on her part. Was she trying to get new customers? Why would she risk doing that in here?

Signaling to get my attention back to her, she asked me, "Do you want to do some?"

In that moment, in that place, with those people, I was damned if I did, and damned if I didn't. After what happened with Rodriguez, I knew if I didn't do it, she would be constantly paranoid that I would tell on her, rat her out—that I had that information over her. If I did do it, it would be my worst nightmare; to be high on methamphetamines in this place. To do a drug like meth in a place where you are confined? I couldn't see it working out well. Meth took away my appetite, and mealtimes were the highlight of the day for me.

Meth made me feel like I needed to move around, smoke a cigarette. I couldn't sit still on it. It was a horrible place to do a drug like that.

Nevertheless, the next day when we were all sitting at desks in a classroom setting, Speedy made it a point to sit next to me. She passed me a note that read, *In the bathroom*. She got up and went to the bathroom.

We had to sign a logbook when we went to the bathroom, even though the bathroom was in plain view of all of the guards. When Speedy returned, she nodded to me that it was my turn to go. I went in, and to my surprise she'd left a line of the drug on the toilet seat for me. I was filled with a sense of heart-pounding shock—it was so careless. Anyone could have gotten to the drug ahead of me. My anxiety went through the roof. I flushed the toilet to drown out the sound of me snorting the drug.

The drug burned my nose differently from anything I had felt before. I instantly felt my eyes open wider, my heart beat faster, and the hairs on my arms stand up. For some time, it numbed my judgment of where I was. But I was also paranoid. *Act normal, Holly. Try and swallow your food, Holly. Don't stare!*

What seemed like twenty minutes later, she rose from her desk and went to the toilet again. I could only imagine how numb she was to the drug. Just as she had done before, she nodded to me to do it again. There was a strange subservient feeling in me. I felt like somehow, we were allies. This second time, however, I flushed it down the toilet. I was just too scared to do more of this Flat Champagne.

It was the strongest drug I'd ever taken. I could feel the difference. I had no appetite for days and days, and I had to hide not eating my food. I physically feared for my safety. All the times I had pushed the limits on the streets, I could have been given anything, yet I was surprised that the one time I feared for myself physically was inside an institution. It was unbelievable.

This went on for a few days. I had trouble sleeping. I had moments of my heart beating too fast and irregularly. I had waves of fear that I would soon have a heart attack, and it worried me endlessly. With all of the time I had to sit and think, having all of those fear-filled thoughts made everything dire. I remember we had a group strip search, and I thought the guards were staring only at me, whispering to one another, noticing my darting eyes and weight loss. Yet, I was in a position where I couldn't say no to Speedy. I couldn't take it anymore. I couldn't handle sitting there feeling like my body was about to break down on me, and all the while having to try and behave normally. My body was starving, which aided my heart palpitations, and I was sure I looked gaunt. That night, I decided I had to get this stuff away from us—from her and from me.

Speedy had brought the drug in by creating a hole in the elastic band of her pants and pushing the bag of meth deep inside. She told me her uncle had given it to her on a visiting day.

My paranoia got the better of me, and in the middle of the night, I got out of bed and walked over to the guard who was at a table, watching over us as we slept. I sat down at her table.

"What do you want, Cohen?"

I signaled I needed to write something down. I wrote on the piece of paper she handed me, *The girl sleeping next to me has a bag of crystal meth. Please don't tell her I told you.*

The officer wrote back, *Where?* and added, *Which side?* I gestured and pointed as an answer.

Where is she keeping it?

I wrote, *In the sole of her shoes.*

Speedy had been very clever. She had peeled out the soles of her shoes, and when she slept, that's where she kept the drugs.

The officer told me to go back to my bed, which I did quietly. After a short while the officer approached Speedy's bed while she slept. The officer immediately searched inside her shoes and took out the bag of drugs. She woke Speedy up. Another officer brought in handcuffs, and they escorted the girl out of the communal sleeping room.

My pent-up stress deflated as soon as she was arrested. I never saw Speedy after that, so I knew something must have happened to her. I spent the next few days wondering whether I was going to get time added to my sentence, but it didn't happen; maybe because I'd fessed up.

CHAPTER NINETEEN
A FAITHFUL REACH

It was so bizarre to have study periods that were so similar, yet so different, to public high school. Sitting at my desk in the unkempt classroom, the walls seemingly trapped me with their fading paint; the fluorescent lighting sucked the energy from my eyes. I didn't know what I should be doing. The teacher handed me a notebook and a textbook.

All of us had different levels of education; some of the girls, no education at all. On initiation at the juvie school, each of the girls received a complete, dissecting interview as to what their level of education was. But it didn't seem to matter; they weren't going to change things up to accommodate any of our learning styles. I oftentimes would stare at those soul-draining fluorescent ceiling lights, and the flicker would follow a beat I created in my mind. Until this day, I recoil under flickering bulbs.

Regardless of anyone's level, juvie students would all get the same book. Girls who didn't know how to read wouldn't even try, and girls who were quite advanced had absolutely no interest in anything that book contained. Instead, they'd throw rubber bands around, shoot spitballs at anyone and everyone, and toss around pencils. No one paid attention. No one understood the lessons, the worksheets, the word problems with seventy-five watermelons. Education did not exist there. I looked around and saw girls carving their names into the desks, scraping their No. 2 pencils down to the eraser nubs just to scrawl a gang symbol or a dick alongside countless other symbols and dicks from girls' past. The room was awash with boredom and anarchy.

"I don't know what this shit is saying. I don't know what the fuck we're supposed to be doing. This is some bullshit," were the words often echoed, and followed up with laughter.

The teacher was more like a babysitter, or, realistically, just a warm body in the room. There was no apparent way to fix it then, and without reform, there's no way to fix it now. The numbers of students in the class depended on how many inmates there were at each time. Classroom rosters varied from fourteen students to thirty-five, even forty at a time.

I'd be sitting in class, and all of a sudden the room would become a house of mirrors.

I saw forty-five of my faces looking back at me. My frozen six-year-old body was sitting next to me. My nine-year-old washed-out face was diagonal from me. My fourteen-year-old eyes were set within each face I saw. And there we all were, a group of young minds filled with a cluster of words we didn't fully seem to understand from the past.

I couldn't ditch anymore; I just had to grit my teeth and sit through it.

Physical education would follow. Each day, the sun would beat down through the material of my thick, V-neck juvie top. It would scratch my skin as my arms flailed up and down in jumping-jack formation. We weren't given any sports bras, which made it all the more uncomfortable, and it made me a bit nervous. The echo of Susan's voice pierced through my thoughts.

"Holly, we bought your very first bra today. I want to explain to you how to further look after your breasts." Susan had a way of pronouncing her t's and s's with exaggeration. It almost made the word "breasts" sound pornographic.

I felt bashful with my newfound female assets; I wanted to hide them.

"Now stand up," Susan instructed. "Take off your shirt and I'm going to show you how to place your breasts in the cup of your bra. You tuck it into the cup. The nipple should be facing up. The strap should be tight to hold them in place. Breasts are made of tissue and fat, so when you do run, you need to wear a different bra so that you don't tear the tissue, so that they do not hang." Susan would refer to Heather's and my bras as "tit slingers." She thought it was hilarious, but Heather and I thought she was weird for saying that at all. Our eyes would meet in a confused teenage glance, silently communicating, *Susan has lost her mind.*

"I'll give you a teenage timeout!" The guard snapped me out of my reverie.

"You bettah jump higher, heffah," a girl muttered.

I had been in juvie long enough by then to know that I couldn't tell her that I was doing them half-assed to protect my breasts.

My new cellmate, standing to my right, quietly mumbled, "Cohen, don't talk back, just do it."

"What's the teenage timeout?" I asked.

"Only forty-five minutes outside your room. That's all they have to give you legally."

One becomes conditioned to their environment. Pavlovian punishment diminished our spirit, made us dogs on leashes and in cages. I wasn't a dangerous criminal—but I acted like one while I was there. The authoritarian control from being a ward of the court made me respond automatically.

We learned how to be worse than we had been when we first arrived. Nothing the juvenile detention system did was in any way conducive to creating better members of society.

In my adulthood, I've checked back on the juvenile system to see if reform has occurred. The last time, I was informed they had a writers' program so that the girls could start writing down their feelings. The problem is: how does a girl who can't write do that? Are they really educating her?

In retrospect, the one thing I gained is compassion for those young girls. I saw how it was, and I know how much better it could have been. I know those girls—still innocent enough for a fresh start—still exist within the system, and as a society, I feel we are responsible for creating a system that helps them do just that; rather than create more damaged, complicated, criminal minds. Those young adults would cycle out and right back in, and there is seemingly nothing in place to help cease the cycle.

It was a Sunday. I looked through the speckled, worried faces of visitors in search of the contrast of pale skin and black hair. And there she was, waving. My mom. She wore mauve lipstick, which was her signature color, and I knew I wouldn't be able to get close enough to her to smell it like I used to. We were only allowed to sit across from one another. I listened to her tell me stories. I soaked in her animation and strength as if to borrow it for a short time while she was with me. I was allowed one short hug before she left.

Staring up at the faithful flickering, fluorescent light, I saw my mom tucking me in bed, whispering in my ear, "Dream big, reach for the stars."

I pulled the rough bed sheet, tucking myself in. Memories of running on the water's edge filled my mind as I closed my eyes. The whitewash of the sea, tickling my toenails, the sun skewing my vision as I turned to witness my twin's sunlit, giggling face. She was such a beautiful child.

CHAPTER TWENTY
SMILING LITTLE NATHAN

When I look back over my life, Boarders was, in comparison with the next stage, a lovely vacation.

Upon my arrival, the guard opened the government van, and I stepped out. I scanned my new home as the handcuffs were removed.

Just down the street, in an upper-middle-class neighborhood, lined with lush green yards and luxury cars in each driveway, my twin existed, living a completely normal teenage life. I wondered what that felt like. Did my friends ask where I went? Were they now Heather's friends? Did they shun the idea of ever being my friend again, now that I was damaged goods? Heather had the rights that had been stripped from me.

Heather was taller than me, with straight hair and high cheekbones. Her thighs were thicker than mine, though she was still a thin girl. Her skin was a paler shade than mine. In the sun, she would burn and I would tan, and her face was freckled with sun kisses that looked like a perfectly symmetrical painting. My sister was quiet, yet you could almost hear her think. There was always judgment behind her dark blue eyes that no one knew about, and dreams that she never spoke of. I believe she was more heard when I was gone, for that I had found some solace. Heather's curiosity was always satisfied within the pages of books like *Little Women*, by words I never understood.

"Holly, time to get up." One of the staff member's voices drifted in from behind the door. I woke up and immediately recognized the smell of burnt cheese and scrambled eggs, and the sound of dishes clanking, showers turning on, and the slow movements of the neighboring girls rising for the day. It was a bit like a dorm. I showered, and I got to choose what I wanted to wear—I was grateful that my mom had packed all my clothes and toiletries. As I picked out each article of clothing from the duffel bag, I could smell the stench of stale cigarette smoke. After my shower, I concentrated greatly on my hair. There was an intricate process: I applied three handfuls of Finesse hair mousse, wet my hair, and scrunched my curls tightly with a towel; I needed hair oil and then hairspray on top of it all. Then onto my makeup while sitting on my bed, facing the natural light to concentrate on correct shading. My favorite part of the day was getting ready and listening to Korn. Not one moment of any of this freedom was taken for granted.

"Wow, Holly, your makeup looks so good today," a staff member said. No more juvie prison garb and a barren face.

There were several little houses for the girls, each containing many separate rooms. And the rooms also had their own TV area. Some girls had their own room, and some shared. The smells of the room were new to me; an array of different female products. The colors were vibrant and shocking, as were the fabrics and ceilings that I often stared at before bed. I noticed it all. Across the campus, the boys had their own house.

Our bedroom windows could open and shut, and they looked out onto the center lawn. I would often enjoy clicking the lock, knowing I had the choice to lock it or leave it open.

Should they trust us enough to have no locks on these windows?
I asked myself.

"Girls, line up for your meds," the staff yelled. We lined up in front of the nurse station, and were each handed little white paper cups with our daily dosages and water. My cup contained only an antihistamine. "Drink it up," the nurse would say, then, "Please stick out your tongue." To break up the monotony, after sticking out my tongue, I would flash a wink at the nurse to make her smile. And then school started at 8:30 sharp, which continued to make me more anxious and uncertain rather than well-versed and confident, but I made sure my thickly-applied makeup and careless rebel attitude hid my emotions well.

Sometimes a few boys, in particular little Nathan, would knock on my bedroom window to say hello and catch up before school. Nathan had short, ashy-brown hair with a fringe cut straight like one of the Beatles. His little petite body was so delicate and cute, as if I could squish him in a cuddle.

The time dragged on with the daily routines. We had our individual therapy sessions three times a week, and two times during the week we had a group therapy or family therapy. I often found myself wondering what the life of my therapist looked like outside of the rehab. Did she garden? Did she drink tea and read a book with a blanket? Was she fulfilled with what she was doing? I pondered these things but I was too shy to ask. I was told my mother and father had to go to parenting classes.

There was quite a bit of freedom to relax in my room and spend time with the other girls. I often roamed around during my free time. There was an old piano in one of the rooms, not being used for any therapeutic purpose. I sat down at the piano, looking at the stained ivory keys. I could smell the felt beneath them and I was desperate for the courage to play well; it ached within an unspoken place. It was the same emotion that would sweep over me when I would watch my ninth-grade piano teacher play. How he, and that class, reinstated worth in my life during 9th grade, he will never know. There were times that the only reason I got out of bed was to go to piano class. I was never too stupid to understand art. I spoke to the silence while sitting at that beaten piano. The quiet allowed me to think. I repented to God, telling him one day I would gain enough courage to openly play. I felt as if I let God down. I apologized for the mess I was in. I apologized for it all. I left the piano there, untouched.

Nathan would sometimes meet me on the grassy quad outside my room, and he would confide in me about his love of music. His eyes were always sparkling, but they glowed a brighter shade of hazel when he daydreamed and planned. He was nine years old, and even with our age gap, we shared a kindred love for lyrics and song. He said it kept him alive and if it weren't for music he would have already been gone. He attested that one day he would openly share his creations. I saw him at times as a younger brother; protecting him felt natural and reminded me of Dustin.

I woke up every morning to my smiling Nathan's happy "Hello." But the fact that he kept cutting himself haunted me. It wasn't so confusing to me, that he was so young and endlessly cheerful, yet he was branded with permanent scars from his internal agony. I related to this—his ability to act happy during tremendous pain was an effort towards survival, a trait in which we shared.

I loved having art class with Nathan. One day, we were tasked with creating an abstract piece that represented an unknown part of ourselves. Nathan and I looked at each other and started to laugh out loud. Everyone stared at us, shocked by how openly we mocked the assignment. But we didn't care; the irony of the task sent us into hysterics. I remember Nathan saying, "I'm in therapy literally all day, what don't they know? I wish I had unknowns." As usual, I completely agreed with him. The mystery of personal unknowns was a luxury that someone in rehab couldn't possess.

One morning, he knocked on my window. I went to the window to greet him and stopped cold in my tracks. Blood was dripping from his fingers and onto the ground, his arm hanging awkwardly at his waist.

"Nathan!" I screamed, pointing at his wrist.

He looked down. "Don't say anything; it will stop bleeding soon. These ones were deeper, somehow."

I flinched. *Who upset him?* Aloud, I asked, "Why do you do this?"

"The cutting makes the pain feel better..."

I wanted to cry, to wrap him in a hug and tell him he would be okay, but he ran off. I remember watching his small frame fade into the distance.

I stopped the first person I saw; it was a girl that I often got ready with. "We need to tell the staff—Nathan has cuts on his wrist."

"Yeah, so do I," she said emotionlessly.

"What? What do you mean?"

She pulled up her sleeve and showed me her scars. "It's been a while, but I get it," she said.

Was I in the Twilight Zone? *How could she want to cut herself? How could Nathan?* She looked like a model out of a magazine. If someone who looked like her wanted to do it, what about this cutting was so pervasive? I didn't bother to further the conversation with her. I thought she may have needed to get her meds; her whole demeanor was so flat she almost seemed like the walking dead.

I rushed straight to the redheaded staff member, Emily, and said, "Nathan, he's cutting himself!"

"Thank you, Holly, we are handling it."

"No, you don't understand, he had blood dripping from his cuts! I think he needs to go to the nurse."

"Yes, Holly," she said with irritation. "We do know—"

"He needs attention! Now!" I cut her off.

"Holly! Get in line." She pointed to the girls queued up for their meds. "We will handle it."

I thought, *If not right now, when will you be handling it? Why aren't you there right now?*

Nathan was back at school within a few hours with a bandage over his wrist, laughing like any normal nine-year-old boy. When I asked him how he was, he sharply told me he didn't want to talk about it.

The next morning, he killed himself. He hanged himself in the shower with his own belt. The memory of his body being wheeled out, a black drape covering him from view, is etched into my mind forever. I had never seen grief as I did from his parents that day; they clutched each other desperately, sobbing and walking beside the body of their young son.

Why didn't the staff listen? Wasn't it their job to respond? Weren't they supposed to know when something was serious? We told them. Not just me, but others. "We have this taken care of, we are aware," they told us. Well, that was a fucking lie.

I did my best to ignore the crass, callous comments and questions from my peers. "Were his eyes bulging? Is there blood when someone hangs themselves? Did the parents keep the belt?"

That night, my tears soaked into my pillow. I couldn't stop sobbing, knowing I wouldn't see Nathan the next day, the shattered expressions of Nathan's parents flooding my brain. I didn't trust anyone in the rehab after that. They had killed my closest friend in that place.

I stared into the darkness. Nathan's dreams were dead. He'd had so much to give to this world. He had been my light, and now it was gone. I remembered his dazzling smile as he painted pictures in his mind of what he was working on. His art. I thought of his empty room across the quad being filled with the next victim's belongings. My heart sank; Nathan was irreplaceable. I opened my window and climbed out. I ran barefoot across the quad, the cool night air soothing on my skin. I went to his room, trying to move carefully through the foliage near his window. Every time the leaves crunched, my heart skipped a beat. I placed my cold palms on the window and slid the window open with the gentlest pressure, then jumped in. Being able to smell him again nearly undid me.

I walked over to his CDs lying on top of his dresser and grabbed them. Then I retreated back out the window, closed it, and ran back to my room. I laid on my bed with his CDs over my chest, and I could feel my heart beat against the cold plastic cases. In a strange way, it felt like I was breathing life back into his love of music. I knew these CDs. I knew that every day he would read the lyrics to the songs. He dreamt one day his lyrics would be there. I couldn't bear letting his dreams go. This was the least I could do to protect them.

From that moment on, their claimed answers for everything—therapy, counseling, psychiatric medicine—fell to ashes. I had watched a young, beautiful family lose everything because they had believed it too.

Yet, therapy was nonnegotiable. It was a particularly bitter experience for me, having to see my twin do so well, despite having the same upbringing as me. Every time she walked in for therapy, the sight of her newly-dyed hair and the sound of her car keys rankled me, reminding me of a freedom I was so far from. I flashed back to the memory of the guards opening my cell doors. Heather was the one with the trust, the power; I was still the bad seed. It was further imprinted upon me in every single session.

Nathan's suicide haunted me, made everything darker, crueler, more infuriating. The urge to run prickled in my palms.

One afternoon, I sat in my room, and I packed my bag. I carefully laid out what little supplies I had and folded up my clothes. I made sure to tuck Nathan's CDs in carefully. I had my plan for him. It was midday and the sun was bright; my JanSport backpack, filled to the brim, was heavy on my back. I quite literally walked straight out of the gates of Boarders. I had money on me for a bus ride—at that time, it only cost seventy cents. I sat at the bus stop, looking in two-second increments to check if a staff member was coming for me. Once the bus arrived, I stepped on with a poker face. As the bus took off down a busy road called Engine Avenue, I exhaled with relief. I was free.

At a payphone, I called a high school acquaintance who didn't know I was in rehab. Lupe and I had been friendly in L.A., and I knew she would let me get high with her.

That very night, Lupe called her dealer. We got to his house, and this guy, Cal, while devilishly laughing, invited me inside. In the kitchen, there was some fluid boiling on the stove. Lupe said it could have been meth, but we both had no idea what it was. On the guy's couch, five friends of his sat, joking and wasting the day away.

Cal was six feet tall, plump, with an awkward posture. He had patches of teenage beard growing unevenly on his face and hormonal acne. Two of his teeth protruded out away from the others, making his upper lip disproportional. He treated his friends like dogs, ordering them around—and I watched their masculinity get chipped away with every demand, the same way I saw inmates lose their self-determinism in juvie. My heart broke for them, but I wasn't there for that. I was there to forget about Nathan, and the fact that, by now, my parents were probably looking for me.

Someone knocked on the door. Two of the guys got up and answered it. There was heated conversation that I couldn't decipher.

"Shut the fuck up," Cal commanded. It took me a moment to realize he was saying that to his new guest and not to us.

I became terrified instantly from the weight of his tone. I looked for an exit, maybe through the back of the house. I glanced over at my friend Lupe, who seemed unconcerned. But my pulse was pounding; I knew there was danger here.

This young boy, who resembled my own age, walked into the room very apologetically, almost like a puppy with his tail between his legs. Then Cal ordered him to go down on his knees.

"What's your favorite song?" Cal demanded.

The kid answered sheepishly. I couldn't hear what he said.

"Put the song on," he instructed one of the guys on the couch. "It's the last song you will ever hear."

I stood up, trying to make a bit of a joke. "This is fun, but I've got to go."

"Sit the fuck down. No one is going anywhere," Cal snapped. He took out a gun and motioned to the couch. I sat obediently.

Bone Thugs-N-Harmony began to play through some speakers. Cal lifted his arm and hammered his fist down on the kid's head. I heard a deafening thud, even through the bass of the music. The kid curled into a fetal position on the floor as the other guys in the room stood up and began shouting.

My heart was beating out of my chest, and my upper lip was wet with sweat. My body could not move; it became stone. Cal beat the guy across the head. I watched as he brutalized him.

Cal reached out for a cloth someone brought over and threw it down on the kid. Then weirdly, Cal stuck his hand out to the kid he had beaten, and said, "Now you know you don't talk me down in the hood."

The kid rose to his feet, and weakly shook hands with Cal.

I sat there completely confused at how beating a boy created reconciliation. But then again, it was the same theory of justice that I had witnessed in juvenile hall.

I realized I was still holding a joint between my fingers, and I gave it to Lupe. I wanted to be all together while I waited for a gap to escape.

Then there was another knock on the door, and someone said "Five-O!"

Some thug entered, saying, "Not the cops; it's me." His jeans were baggy. He had a neck tattoo and a toothpick protruding from his mouth.

I took the opportunity and dashed out the back door. I ran as far as I could.

CHAPTER TWENTY-ONE

VENICE BEACH, SEVENTY CENTS TO FREEDOM

I sat down at the bus stop, trying to act normal. It felt like hours before it came, but in reality, it was probably only fifteen minutes. Then I got on the bus like it was any other day, just like I used to do when I was in middle school. And the bus took me directly west to Venice Beach Boardwalk. On that bus, I looked around at all the people, thinking, *None of them know I am a runaway. No one knows me; this could be the end, or it could be the beginning.* I knew I could turn back if I wanted to, but I didn't want to. I felt the opposite. I wanted to be as far away as possible from anyone who knew me.

I thought back to trips to Venice with my dad and Susan just a few years ago; I remembered all the teenagers lounging along the boardwalk. They had looked weathered but free, laughing back and forth carelessly as if they had all the time in the world. They carried an attitude, despite the dirty clothing and unwashed hair, that they knew something more about the world than anyone else. I went to them.

Every block the bus passed, I was further and further away from Cal, Nathan, therapy, and endless forced regimes. All of it melted away like ice in the spring. I got off the bus and let myself get lost in the crowds of Venice Beach.

I instinctively became hyperaware, like my mother.

I noticed a group of kids about my age, and I sat down next to them. They looked a little dirty and unkempt, and they were selling bracelets; I asked if I could bum a cigarette. That was my gateway to a conversation.

I started to ask about the bracelets, which they were braiding by hand. I was impressed by the intricate and fast movements of their winding fingers. And that was the first time I saw Jesse. I noticed him through a stream of people slowly walking by the shop stalls. I saw him see me. We held a stare for a moment.

He looked like a surfer boy, and his hair was about shoulder-length. He was beautifully and confidently disheveled. And he had this sway when he walked, this carefree swagger. His radiant blue eyes looked like they had a million untold stories, filled with wisdom he didn't even realize he had, and they contrasted against his beachy, golden-brown skin. His eyes were wide-set against his dramatically v-shaped face. He had broad surfer shoulders with a tiny waist. His jeans hung low, and he didn't mind it. He sat down next to me.

"What's your name?" he asked, all mellow.

For a moment I thought, *Do I give him a real name, or do I give him a fake name? What identity am I going to have here? What's my story?* I didn't know what I was going to do, but no one knew me, and because of this, I felt free.

I made a decision. "My name is Holly, but I don't want people knowing that."

"Why?" he asked, searching my eyes for answers. I could feel that and it was enticing. It was the first time I felt that someone truly wanted to *know* my answer.

I didn't hesitate. "I've run away from home."

"Do you know anybody here? Do you know where you're going to sleep?" he asked.

"Not really, but it's okay," I shrugged.

"I can help you, if you want," he replied, no pause in between for pondering.

We were like an automatic pair, almost like when you find a girlfriend at school that you click with. I was reminded of the goodness in people and how valuable it was to have a friend. We chatted about the people sitting next to us and Jesse pointed out the ones he knew. He said the owners of the Chinese food shop would give him leftover rice and teriyaki chicken at night. He would save me some when he got his. I thanked him. I learned to beg outside the local liquor store. Oftentimes after ten minutes I would be asked to leave. I would wait until the shift change and go back again until I was asked to leave once more. Every now and then, I would look around and think, *Look at all these free spirits, entertainers of sorts, misfits... I am one of them.*

It was a quick connection, and I realized from that moment that people on the street, once they see that you are in the same survival band as them, will group up because being together is better than being separate.

Jesse's voice sounded smooth; it soothed my nerves like a lake on a winter's morning, but it had the warmth of the summer sun in North Carolina. He spoke to my being, not my looks, or my boobs, or navigating how to get what he wanted, which I now had a knowledgeable radar for. As I looked at him closely, I noticed dirt under his nails and that his hair, often up in a messy bun, was unbrushed. I could smell the salty seawater and somehow, I didn't mind it; somehow it smelt familiar. He picked up a little rock, inspected it, and tossed it. When he was speaking to me, he ignored any passersby that would say hello to him; his attention was purely and solely on me. I felt special when he did this.

As nighttime approached, the reality of what I had done started to set in, and I began to feel unsafe. I instantly thought to myself, *What have I done?* But I couldn't turn back then because I was afraid to, and I didn't know what consequences I was going to be facing. I didn't want to go back to juvie.

The sun was setting deep over the horizon, almost completely gone; I silently looked at Jesse for answers. He noticed. "We'll find somewhere to be tonight. I have an idea."

I may not have known this guy, Jesse, but he was my safest bet. His kindness guided me. He moved slowly and confidently in motions that swept away my apprehension. I looked at the Venice Beach Boardwalk, and I saw people packing away their stalls, shutting their doors on their boardwalk stores, and chaining up metal doors as the sun set. The sounds were harsh. Venice Beach Boardwalk was like a circus, closing down nightly. I had a relentless jitter in my stomach that I can only describe as being inherently different than any other nervousness I had previously experienced. This time, it was true fight or flight.

Jesse walked and talked, "I know of an abandoned parking garage that we can sleep in; and you can borrow my friend's sleeping bag."

My initial thought was, *Oh my god, is the sleeping bag clean?* But how could I complain? I didn't have a choice; all I could say was "Thank you." I remembered a time when I was a child and my stepmother took in a homeless man for Thanksgiving dinner. He would sleep under a bridge, so that night she gifted him a sleeping bag. He opened it, and he cast it aside as if it were a dirty rag.

"What's wrong?" Susan said. "This will keep you warm!"

"It's red; I don't like red. If it had been blue, I would have taken it," he bitterly replied.

I watched this and thought maybe he was worried red stood out more and would alert the police. Or maybe it was the color of blood, and it reminded him of war.

Regardless, I tried to not be like him.

"Don't worry, I'll show you how we do this. We're going to go squat in a parking garage; at least it's under cover," said Jesse.

"What does squat mean?" I questioned, hesitating to ask out of my fear of being judged.

He explained the ins and outs of not having a place to stay and trespassing for places to sleep. I understood now that it wasn't going to be easy. There was no sense of security, and everything about Jesse's lifestyle was the complete opposite of the strictly structured world from which I had just escaped. Amid my fear, I faced the fact that I wanted to be homeless. I chose it. I also needed to set Nathan free.

So we found a parking garage and I watched a group of people start to place broken-down cardboard boxes down on the ground. No one really spoke as they were doing this. Maybe just a nod here or there for an acknowledgment.

I asked if I could help, and Jesse said, "No, I will do it tonight, but in the future, you'll know what you're doing and be able to help." He handed me someone's sleeping bag, and I had to suppress the instinct to sniff it.

He ended up sleeping next to me; we didn't touch each other. I tried to relax. Everyone went quiet, as the sun was already down.

In the middle of the night, a flashlight beam wavered toward us. We heard a voice talking to some other homeless people and then realized it was a police officer questioning them.

Jesse turned to me and said in a whisper, "Don't say anything unless they ask, and if they do, you are over the age of eighteen and have nowhere to go."

I breathlessly whispered back, "Okay." I couldn't get enough oxygen in my lungs. *Oh my God, I'm caught,* I thought, *Do I run? I hope I remember what he said.*

Next thing I knew, the police officer had his light shining in my eyes. I saw his shiny badge on his uniform. He asked me for my ID.

I scrounged around in my backpack, and from one of Nathan's CDs fell my fake ID. It said my name was Vicky and that I was eighteen.

He looked at it suspiciously, and he said, "What are you doing on the streets?"

"I—I don't have anywhere else to go," I replied, trying not to shake with nervousness.

"You don't have a parent you can go stay with?"

"No," I shook my head.

"Well, you need to figure it out, because you can't stay here."

Although I was terrified, I realized then that it was a game to play, and I was going to play it well. The way I saw it, I had no other choice. No one was there to tell me what to do, and as far as the cop knew, I was a legal adult. It was somehow thrilling. I had an urge to survive it.

The cops waited and watched until we packed up all our belongings. As we walked away from the garage, I felt fear of the unknown, but even among that, I internally held a space of warmth at the idea that Nathan had stolen my ID as a keepsake—and how ironic it was that I had done the same to keep him close, too. As a group of beach bums, we relied on each other. We all needed help, and there was mutual comfort in that; we banded together to solve problems like finding food, toiletries, female products, and bedding. Jesse's friend helped locate an extra sleeping bag. Another friend had a few extra coins to wash it at the laundromat, and someone else contributed the laundry detergent. The value of a friend was never lost on me after those experiences.

There was an older lady who was basically the leader of the pack of all the younger kids. They would report to her; she used to call them "Children of the Corn." And if anyone really needed something, they would go to her. She used to get a check for her husband having served in the war. I didn't know if he'd died in battle or sometime after, but she frequently remarked that his service had killed them both, in one way or another. There were a lot of war veterans that were living on the streets—they were often either injured or mentally deficient. They would wait for their government check, which fueled some of the circulation of money.

At night, people used to hang out with her in her tent because they knew that she had drugs and money. She was very popular, and I went by one evening just to see what she was all about. If too many people were in her tent, she would deny you access, and you would have to find somewhere else to go. Thank God I was denied that night, or else I may have never seen the light of day again. I later learned she would shoot up heroin and offer it to others, and then they'd be hooked and she'd have customers. Had I tried it, I know I would have wound up dead.

My youthful ignorance was my emotional protection; I was incapable of understanding all the possible dangers of my circumstances. But my imagination often took me away from reality. I would daydream all day. The sound of the waves soothed me. The sunlight and her warmth relaxed me, but never enough to ward off all my worry. I wished at times I could go back and shake myself awake.

How I worried those I love; I can never take that back. It hurts me now to think of it. They didn't understand how responsible I felt for Nathan's death. I couldn't have put it into words back then. The thought that—if only I had been a better friend, then maybe he would have still been alive—was shackled to my soul.

As time went on, Jesse and I became basically an unspoken couple. We used to watch the sunset together every night on the beach. We'd smoke a cigarette and talk about life and goals, about people on the boardwalk, and sometimes not talk about anything at all.

Eventually, we stole bikes and bike parts for money, scavenging Venice and its interconnecting alleyways and side streets for anything of value. We'd be high, often stopping to make out or twirl and spin, holding hands and dancing. This delusion was derived from my hallucinogenic state of oblivion. Nevertheless, it was our secret world, and nobody could get to us.

Jesse knew a lot of people. He'd been there a long time, and he knew what he was doing. He sure knew a lot more than me. I remember him saying, "I have to take care of a few things," and he would go away for the day, but then he would return later with some money for drugs to escape our inner demoralizing narratives we were desperately trying to leave behind.

One guy would make money off of creating sand sculptures of mermaids. His art was so spectacular that people would actually drop money to see it. Another guy had lost his arms and legs, and he would do tricks on a skateboard and get tipped by crowds of onlookers. Another guy, who actually became famous, would wear a huge turban and rollerblade in a weird outfit with a boombox, and do really amazing tricks with his roller skates. This was the group that I was in. I didn't offer any special talents, but I was friendly, and they allowed me to kind of bounce around. After sundown, Jesse would take me to his friends' house parties, normal people with normal lives, who'd occasionally help us out. We'd get into philosophical conversations, and at times I believed they used us as muses. Among our ragtag group, there were true artists invoking incredible emotional responses with an authenticity I've never felt anywhere else. They were the people who would hold your hand until the end. It bred a passion in me to listen to those that often went unheard. This is what I instinctively came to the boardwalk for.

I took what my mother called a "bird bath" every morning in the public restroom. With bar soap, I'd wash myself only where necessary, and dry with a paper towel or toilet paper. I had toothpaste and a toothbrush that I'd bought with my begged-for change. I made sure to brush my teeth at least once a day. Some people would joke that I was the cleanest homeless person on the Boardwalk.

That was how I spent those Venice Beach days. Moving in and out of crowds, the sun coming up and the sun going down. I people-watched; all day I made up stories about the families I saw walking, *ooh*ing and *ahhh*ing about one trinket or another at a stall owned by someone I most likely knew.

My nascent instinct for danger only strengthened. I earnestly searched people's eyes for indicators of who they truly were; sometimes, my survival depended upon it. Once, while begging alone for spare coins outside a liquor store, a man came by and asked, "What are you doing here?"

"Oh, do you have twenty cents? I'm trying to catch the train back home." There'd always be a new story that I'd come up with as to why I was asking for money.

Instead of offering to help, he said, "I'd love to photograph you in a field of flowers." Unease crawled up my spine. I made some casual remark and left, making sure to take a winding route so I would know if he followed. Despite moments like this, I was still willing to live on the streets. It was a weird push and pull of experiencing fear, overcoming it, and being fierce.

That night, I told Jesse about the photographer, and he sternly told me, "You need to be careful of people. You need to watch out." I knew this, but I basked in the sound of his protective nature. It was like exploring a new frontier; we lived in an obscure city version of the Wild West. I would wait for Jesse through the day; he was my beautiful distraction.

Later, I went to our tent and crawled inside to find Jesse already there. I laid down next to him. I slept with my head on his chest. I could hear his heartbeat; I could smell his familiar scent, the same as the first day we met. All this time had passed, and we didn't require too much conversation. We knew each other's ways. At least that's how it felt to me.

I slept well and woke at sunrise, well before the stalls were set up and anyone was around; I could hear the waves crashing and the sound of goggling pigeons. In the mornings, I would lift a small portion of the tent and let myself be amused by the movement of their little feet. The way their necks would forge forward as they bobbled around looked like a dance. I watched them like I watched cartoons on the TV as a child.

Jesse woke and said, "Have you said 'Good Morning' to your little friends?" The sound of his chuckle made me smile.

I replied in a whisper so as not to disturb them, "Not yet, just watching them. I wish we could feed them." I wondered why pigeons were so rudely disregarded. They could fly as high as any other bird, and offered beauty and beautiful song. I had heard stories of pigeons and how smart they were, yet to everyone else, this information was deemed unimportant. Pigeons used to be our messengers, and now we treated them like pests. I felt kinship with these pigeons. I whispered to them, saying, "You are not a meaningless little bird; you are not overlooked. I still see you even when the world doesn't." In a way, it felt as if I was speaking to the old houses we used to leave behind. Soon after, Jesse had a new nickname for me: "Pigeon." I smiled every time I heard it; it was now the little things I appreciated.

We packed up our belongings and stashed them with a stationary homeless friend who we knew would be in the same spot all day. I kept only my backpack.

Jesse said to me, "Hey, I'll be back in a few hours. I'll get cigarettes and try to find some weed."

I said okay, and off he went. No one was out yet, so I wandered to the water's edge of Venice Beach. It was time to do what I'd come here to do. Then, I heard an echo of a man screaming angrily at what looked like the ocean itself. His body was lean, and his arms were flung wide.

"What the fuck, man, what the fuuuuuckkkkk? Is this how you treat me, God? Is this what it is supposed to be? What the fuck, man?" He repeated this over and over again, arms stretching further and further out, as if he was trying to touch both sides of the beach while he waited for an answer from the heavens.

As I treaded closer to him, I noticed he resembled Jesus. I thought that was funnily befitting. His lengthy white beard only added to his Messiah-like appearance. His nails were yellow, long, and sharp, which somehow frightened me. He had the same skinny torso as the notorious one hung from a cross, and his arms extended out in the same manner as if he himself was invisibly hung from one. I cautiously moved towards him.

I gently asked, "Are you okay?"

He turned to me, his long white hair following. I wondered about the danger here in this moment, as he felt unpredictable. He looked into my eyes, scanning me, pausing for an uncomfortable length of time. He then slowly lifted his arm up to point at my face, all the while keeping his gaze at my eyes, and said, "It's you." I was startled. It was as though he had held a conversation with God that no one else could be a part of.

He continued, "It's you who's going to be okay. I can see it in your eyes." To me, it was a sign like many others I had experienced. It wasn't the first time someone had looked into my eyes, and maybe even into my soul, and said I would be alright. It somehow fortified this protection I had. The contracts I made with God were forthcoming in mysterious ways. The thing was, if he had been a well-groomed man, or another white-coated doctor, or even a therapist, I wouldn't have believed him. It was because he was homeless, screaming at the ocean, living in some other dimension, one I didn't know of, with nothing more to offer than his own knowing, that his prediction felt sound.

I thanked him. He smiled back at me as if he knew he had given me a gift. Then he turned back to the vast ocean and went about cursing the waves. And I felt his anger. It awakened the injustice of the death of my beautiful Nathan. I pulled his CDs out of my bag and flung them as hard as I could into the ocean. I was surprised at my own strength and passion. For a split second, a glimpse of sunshine caught the closest CD. It flashed a single sparkle into the sky. It was the same sparkle I would see in Nathan's eyes when he spoke of his dreams. It was unmistakable. He was there. I said my goodbye and I freed his dreams to the world in my own way. I felt unshackled.

That night, I heard my name being called. "Holly," echoed from a distance. The voice sounded familiar. So familiar. I almost couldn't believe it; it was my stepmother. There I stood, in tattered clothes and unbrushed hair, in front of Susan, my father, and my sister.

"Holly, come away from here! You are ruining your life!" said Susan.

"Please, Holly, just get in the car with us," pleaded my sister.

Somehow Heather's pleading further angered me. How perfect this must have been for her, to have to come and rescue me. The bad twin. I remembered the times I intimidated or pushed back any girl who bullied my sister. I had been her protector, yet I had never been praised for it.

"Holly, please, you are ruining your whole life," Susan repeated.

"This is not me," I said. "This is not my future. This is just what I'm doing right now. You can't see what I see. I will be ok."

I was more at home on the boardwalk than with my family, so I forced them to leave without me. I laid on the concrete bench, looking into the black sky, and in my own silence I automatically felt apologetic. The conflict of being stubborn and sorry was a curse.

I felt relieved they left me. I needed the boardwalk, and to rebel. I didn't care what I looked like or how illogical my decisions seemed; they were for me and only me. It was the only way I felt like I could breathe, to be away from everyone that had some type of "fix-it" philosophy for me.

If I could go back, I would have wrapped my arms around my stepmother, sister, and father. I would have told them how much I needed to feel part of a family and not like the bad seed. How it hurt the way Heather did everything with such support and approval. How I yearned to be accepted as an artist. How I wanted them to show me they had hope in me, even against all the odds I was throwing at them, deliberately or not. The guilt I felt for everything, and the anger. I wish I would have had the words. But I didn't then.

I didn't sleep that night. Neither did Heather, my stepmother, or my father, I'm sure. The thoughts circulated my mind relentlessly. I didn't feel fully justified in my decision to stay, but it didn't feel right for me to go back with them, either.

The next morning on the boardwalk, tourists and shoppers and runners started to fill the street. I looked down at the clothes I was wearing and thought, *God, I am dirty; dirty and torn and gross.* I occasionally borrowed clothes from girls I had met, but it was time for something new. If I could get a new dress I would wear it for Jesse, and find a flower to put in my hair. A yellow one from someone's yard. We could have Chinese and watch the sunset like a real date. I walked into a store and asked if I could try something on.

The Asian clerk, not blind to the crime in Venice, and looking a little rough around the edges herself, said, "Don't you go stealing any of my clothes. I know your kind."

I replied, "Excuse me? I have money; I don't know what you're talking about."

She said, "I've seen you up and down the boardwalk."

I replied, "Yes, my sister works here, so I come to work with her sometimes."

She suspiciously and reluctantly said, "Okay." I grabbed four dresses and brought them into the stall with me to try on. I felt somewhat guilty because I knew she was trying to make money. I put on the dress with the least amount of fabric underneath my dirty clothes. I came out of the stall and handed her back all the clothes in a messy bunch, and before she had the time to count how many dresses I had given back, I ran out of the store. The lady ran after me, and she started calling me names.

I waited for Jesse in our usual spot. I found a yellow flower and put it in my hair. The moment I saw him, I dashed towards him and we embraced.

He asked, "What's wrong, Pigeon?"

"Nothing, I just want to dance with you."

He smiled and I melted into his warm eyes. He looked at me with such love. I was trying to replace the heaviness from the night before with something beautiful. I knew my time at Venice was coming to an end soon.

He twirled me like his own tiny dancer and asked, "New dress?"

"Yes," I said girlishly. We sat side by side near the water's edge, watching the sunset and slowly picking at our food. I hummed the melody of Sarah McLachlan's song "Angel" with my arms casually resting over his shoulders, and we swayed to the rhythm of the ocean with the crashing white sea foam as our backdrop. I learned from the people on the boardwalk that when you can dance despite the pain, you have truly learned to survive, and for that I will always pay tribute to them. They provided the education that you can't get in college. They are the ones that taught me money truly doesn't mean anything.

Another week went by. I started feeling lifeless, even with all the freedom. I walked by the restaurants and stores and noticed all the Easter decorations in the windows, marveling at the passage of time. I couldn't shake my despondency. Maybe I had learned all I could from here. I missed my sister, despite my resentment, and if that isn't the power of family, then I don't know what is.

So, I took the twenty cents that I had from begging in front of a liquor store and put it into a payphone. I called the personal line that I used to have in my room at my dad's house to make sure I wouldn't get my dad or stepmom. My sister answered the phone.

Grateful to hear her, I said, "Heather, it's Holly, don't tell Dad and Susan. You promise?"

"I promise. Are you okay? I'm so worried."

"Yeah, I'm fine. Would you meet me for lunch?"

"Yes, of course," she replied. "Yes, I'll meet with you. Where?"

"Would you be able to get away and meet me at 28 Sands Café?" I asked.

"Yes!"

"What day?"

"In three days," she responded.

"Okay, in three days' time, I'll meet you there at noon." I hung up the phone, happy I would finally be able to see her.

I waited for those three days, thinking about her constantly, what she would tell me, what I needed to say. The three days crawled by.

I went to the restaurant. I was purposely late because I wanted her to get the table first; I knew I didn't look like any average Joe walking around. They may not have let me in without her.

And there she was. "Hi!" she exclaimed, and we gave each other a tight hug for a few moments. "Do you want to order anything? Are you hungry?"

"Yeah," I said eagerly, "I'll have an Arnold Palmer." It was half lemonade and half iced tea; it was a drink that my dad liked drinking, so I ordered it.

Before I could taste my drink, before I could settle into the moment, Heather looked up. "I'm sorry," she said.

"For what?" I asked.

After a heartbeat, I looked behind me. There were two uniformed police officers muscling their way into the restaurant.

I looked back at her, dismayed. "Why would you do that?" Truth was, I knew why. I knew Heather had to follow my dad and Susan's rules. That was what Heather did.

"I'm so sorry. I'm so sorry," was her only response.

The two police officers approached the table. One was tall and African American and the other was Caucasian and redheaded. They had a high school photo of me, and they asked, "Are you Holly Cohen?"

My sister exhaled a short breath and said to the officers, "I'm sure you know it isn't me."

The redheaded officer said, "You do have to come with us. Can you please get up?" They handcuffed me in the middle of one of the busiest restaurants in Venice Beach. The restaurant was dead silent, and every single person was watching me. In utter shame, I thought, *If you look at the floor, you won't see anyone looking at you...* I didn't know what else I could do. They spoke to me outside the police car in plain view for all to see.

The tall African American officer said, "Your dad has requested that we drive you to his house."

I replied, "Please, I'm not going there."

"Well, we're going to call your probation officer."

"I'm not going anywhere."

The police officer then said, "You have the opportunity to go back into Boarders. We can take you back there."

"I'm not going anywhere."

My assigned probation officer drove from Long Beach to Venice Beach, where he said he wanted to speak with me. I was escorted and made to wait on a bench. I had recently been high; everything felt a little like a dream.

All I could focus on were the homeless people, many of whom I was friendly with, who had watched the police walk me out of the restaurant to a bench. My reputation was already ruined and known now. Gossip spread like wildfire along the boardwalk communities; I was too hot now, identified by the cops, so if I stayed, they all would have avoided me in effort to protect themselves.

My probation officer arrived. He had a short chat with the two officers and walked towards me. His belt was thick with lots of compartments, as if he was a police officer but without the uniform. He drove a baby blue four-door sedan, which to me looked inconspicuous. He sat beside me and told me, "I need you to take a drug test."

I replied, "How am I supposed to do that?"

He handed me a plastic medical cup and instructed me, "I want you to pee in this."

"Where?" I asked.

He gestured with his pointer finger. "In that public bathroom over there. I will be standing outside the stall, and you can hand it to me after."

I did as I was told and handed him the filled cup. I wasn't

hydrated, so it was dark gold. He then sat me down on a bench and we waited. Afterward, the tall police officer came back and told the probation officer something, and the probation officer looked at me and said, "Your drug test has come out clean."

Flabbergasted, I stared at him. "That's not possible. I've taken drugs."

"Well, it's clean," he replied. "There are no drugs in your system."

"It's not possible. I'm telling you I've taken drugs."

"Sometimes if you don't have any fat cells in your body— looking at you, you're very thin—the drugs don't show properly and it won't read on the test. As far as I'm concerned, you haven't been taking any drugs. And that's what I'm putting down in my report."

Years later, I realized he was trying to help me. If I had a violation of my probation, I would have been sentenced to my full five-year sentence.

He was doing me a favor. He was being a friend.

After the drug test, my probation officer said to me, "I need you to walk yourself back into Boarders. I need you to walk yourself back there, because then it won't be a violation, and we won't take you back to jail."

"I don't want to go back there!" At that point I was becoming frantic and frustrated.

"Listen, if you don't do it, you could possibly get more time added to your sentence, and that is not what you want. Five years in jail, Holly, was your full sentence. Five years. And you will have to do that full five years, if not more, if you don't voluntarily bring yourself back to Boarders. It is better than jail, isn't it?"

I looked down and spoke quietly, "Yes."

"Then go. I will drive you. They're willing to take you back. Your dad has already talked to them. If you voluntarily give yourself back, it will have been a motion of you wanting to get the help, and they will see it that way, and they will take you back."

"You don't understand why I'm in this situation to begin with," I said pleadingly. "My dad put drugs on me, in my bag." This was my first time admitting that fact to anyone outside of my mother. "I shouldn't even be in this situation."

"Look, I'm not telling you that what he's done isn't wrong. But it's water under the bridge; just go back."

The phrase confused me, so I asked him what "water under the bridge" meant, but he just repeated, "It's just water under the bridge at this point. You need to walk yourself back into your rehab."

And that's what I did. The police officers drove me back to Boarders. I sat in the back of the police car, separated from them by the wired partition. I played with the frayed piece of torn leather on the back seat. The cuffs remained on my wrists. I made a joke asking to be taken to McDonalds for a vanilla shake before arriving back at Boarders. I was ignored.

I was dropped at the gates of Boarders and I walked back in.

Everything was a blur; I didn't want to be present, and I definitely didn't want to remember Nathan's death. There was loads of therapy, none of which I trusted. I had adopted the attitude of the Boardwalk misfits; that I had wisdom they couldn't begin to understand.

"We were so worried about you; what happened? Why would you run away?" the kids asked.

I tried to get back into the routine of Boarders. And I admit it was nice to have a bed to sleep in, to take a long hot shower, and to know that the next morning food would be cooked. And it was nice to have my room back—they kept it just as I had left it. But every night, I thought of Jesse, and every morning I woke thinking of Nathan. I would lie in bed waiting for his cheerful greeting, but it never came.

I was told I needed Prozac because of my behavior. Now my little white cup had an additional green-and-yellow pill; I winced at the sight of it. To me, this said I was far from capable of handling myself, and that there was no natural solution either. I didn't have the choice to argue, so I shut my eyes and swallowed.

On my first Sunday back, family therapy was scheduled. I heard Heather's grades had dropped in high school due to the stress of me running away. I hoped with me being back, her grades would rise again. She was always an amazing student and daughter, and her future looked bright. I wanted it bright, as much as it hurt for me.

I met with my therapist in the sterile therapists' room, and then my dad, Susan, and Heather all entered. They all sat there, attempting to help me, and I looked up at my therapist, hoping she would say something that made sense.

"Holly, is there something that you wanted to say?"

I had told my therapist that I wanted to bring up the fact that cocaine was put in my wallet. I had rehearsed this with her, yet fear paralyzed me at every attempt and I couldn't get the words out.

CHAPTER TWENTY-TWO
IMAGINARY FRIENDS

At our next therapy night, a Wednesday night, my sister had driven herself to the session. My father and Susan followed in after her, and I clenched my jaw as I saw Heather jangling her car keys and daintily swinging them around her finger. I noticed every little thing, and every little thing was a jab at me.

My father started talking about how, now that I was back again, he hoped I would stay, that I was troubled. My father meant well, but his sergeant-like demeanor of delivery did his message no good. I now wonder how this made him feel, having to come to therapy in the first place, and the therapist declaring his offspring a "troubled child."

But in my teenage mind, I had no empathy; I was fully exhausted in their ceaseless observations. "Dad, you know it's not even fully my fault that I'm here," I said. I knew it actually was, but I needed them to be honest. It was strange, using a partial lie to try and coax out truth. I did want change. And from what they had taught me, that could only come from total truth. So I demanded we all be truthful.

Silence fell. I continued, "Dad, you put the cocaine in my wallet so you didn't have to pay for the drug rehab." I was terrified to say it, but I managed to get it out.

My father calmly looked at my therapist and said, "I'm not sure I've told you, but our daughter has been—for a very long time—a pathological liar."

Susan turned to me and asked, "Why did you say that? Of

course we didn't."

All those times my stepmother had warned me about the boy who cried wolf; now I was living it.

Why would anyone believe me, anyway? The girl who had lied, the runaway, the troubled one. *Fuck it!* I thought. I felt betrayed as I looked over to my therapist, who did absolutely nothing to defend me.

My father stood and walked out. I did too.

I made my way to my room. I kept hoping my dad would come back, but he didn't. The staff walked into my room and stared at me as if I was a foreign object, and then eventually they left. My fury and pain was all witnessed. I felt I was on display. Every minute that passed with the stubborn absence of my father, my anger grew.

I ran into the bathroom and locked myself in it.

I remembered the beauty model who used to cut herself. She said it made her feel better. I remembered Nathan. I felt the same betrayal from this place as I felt when he died. I looked at my arm and then to my razor in the shower. I took it and in a pathetic attempt, I tried to cut my wrist. The skin was tougher than I had imagined it to be, and I struggled to draw blood. The pain in my wrist didn't feel better than the torture I felt inside of me. But maybe they would all see what this was doing to me...what they all were doing to me.

The action of cutting was my cry for help and not a suicide attempt. The staff and the therapist knocked on the bathroom door, calling my name, so I came out. They allowed me to go to my room, and they realized I had cut my wrist. I climbed up to the top of the open-standing closet and just sat there. I refused to speak to anyone that entered, and I defiantly would not get down. It was my attempt to exercise control, even if it just was over what I did with my own body. All the staff took this as a sign of "having a fit" and warned me that they would call the paramedics to take me to the ward. I didn't care. I didn't care about anything now.

Two men entered my room dressed in white, short-sleeved uniforms, demanding I get down. I refused. One grabbed my arms, the other grabbed my ankles, and they pulled me down. I began contorting my body, but they kept hold. I turned my head as far as I could, and I bit one of the men on his thumb.

"She bit me!" he said.

"She's a feisty one," the other responded. Somehow this left me feeling satisfied. I had done something: my act of rebellion.

I was escorted in an ambulance to the UCLA mental institution.

"Here she is," the paramedic said as he walked me in.

I was escorted inside. Each sliding door automatically closed and locked behind us. They took me to a room, and a staff member knocked on the door. It opened just enough for me to see one large, dilated eye. The girl inside had an unnervingly soft voice the pitch of a ten-year-old's.

"Hello," she said, "My name is Claire."

"Hello, I'm Holly," I automatically replied. A long silence dragged out as she vacantly stared at my face.

The staff stood behind me and prompted, "Okay, Claire, let's show Holly her room."

That's when I realized she was my new roommate. The way her fingers curled around the door caught my attention. It was haunting. She was so pale, so ashy. She had a bob cut, dark brown hair, black empty eyes, and veiny skin. She was tall and extremely skinny, which made her skin appear paper-thin. She slowly moved to sit on her bed; it was like she was walking through quicksand.

As I stepped inside the room, she recited all the medications she could, counting them. I tried my best to not stare but I couldn't help myself. She didn't notice me scanning her.

The room was stale, with medical beds and large course facility-textured sheets. The floors were white. The walls were white with silver steel shelves that held various medical equipment in the room, but nothing that you could use to harm yourself with. By now I had become accustomed to this type of pharmaceutical room, and I didn't feel anything from it anymore. It was now just a numb observation.

The staff said I could walk around. They said I had free time to see where things were. I was shown the art room, and a therapy room, all stark white, and across the hallway there was a kitchen, and then a game room.

It was nighttime now, and we soon would be sent to bed. The staff allowed me to have a piece of toast before changing. I was concerned about falling asleep. I wasn't sure if it was the right thing to do. What was Claire capable of doing? She obviously wasn't all there, even if she once was, with all those pills she had been prescribed. Who knew what her impulses were? Eventually, after lying in the quiet and listening to Claire's steady breathing, I got some rest. When I woke, I blinked my eyes repeatedly, forgetting where I was for a moment. The ceiling looked different than Boarders. White cardboard cottage cheese-textured squares aligned side by side. I started to count them. My thoughts were interrupted by a sunken emotion as the memories from yesterday flooded my mind. *What does this mean for me now? Will my family visit? Will my dad ever speak to me again? I was never supposed to do that. I promised him I wouldn't. But it wasn't fair. I shouldn't have bit that man. I should have gotten down from the cupboards when they asked me to. Now they all think I am a liar.*

I had nothing now, not even my truth.

I got dressed, trying to ignore Claire counting aloud her medications. *Does this girl like all these pills?* She said her parents were coming for a visit today.

"Do you have anyone visiting you?" she asked.

"Not sure. Maybe. I hope not."

I didn't trust that I could make some kind of lasting connection with Claire. And I knew I was most likely only going to be in there for seventy-two hours while they examined me. *Three days, that's all... Be good, Holly.*

I stepped outside my room, squinting as the bright light bounced off of the blank walls. I heard a hollow ball being hit back and forth. I walked towards the sound. There were kids playing Ping-Pong, and I approached the green plastic table. Also in the room was a young boy, several years younger than me. He had round, rosy cheeks, and when he would smile, it made his eyes curve like they were mini rainbows. He was the same height, and had the same shade of ashy brown hair, as my Nathan. Was he trapped like Nathan was? I felt like it was yet another sign to not trust this place. He let out a belly laugh while talking to an empty space. I watched him as if he were an enchanted puzzle.

"Who are you speaking to?" I asked him.

"Mickey Mantle," he replied, his voice chipper. I knew the long-dead, famous baseball player because my father loved baseball and Mickey Mantle.

I understood him; he had found his own invisible friend. I remembered being a little girl and having an imaginary buddy.

"What is he saying? What are you asking him? " I asked, intrigued by this sacred chat.

The boy's smile never faltered, his blue eyes sparkling. Compared to the dire crowd lifelessly sitting around, he was the most interesting kid by far; I could be his friend.

A staff member came up and politely said, "Holly, please don't speak with him in this way."

"Why?"

"It would make things worse!" he warned me.

I refused to listen. I whispered to this boy, quietly asking him more questions, and he softly responded as if it was our precious little secret.

Just as I was about to be escorted out for my intake evaluation, the boy turned to me and said, "I have never felt so happy." I felt honored, and I wished I could have been this harbinger of joy for Nathan. Maybe he would have still been alive.

The staff walked me out, showing me the psychotherapist's office. "Please, sit down here, Holly. How are we today?"

We? I thought to myself, *That's weird.*

"I'm okay." I shrugged.

"We are here to take a few tests," the doctor said. I scanned the off-white walls of the bland room and noticed they matched the doctor's bland lab coat. His skin complexion looked washed out, and I wondered if maybe it was the florescent lighting. He had a warm smile and a welcoming demeanor, but it all felt like a farce. Was I a lab rat?

A female and male nurse entered, also dressed in white coats. They had me thread a needle through holes bored into a piece of leather. The woman scribbled notes the entire time, and I tried to appear as calm as possible. The second test was a Rorschach test, although I didn't know at the time that's what it was called. They showed me a series of cards with blotches of watercolor paint. With each card, the doctor asked, "What do you see?" I was irritated at that point.

I felt dissected, the way Susan would pick my brain at night before bed.

The rebelliousness flared. Eventually, I reached a point, during the strange testing, when I overcame my complacent silence, and I asked, "What are you looking for in your test, with the blotches of paint?"

The therapists explained they just wanted to understand my

perceptions. Once they finished assessing me, they determined I wasn't clinically insane, and then they sent me back to Boarders. But now I was prescribed a higher dosage of antidepressants, to take the edge off my anxiety; I was also prescribed an additional pill to calm me. Now I could be more easily controlled.

For roughly the next thirteen years, I started each morning by taking a narcotic, numbing myself with a legal drug.

They tried to solve the invalidation I felt in therapy. From my perspective, pills did not have the ability to help anyone; they were a tool used to control people into submission— through various gradients of emotional vacancy.

Initially, I became smugger every day at Boarders. Everyone was extra careful in their demeanor towards me. I held onto the belief that they were all going to realise how much better I was than all of this, how above it all I truly was. I think it was the only thing keeping me going. But only a few weeks later, I too became desensitized. I never felt too happy, and I never felt too sad. Life wasn't too great, life wasn't too bad. My natural ability to respond to life, and its emergencies, was blunted. Our bodies, our minds, our souls are designed to respond to emotions, to resolve problems, and to love with feelings. That innate gauge for me was gone. Because my dosage was somewhat low, compared to the others, they figured that I would still have emotions, still be able to feel things like a normal teenage girl. They claimed they were just trying to calm me, dull my anxiety and depression, but that wasn't a problem with a one-size-fits-all solution. They wanted me to be malleable. They were playing

God.

There was one thing the psych meds couldn't seem to numb: my resolution to never sit through another false therapy session. I wouldn't do it if I couldn't truthfully speak. Several weeks had passed and I was given a stern warning during my private therapy session: "Next Tuesday, your family will be coming. You must participate. This is a requirement for your stay here and from the courts."

Fuck your requirements, look where that got me before. Look where that got Nathan.

"Yeah okay, I'll participate," was all I said.

Later that day, without further consideration, I simply opened the window, crawled out, and walked out of the front gate. I got on the bus without a worry and left Boarders. I wasn't met with any of the same emotions as my first escape. This one was less calculated, almost zombie-like.

I returned to the boardwalk, but things were different. One problem was that I wasn't getting proper nutrition out on the street. The only full meals I was getting at Venice Beach were on Sundays, when I would stand in line with other homeless people to receive my free Sunday meal of KFC leftovers at the park. The food was donated and arranged, I believe, by the Salvation Army, but I never really asked.

Whether Jesse was present or not, I experienced huge emotional rollercoasters. I struggled immensely. I spent about three-and-a-half weeks on the run at Venice Beach, and finally I couldn't take it anymore.

Another major issue was the fact I no longer had access

to my psych meds. No one had sat me down to tell me what could happen without the meds. My withdrawal, unsupervised and vicious, was a monster. While on the streets, the depression began to grab me and wave me around as if I was a ragdoll. Something felt persistently wrong no matter what was happening. The depression wasn't simply feeling hopeless or sad, but the never-ending sense that it would be easier to simply not exist. There was a void within me that nothing was able to fill. Physically, I had diarrhea, I had debilitating headaches, and I had waves of dizziness that would pass over me with no warning. I lacked the ability to create an honest smile, and I had to find a way to survive—and to feel some sort of wholeness come back to me. "Normal," "good," "socially acceptable" doctor's drugs had done this to me, so I went out and found my own drugs. I went from psych drugs to street drugs, and it was based solely on my will to continue surviving. The rush of chemicals was a means to an end.

CHAPTER TWENTY-THREE
THE GIVER

Running away does not produce the euphoric feeling of freedom that movies and television shows make it out to be. It's not an immediate sense of being able to do whatever you want with your life; there isn't really a sensation of starting anew. There is, instead, an innate desire for comfort, for some sort of home.

Jesse had been that for me, before. The thought of him was a magnetic pull. I loved him, for what I knew love to be at that time, and as a teenage girl, that can be one of the most powerful feelings. He was willing to nurture me with whatever he had—which was practically nothing. We were friends on the deepest level and under the harshest of circumstances.

Night fell, and Jesse was nowhere to be found. I was all alone. I couldn't see anyone on the boardwalk.

I began to weigh my scarce options. I knew there was an AA meeting being held nearby. At Boarders, one night a week, we were to attend. We would shuffle into the Boarders van, wallet chains clinking, extra black eyeliner donned, and the scent of Aqua Net filling the air. Two staff members would accompany us, eyes nearly glazed with boredom. During break time, we rehab kids would camouflage ourselves amongst the crowd as we bummed cigarettes from the other attendees.

I made my way to the AA meeting. I knew there were free doughnuts and coffee, and there would be someone to help me out. As I found a seat, people were getting up to receive their chips. They were telling their stories; they were introducing themselves.

Interestingly, the AA meetings confused me as I never truly agreed with having a disease for the rest of your life. I knew there was so much I didn't understand. I strolled over to the hot coffee and picked up a doughnut out of the box, searching the faces around me. I nodded my head at one guy that was there and poured myself a cup of coffee. I looked over at that same guy again, and I noticed that he noticed me. Then I sat down again.

I listened to the stories of a few of the people. One man had lost his mother and had just gone on a cocaine binge for a year.

There's always a fifteen-minute break at these meetings. Everyone goes outside and smokes, and everyone knows everybody. And I had no one to talk to. The guy who had made eye contact with me approached me and offered me a smoke. At that point, I'd had a doughnut and a cup of coffee, I was in a warm church, and I'd been gifted a cigarette. For me, at that moment, it appeared that things weren't all so bad.

He looked at me and asked, "How long have you been sober for? And what's your drug of choice?"

That was always the biggest question.

I exhaled smoke gently out of the side of my mouth. "Some of this or that, and weed."

He nodded and replied, "Mine is alcohol. Are you here with anybody?"

"No," I answered. "It's only me and my backpack." I motioned to my backpack slung over my shoulder. "This is basically all that I have."

He seemed concerned and narrowed his eyes at me before he replied.

"Well, you know, my wife is coming home from work soon, and if you need to wash your clothes or whatever, you're welcome to come by and use our washer and dryer. We all kind of help each other in this group. It's what's great about going to these meetings—people helping each other."

That's amazing, that's exactly what I came here for. And he has a wife, so it's safe. So, I smiled and said, "That would be really great."

"Maybe if it's okay with my wife you can stay the night."

Surprised, I replied, "Oh my gosh, yeah, cool. I'll probably know more tomorrow about where I could go."

"I'm sure that's okay. Let me just call my wife and make sure."

He said his wife was a nurse. I got the sense that he was a nine-to-five guy working a desk job. I think he mentioned he was in tech. He told me how long he had been sober for: over six years.

He was dark-haired, and chubby-faced, as if he was well fed. Old acne scars dotted his face. He had brown eyes, a sharp crew cut, and wore an untucked crisp white button-down shirt. I noticed his hand perpetually pulling the bottom part of his shirt towards the ground in an attempt to conceal his middle-age potbelly. He wore iron-creased blue jeans and clean white shoes. The shine of a gold wedding band flashed on his finger. Funny as this may sound, observing these characteristics was a part of my assessment if he was safe or not. He passed.

After the meeting, he gestured to me and said, "Come on, my wife says it's okay. You're welcome to come for the night. We're good people; you don't have to worry." *This is really good for me,* I thought. *Tomorrow I can find Jesse.*

We walked side by side over to his car. He had a cool, classic powder blue Mustang in pristine condition. The rims shined brilliantly in the parking lot light, reflecting the dark yellow streetlights. Once he cranked the engine, he looked at me with a rev in his eye and asked what kind of music I liked. He had all these tapes; I chose Led Zeppelin and that was the soundtrack to the ride to his home.

Zeppelin in a Mustang. He kept giving me cigarettes and I believed I was the hottest thing ever. There I was, having just gone AWOL from my rehab, full off a donut and a cup of coffee, smoking a cigarette, with a place to stay.

Once we arrived at his house, I met his wife. She seemed like a tough lady. She was taller than him. She spoke in a low-toned voice, and had loose skin around her mouth and dark magenta hair. She wore thick black-rimmed glasses that slanted up at the tops resembling a cat's eye. She wasn't attractive; she was bulky in frame, with a pasty skin color. She invited me in and showed me where the washer and dryer were. She asked me if I wanted to help cook. The house was really warm. I didn't have much of an appetite; I was stressed out about Jesse. But I ate a little bit, and I realized there would be no drugs and no alcohol; I was in the house of sober people.

After finishing her meal, his wife stood up and said, "Listen, I just got off work. I'm just gonna take a shower." She winked at her husband on the way out.

She took quite a while. I was folding my washed laundry on the floor next to the heater. I sat there, folding my dry soft clothes, and I smelled them, inhaling deeply. Being able to fold each article slowly was so different than my usual harried rush to shove everything in my pack and get on the run. I glanced up at the guy, and then did a double take, not trusting the visual I just saw. The spell of the laundry and heater disintegrated into thin air as I saw him on the couch, his pants unzipped, his hand shaking his penis and dangling it out of his pants. *What the hell?*

I was dizzy with confusion and blurted out, "What are you doing?" He was fondling it and it looked like a loose, wrinkly noodle.

He looked at me and smiled. He whispered in a desperate

tone, "It's okay, trust me. It's okay."

"No! And your wife is in the shower!"

He only replied with, "It's okay. Come on. It's okay." He gestured with one hand to come over.

I gasped and stood up. "I don't think so!"

In the middle of that conversation his wife walked out. She flung up her arms and exclaimed, "You didn't wait for me!"

Oh my God, she's in on it too! I thought. It took me a minute to get out of the confusion. It was mind-blowing. Oftentimes at the AA meetings, we would hear people exchange one addiction for another. *They're sex addicts. What kind of marriage is this?*

His wife, in a tone of bitter derision, mumbled, "I leave you alone for twenty minutes while I am taking a shower, and you can't wait for me?"

"It's no big deal, honey, you knew what was up," he replied.

I sat back as if I was an audience to a freak show that involved me, yet I had no idea my role in it all.

She prodded him further, tensing her already thin lips. "I can't trust you. Get her out of here, and you too. We had a deal." *It must have been a deal about me?* He must have broken a rule that they had around these things, and they assumed that they were going to have sex with me.

I started shoving my clean clothes back into my backpack. I was worried because I didn't really know where I was.

"Look, don't freak out on her," the guy said. He was making some odd attempt at protecting me. He turned to me as his wife watched with beady eyes. "You can't stay here anymore. Maybe there is someone else who could help you out at the AA meeting. Hopefully there will still be some people out there, and you can ask somebody else for a place to stay."

I scoffed. "Are you kidding me, man?"

He rushed me outside.

"Well, you can stay in my car."

"No, that's okay."

He profusely apologized over and over and over again. "I would have never put you in an uncomfortable situation; I thought you knew. I am so sorry, please believe me," he pleaded. I did believe him, actually. He offered me twenty dollars and I took it. I made my way back to Santa Monica.

The church was closed. The sky was black. Not a person in sight. The Starbucks, where the AA attendees would hang out at after meetings, was shut down. No one was there, and I thought, *Holy shit, I'm really screwed now*. I walked back to the boardwalk to look for Jesse. It started raining.

Jesse had a friend he knew who had a real apartment; a girl. He would tell me it's where he could score from time to time, but I suspected it was more. I would shun the thoughts of them together. The first time I had run away to the boardwalk I would occasionally walk past the building and stare. She had ceiling lighting, which looked expensive. I thought she had money or a real job. I would see a glimpse of her when he would tell me he was going to be meeting up with her. She had long, well-groomed brown hair. I was shattered when he was with her, but who was I to claim him? He was such a free spirit.

I had nowhere to go. I was desperate, and in a desperate act, I started yelling Jesse's name from the street, up at her window. And the shame I felt in doing this was humiliating. But I needed to survive, and it was either getting him to come down for a moment so he could tell me where to go or me just staying on the streets. I stood out there for over half an hour in the pouring rain—my hair, my shirt, and my shoes were drenched. All the stuff I had just washed became wet and cold. The colder

I felt, the louder I shouted his name in tears and desperation.

Instead of Jesse coming down to rescue his pigeon, he sent a friend. I heard the skateboarder approach in the distance.

He asked, "Are you Vicky?"

"Yes," I responded, wiping my face.

"I am Jesse's friend; he asked me to come and get you. I know where I can take you."

"Thank you," I replied in desperation.

"You must be cold; come with me and we can get you into some dry clothes."

I thought to myself, *Oh, thank God.* But while waiting there, my heart was shattered because I knew Jesse was with her. Their relationship was fake. I knew the real Jesse. But he went to her after I left the boardwalk? As if he and her were a normal couple now? He knew I was outside. Why would he choose her over me...? I must have been a second choice, and I was utterly heartbroken. Didn't he realize how much I had risked to come back to him?

"I have an apartment—my girlfriend, Amber, and I live there."

I was greeted at the door by Amber. She had blonde dreadlocks, and a chubby stomach confidently displayed in a midriff outfit. She lit a stick of incense while talking a million miles per minute, bouncing to all corners of the room.

"Would you like to make jewelry?" she asked, pointing to her eclectic art table filled with various hand-painted glass beads. She said it was my way of paying for a night of room and board: I made jewelry, and she would sell it on the boardwalk. I thought her name fit her nature; she was kind but she was high, seemingly on more than weed. All I wanted was a calm night with Jesse in our little tent. She let me take a hot shower and borrow a T-shirt and some jeans. I rolled her jeans at my waistline for a better fit. I was reminded of my mother, in a panic, dressing me for my courtroom arrest. How worried my mother must have been that day wasn't lost on me.

"Here," Amber said, interrupting my vivid memory.

She handed me a bowl to smoke. I wasn't sure I wanted to. I pondered, *It could be worse. But I hope I don't have to have sex with these people.* I wandered about the apartment, sussing out my surroundings.

I thought maybe I had gone too far, running again. The consequence would definitely be jail; why didn't I think of that earlier?

I was alerted by the sound of a girl talking. I entered a dark room, and I saw two girls in a corner quietly conversing. One had warm eyes, a petite face, shiny brown shoulder-length curly hair, and mocha-colored skin. Her eyes were brown, round, and smiling. I listened to her speak. She sounded educated, and when she looked at me, I felt a small jolt of electricity. Her well-cut hair and clean clothes told me she didn't belong anywhere on the street or at this apartment. She politely excused herself from the conversation, and I took notice of her manners, a foreign attribute in this environment.

She approached me, saying, "I heard you just came from the boardwalk. Why are you on the street? You're so young." She was direct.

"Well, don't be shy or anything," I sarcastically replied. "I might be young, but I've probably been through more than what you would have any idea about. You're older than me, I assume?" I wouldn't allow patronizing.

She smiled, almost smirked. Her tender, earthy eyes, and her perfect, poreless skin distracted me. "You might be right. I'm not living on the street, so your life is probably more exciting than mine." We started to banter. Her name was Lauren. After talking for over an hour, we both started feeling restless in the apartment. It was as if we found a bubble that others didn't belong in.

She asked, "Do you have some place to go tonight?"

I replied, "No—but I really don't want to stay here."

"You can come to my house and sleep on the couch, or we can stay up talking all night."

My smile was enough of a reply; we locked eyes, beaming back at one another. She knew that meant "yes." She grabbed my hand—her hands felt like silk in mine. I went to stay at Lauren's off-campus apartment, and we did exactly what she had promised: we stayed up all night talking. I wondered why she was escaping through drugs, seeing as she was seemingly legitimately educated. That was when I realized that drug users came from all walks of life. She was an anthropology major at UCLA, and yet we were in the same environment, doing the same thing. But she was safe, and her apartment was safe. I stayed with Lauren. And we became very close, eventually becoming best friends, and for a brief time, lovers.

She would wake and quietly get ready for school. In a funny way, her routine made me feel grounded because, in my mind, at least one of us had something going for them.

I would wake up slowly, usually in a daze from a late night, and would find a bowl of weed next to the bed and a note that read, "Try and leave some for me" with a smiley face.

I hid behind Lauren and she supported this. I would turn on The Fugees and dance in her living room. The gold sunset shimmer would pirouette across her walls right at five p.m.; the moving lights inspired me to dance—as if I was never running from something, but only dancing amidst the storm. Lauren watched me as if she had found a wildflower on a cold, rainy night. It felt so good to be admired like a muse of sorts. She found the beauty within me, encouraging me to blossom before her. I hoped I did the same for her. These moments I could never forget, even if I tried.

Lauren's drugs never quite dulled my worry enough. I feel guilty admitting that at times, when she asked me to withdraw money from her account, I withdrew a little extra for more drugs.

I dyed my hair dark chocolate brown to disguise myself, and I would go back to the boardwalk out of habit. I felt more comfortable being free at the beach. Maybe it was sunlight and the beach air that helped my serotonin levels. I'd look for Jesse.

One evening, Lauren had a family function—a dinner with just her mother–and I was left alone in her apartment. But I wasn't just by myself; I was profoundly alone. Nothing was around to distract me from my undoing. My mind would wander, and I thought about Lauren's mother and whether or not she was trying to convince Lauren that I was a bad influence. Lauren had mentioned that she was usually not invited for a dinner with just her mother. Lauren's grades had started to suffer. It was probably better if I did leave Lauren alone.

I left her house that night and went to the boardwalk to meet with Jesse. I wanted to let him know that I was okay without him...but I wasn't, really. And in total truth, I wasn't gay, I was experimenting, but it became extremely uncomfortable to give Lauren what she needed. It never quite fit. It never felt right to me, and I started to feel overwhelmed by the weight of her wanting to be pleased. I knew it would have never been enough for her to only be friends.

I went to the small, humble abode that some people saw as a cart holding up a tarp, but to me was a room I shared with Jesse, right smack in the middle of the world. I crawled into the tarp to see him there sitting cross-legged, rolling a cigarette. The blue tent cast a cool-toned light upon him.

"May I have one?" I asked. It was as if he knew it was me crawling in.

"Hey," he said with a big smile, showing his straight and

wide-toothed grin.

"Hey," I replied.

"Where have you been bouncing around?" he asked.

I perched myself beside him, our outer thighs touching. "I was at that girl Lauren's house; you know, the one from Amber's?"

"Oh, yeah." He nodded and reached his arm around me. We kissed as if we had been torn apart for years.

"I've been waiting for you," he whispered softly.

I smiled and leaned into him. "I've been waiting to come back to you."

We tried to be intimate, but his body wouldn't work—this is the real side to drug use that nobody shows in Hollywood movies. It was so demeaning for me as a female to not have the power to change it. Was I not pretty enough? Was he in love with that other girl? Was he with her earlier and now he couldn't be with me? I started to ask, but he cut me off.

"It's not you, I promise; it's me and what I took earlier. I'm sorry." He paused and kissed my forehead. "The only other time this has ever happened was when I was in love." He kissed my forehead again.

I was confused by this. *Doesn't being in love make you want to be intimate? Is he in love with me?* I laid on him, content to breathe in the familiar scent of his scalp, his salty hair. I found it all primal and intoxicating. I fell asleep next to him after he said he would stay up all night and watch if anyone was going to come.

The next morning, my eyes slowly peeled open to the sound of a familiar voice calling my name repeatedly. Again. Only this time, it was my *mother*.

I heard her voice calling, "Holly, Holly, Holly!" I should have known it wouldn't be too hard to find me; the boardwalk wasn't that big. In a way, I think I was ready to be found.

She lifted the end of the blue tarp and found me lying between two carts beside Jesse.

She shook my leg, and in the softest, most merciful, tender tone, she said, "Baby, it's time to come home. Come on, honey, come home, baby, I'm here." She reached out her hand, and like a young child, I felt rescued. I purged all apprehension and allowed myself to be taken. I didn't realize it then, until I felt my heart break wide open, how much I had missed and needed my mother.

I turned to Jesse. "Come with me."

"No, you go with your family." He paused to look at the ground and cleared his throat. "You're lucky. She came to get you."

I interrupted him. "Jesse, stop, come with me!"

"Holly, honey, come on now!" my mom cut me off. She didn't acknowledge his existence.

"Jesse, come on, come with me?"

In the same way a protective elder would speak, he simply said, "Go."

I crawled out of the tent to my mother. She held my hand all the way to the car. She never asked for details. She never made me wrong. The ride home was silent; we both felt the seriousness of what was to come, me going back to juvie.

I got home. My little brother greeted me with a tight and lengthy hug. He had a million questions that I couldn't answer. I was tired—beyond tired. I took a long shower. I saw the light brown water from my body being sucked into the drain. I stood there, letting the hot rinse wash away Venice Beach. Where was Jesse now? *I hope he is with that girl. It would be better than alone in a tent.* The way our relationship had turned wasn't lost on me. I once detested the idea of him being sheltered by her; now I was wishing it for him.

Mom called my father to let him know I was safe and at

home. I overheard the call. My nerves were wracked. My feet felt like slick, sweaty ice. I was terrified. Running distracts you, but you can't run forever. Within forty-eight hours, my dad alerted the police to where I was. He thought I would run again. I had time to call Lauren to let her know I would write. I could feel the waves closing in over me.

On went the cuffs, while the neighbors were watching, and my little brother waved goodbye at the front door. My mother couldn't look. Off I went back to juvenile hall for a week. At that point, I became one of the girls that I had judged during my first intake: a not-so-polished-anymore girl. My language had changed. I understood their slang and what the tattoos meant. I knew the gangs around Venice and maybe we knew some of the same people from the boardwalk.

The probation officer said, "Hi, Cohen," like we were old friends.

I was transferred from juvie to a lockdown confinement boot camp. Being shackled at the wrist and ankles wasn't shocking anymore. Confinement boot camp was the last resort before complete Youth Authority prison.

In admissions, waiting for the probation officer, I did a double take as someone walked by. It was Speedy. I saw her face and tried to look away, but she noticed me immediately.

How can they do this? How can they put us in the same facility? It was then I was roughly reminded that I was just a number in the system. Why would they care? It was the taxpayers' dollars. None of this was geared for rehabilitation.

Speedy jerked her body towards me, lunging like some wild beast, and luckily for me—and for her—her probation officer held her back.

"It's not worth it," she snapped at Speedy. "You got three more days, and I am sick of seeing your face."

She asked Speedy who I was and what beef she had with

me.

"That's Holly," Speedy snarled.

The probation officer looked me up and down and retorted, "She ain't worth it, Speedy."

It felt like my juvie-karma for ratting Speedy out, but I thought those drugs were going to kill us both.

I was shown my bunk bed. For the next three days, I was looking over my shoulder in paranoia of what Speedy might organize to punish me. I thought she might have others do her dirty work and jump me. Luckily, I was smart enough to make friends with a girl named Raven, who said she would look out for me.

"Ladies, get up!" It was five a.m. We would groggily get dressed in desert fatigue, lace up our black boots, and make our beds military style in a timely manner, ensuring the corners were tucked in properly. I still make my bed like this. It's sensible.

The clothing clung to our skin as we sweated, jogging in 105-degree weather. We marched everywhere; to PE, to meals, and around the yard. If you were caught doing anything out of order, even laughing with another girl, you were made to do push-ups publicly.

The officers yelled every command as if we were twenty feet away. I would see their neck veins pop. Our beds, hair, cubbies, and clothing were checked every morning. If you had any contraband, you were to jog around the yard for an hour in the midday heat for the next few days, wearing a clown costume; a way of furthering yourself from the group, becoming more of an outsider. Everything was cold, routine, and rough. Every day while jogging, we would sing marching songs. One was a classic, "If you know you did the crime, let me see you double time," which meant we jogged faster, always leading with our left foot.

I remember the dim night light cast over those sweet girls' faces while they slept. Those were the faces parents would admire when they were babies. I saw the vulnerable expressions of beauty on my fellow inmates. In early hours, from my top bunk, I could see who they really were until morning light broke and the tough masks would shift into place.

There was one desk in the front of the cell room where an officer would sit. Her letter opener made the tearing-of-paper sound over and over again. The sound of the letter opener cutting through paper was rhythmic, almost like the ocean. I would watch her read all our mail. I hoped maybe one of those letters was for me. Maybe my mom wrote me this time. Maybe Lauren. Anyone... I quietly pondered if the officer ever read inappropriate sexual content. From some of the stories I heard, it was bound to have happened.

Lauren's letters were always beautiful.

"Dear Holly,

I miss you so much. I listen to Lauren Hill and think of you dancing in my living room, so free. I saved all your stuff. I made scrambled eggs this morning, wanting to ask you if you would also like some. I hope you are okay in there, and please know I love you and I miss you so much. Life is boring without you. Guess what? My roommate has a boyfriend... Can you believe it?

It's okay, you went to Venice to see Jesse; I know things can be confusing sometimes.

There will be so many Judge Judy episodes to watch when you come home.

I love you and I am waiting for you,

Lauren

P.S. I went to look for you at Venice Beach that night. I

didn't want you to think that I didn't care if you left. I do care and I always will."

She called her place my home. I missed her.

Other girls would be curious about who was sending me letters. It was all we had, wondering what was going on in each other's lives. It helped my image that I had a girlfriend on the outside, because it meant that I wasn't an impostor. I wasn't a "poser."

Having something to look forward to kept me going; having a friend. I never once received a letter from my sister while I was there. I wondered if Susan and my dad were protecting her from me, or if she was angry with me, or just didn't care anymore.

Sometimes at night, I would reminisce on looking over at Lauren sleeping, at her long black eyelashes and small mouth that was permanently curled up in the corners, as if she was forever smiling. *What is this beautiful person dreaming about?* I'd wonder. She would feel my stare, wake, and turn to me, wrapping her arm around me.

She would whisper, "I love you; come here, you're safe, beautiful girl."

Being with Lauren intimately was like making love to silk. Her kisses landed on me with gentle intention. Her ringlets would curl themselves around my index fingernails, our soft bellies collided, and we would take turns blinking our eyelashes against each other's cheeks and giggle. We were at times fulfilled by a mere hug, falling asleep in each other's arms after admitting our deepest thoughts. Our bond was emotional, and it felt satisfying to feel companionship safely. There was only one secret that I never fully admitted, maybe because I didn't know completely for myself, but I was unsure as to what we really were.

It broke me in two to be cared for in a way I couldn't

reciprocate. How could I say it back when it wasn't true for me—but, then again, wasn't it? I did love her for so many reasons, but *in* love I was not.

My relationships were skewed; what I knew about relationships was skewed. I was in such a confused state about what a healthy, loving bond actually was. And I was confused about myself, but I was not confused about her loving soul. And she was not confused about mine. We gave each other something intangible, which was vital to our survival at the time. I still carry her with me; how special she was. I thank her for her rescue, she was so patient and loving to such a lost girl.

CHAPTER TWENTY-FOUR
REHAB PROM QUEEN

Sweat gathered under my handcuffs and ankle cuffs in the stuffy van. The vehicle slowed to a stop in front of my new rehab center. Tall Manor Academy's entrance loomed before me; after I'd finished boot camp, my father told me that he'd arranged for me to be released to this particular rehab. His research convinced him this one had the solutions to fix my problems. For a fleeting moment I remembered being little and the way I would sneak into the room where he and my mother slept, and, with my two little fingers, I would peel his eyelids open to wake him up before I had to share his attention with the rest of my siblings.

My parole officer helped me to my feet and opened the door. I shuffled up to the building into a huge facility with two long hallways splitting from the front entrance. One was for the boys and the other for the girls.

I was eventually uncuffed and given a brief tour of the grounds. I was introduced to my therapist, and I sat down with a staff member who created a tailor-made program for me. I would go to school during the day in co-ed classes. After school, I would go see my therapist, and after that we would have group therapy, then dinner; and after dinner we would shower and get ready for bed. It was orderly but I felt I could do it. I was shown to my room—a simple room with two beds and a bathroom. I was very grateful to have a private bathroom, even if it was shared with a single roommate; I wondered who she might be and if the other girls were going to be nice. Family visits were on Sundays, and I was genuinely looking forward to them.

I remember sitting in class and looking around and realizing that a lot of people actually understood what they were being taught. At least that is how it appeared. The attention of the students was fixed on the teacher. I was embarrassed in every single academic class. I had so many misunderstandings in the work. However, I did see a boy who sparked my interest—in what seemed like a desolate world. I quickly developed a crush on him—his name was Alfie.

It didn't matter where I was, or what freedoms were given and taken, or what heavy psychological issues I had; I was still just a teenage girl. Alfie and I caught each other's stare, and the spark lit within me. It breathed life into that stale place.

We navigated to each other at lunch and dinner; it was all I looked forward to. Over the next few weeks, we talked so much he became my close friend. Alfie showed me the ropes. He told me which teachers were strict, and which teachers were cool, which counselors were jerks, which counselors were kind. He'd been there a while, finishing off his program. He had a history of alcoholism.

Instead of bonding over our abilities, we all seemed to be bonding over our inabilities. But I saw through him, he was pretending to be less studious than he really was, and he was insatiably intelligent. He understood everything; he passed every subject with an A or A+, and that attracted me to him even more. We were very sneaky and would figure out times when we could meet in the hallway for a quick kiss, then both of us would dash back to our rooms. I would lie on my bed and have something to daydream about, smiling and giggling into the air like a normal teenage girl. I knew I was getting out of there someday, and so was he—so I dreamed that maybe we could be together on the outside as well. It gave me happy thoughts, something to enjoy within the stale reform. I didn't mention it in regular therapy or group therapy. I didn't want it to be taken.

Two weeks before he was due to be discharged he snuck into my room. All the other girls had lined up and walked to breakfast. I was a little behind. I was almost ready to leave my room when he darted into my bathroom, pulling my hand to follow him. He shut and locked the bathroom door.

"What are you doing?" I gasped. It was one thing to kiss in the hallway, but it was another level to be in my actual bedroom.

"Getting some alone time," he said with the cheekiest smile. I giggled and we embraced. The world was spinning as if I was on a carousel. He put his hand on the small of my back and the other held my hand; we intertwined our fingers. There was a knock at the door.

"Holly, why are you still in your room?" a staff member's voice called. My eyes opened wide and Alfie gestured to hush.

I blurted, "I'm going to the bathroom!"

"Okay," the staff said, "I'll check back in a few minutes; otherwise, get down to the cafeteria soon."

"Okay, sure," I replied.

Alfie waited until he couldn't hear the footsteps any longer, kissed me again, then opened the door and crept out. This was the best morning I had had in five months. Between the time in juvie and the boot camp, I had received no physical contact with anyone other than a quick monitored hug from family. You forget how essential human touch is until you are forced to live without it.

Later that night after dinner, we were instructed to sit in a big circle facing each other. In this particular group therapy, everyone was told to bait and yell at each other. I was told the rules, and for the first few sessions, I watched in horror that this was called therapy—to brutally scream at one another? I hadn't been there long enough to upset anyone yet, so I was a spectator. They had three minutes to do it. It was a way to get everything off your chest. Then the roles would reverse, and you would be the target.

This was one of the most anxiety-fueling experiences. I didn't know anybody, and it was a pretty tough crowd.

A few days later, one of the counselors found out that Alfie and I were boyfriend and girlfriend. The counselor cleared her throat and announced, "I have somebody I want to talk to."

She pointed right at me. "You are here, lucky enough to be in this program, and all you think about are boys! You're wasting all our time, being spreadeagled in this place, doing this and that with boys! If you aren't taking this program seriously, maybe you need to go back to juvenile hall. And that's how I feel about that," she finished, smirking just enough to where I couldn't tell if she was ousting me for her own personal reasons or simply wanted to use me to teach everyone a lesson.

Did she just publicly say I was having sex? With multiple people? In front of everyone? I was emotionally and publicly shattered. I wanted to fall into an imaginary hole and die. I could feel my heartbeat thumping in my ears with each agonizing word she threw at me. My palms were moist, and I felt flushed. I kept my eyes low, completely unable to look at anyone else in the group—a group of thirty kids. They all stared at me during the deluge of accusations. I could feel it. I was drowning.

Then I had three minutes to yell back at her, but I had no idea what to say because I didn't know her. I didn't have any reason to yell at her in front of everyone. Even though she had called me out, it didn't matter. I didn't have a thing to say.

Not meeting anyone's eyes, I finally spoke up. "What's the purpose of this? I don't even know you."

"This is Tall Manor Academy, and we break you down so

we can rebuild you," she replied with a tone of rehearsed pride.

I thought, *This is fucking ridiculous; now I don't feel like facing anyone ever again. I don't feel like I'm rising from the ashes. I feel like I'm nothing.*

"Do you have anything else to add, Holly?"

"No," I replied.

She continued, "We are moving on then."

The held breath within me deflated when the turn was passed on to somebody else, yet my eyes stayed at the ground. I hoped Alfie would still be with me after this public embarrassment of us. We couldn't sit next to one another anymore. We would now be monitored.

I could never understand how that process, done like that, could help anybody. People blindly believed that was healthy? It did nothing but crush my spirit. No matter how tough a young person might appear when this is done to them, I guarantee it profoundly crushes them, even if it does so silently. That night, I met with my therapist. She was a short lady with a gaunt, sunken face and weathered eyes. She had gray hair and a chopped bob cut. I pondered how straight her hair had to be in order for the cut to be as edgy and precise as it was. We sat across from one another in an open-doored room. I sat down in a plastic chair.

"Do you know why you are here at Tall Manor Academy?" she asked condescendingly.

As I bowed my head, feeling ashamed, I peeled a frayed nail and replied, "Yes."

"Why?" she asked.

"Can we close the door?" I asked.

"Unfortunately, not today, but maybe in the future."

Does she think I'm violent? What is she thinking?

With a deep exhale, she said, "Holly, we've decided to give you a haircut."

I sat in silence with my questions. *What? Why my hair? Why is this about my hair? Who was "we?"*

I had really curly hair, and chopping it would make it frizz. I'd always worn my hair long, otherwise it would look horrible; it couldn't be chopped.

And she continued, "We just feel it's something you hide behind. It's distracting to your program."

"Am I in trouble?" I asked.

"Of course. This isn't a place to have boyfriends. You do know Alfie is leaving soon."

Feeling embarrassed, I replied, "Yes." *Does she think I'm a slut?*

I cared tremendously about what she thought of me. She was cold. Clinical and to the point. She cupped her hands and rested them on her lap as she spoke impersonally to me. Her legs crossed, and not once did she shift positions. It was as if I was one of three thousand others she had broken down.

She continued as I stared at my own hands, utterly affected by the control being enforced upon me, even on my body. I was a ward of the court.

"We have a program for you, Holly, and a part of this program is to erase what you were to build a new you. One that doesn't rely upon the tools you used before."

I sat silently, taking it all in.

She continued her admonishment. "This is one of the ways we are helping you; the hairdresser is outside and waiting to cut your hair."

She was nothing like the therapist at Boarders. The only thing they had in common was tearing down my trust.

I nervously asked, "Does this hairdresser know how to cut curly hair?" She waved for a staff member to get me. She never answered any of my questions.

The staff member walked me down the hall to the

hairdresser, and they chopped my hair off at my earlobes. Lock by lock, I watched as my hair fell to the floor. I remained quiet as the tears left my eyes.

I sank in utter defeat. I was crushed, and I felt sabotaged. *How will I style my hair now? What celebrity has short, curly hair? I don't have any mousse here to tame it with.*

As I walked back to get to bed, my roommate gasped and asked what had happened. I couldn't even answer; I just wept myself to sleep. A piece of my identity had been murdered, and I was in mourning. It was a part of breaking me down. It was suppressive. To this day I don't understand how that ever served me. I couldn't bear the stares of confusion over the next week from my peers. I kept what was left of my hair up in a tight bun. I looked forward to my daily dose of psych meds. I started to wish they would up my dosage. I couldn't raise my head to look at Alfie. He finally caught me in the hallway, walking to class.

When no one was looking, he said, "I told you they were fucking stupid in here...and I still think you are the most beautiful girl in the world."

I loved Alfie, from what I understood about love. Love, in whatever shape it came in—admiration or appreciation—remained my warmth within the dark, cold water.

During this time, the rehab center began preparations for prom; the academy wanted to try and give us a normal high school experience. My roommate signed me up to be on the ballot. When elections for prom queen and king opened, like most teenage girls, I wanted to be the prom queen. I had only admitted this to my roommate, and she had signed me up for it. The nominees sat in a room, and we waited as two long-residing girls counted the votes.

As the last vote was counted, the girl carelessly tossed it on the table and said, "White girl won." Despite her blasé disappointment, I couldn't believe it—I'd won something!

The prom king was a short Caucasian boy from juvie as well. He secretly had a Latina girlfriend. I think she really wanted to win prom queen, so I felt a little bad, but as a teenage girl, I couldn't wait to call my mom. This was now a major distraction from the reflection of the girl staring back at me in the mirror everyday; the short-haired identity of a girl I did not know. I went to bed every night dreaming of my prom dance with Alfie; we couldn't get into trouble for it, and everyone would finally see that I truly cared for him, that it was real and I wasn't just a slut. Oh, to see Alfie in a suit. I wanted to be dressed up for him; I was told that my mom could come visit and that she was allowed to bring me a dress.

When I spoke with her on the phone, my mom repeated the counselor's advice: the dress could not be too lavish, too flashy, or too expensive.

A few days later, Mom arrived at my bedroom door with a long, cobalt blue dress. It was a close-fitting dress made of thick fabric. It was see-through mesh at the waistline and arms. I hated it. I couldn't help but show my disappointment. It wasn't the dress, really, it was me. I felt ugly. I wondered if Heather was having prom with a hairstyle and jewels of her choosing.

"You don't like it?" she asked.

"It's okay, Mom." I was always afraid of telling my mom when I didn't like something. I didn't want to disappoint her.

"Holly! They said it had to be minimal, honey. I had to do what I was told, so I brought you one of my own dresses I had. I love it, and the color will be great on you! Holly, once your hair and makeup are all done, you will look great. Let me start with your hair."

"Okay," I replied.

I sat on the bed looking out the window. Mom pulled the elastic band off, and my hair sprung out to the tips of my ears.

She gasped as if she had been shot with an arrow. "What have you done to your hair?!"

I had forgotten she hadn't seen it yet. Her face was red with anger, lips pressed in a tight, hard line.

"They made me cut it off."

"*Who* made you cut it off?" she asked.

"The staff. I couldn't do anything about it."

She grabbed my hair and angrily yanked my head back to face forward. She sighed, letting her hands drop to her sides.

"Holly, what am I supposed to do with this now? I have no idea what to do with your hair. The whole look is ruined."

"It's okay, Mom, don't worry." In a bizarre reversal, I felt the urge to quell her anger and disappointment.

"I can't believe this shit, Holly. There's nothing I can do. Your father took all that away from me."

I sat there while she angrily yanked my head around, trying to find a way to make my hair look decent for the night. We didn't speak. She brought small butterfly clips that were lined with cubic zirconia. She placed them in my hair and said, "This was the best I could do. I'll be back later tonight. Here are the shoes."

She left the box on the bed, hugged me, and left. I knew she was still upset. I felt ashamed of my hair, and every time I looked in the mirror, the girl looking back at me was an ugly version of myself. I tried to ignore the thought. I knew my mom was doing as she was told. Her anger was the loss of control over her own child. Her anger was her helplessness.

Prom started, and I waited for my mother and brother. I saw

a red Mercedes Benz convertible pull up, and I instantly knew it was them. I was proud that my family showed up in such a nice ride. My mother had worked hard for what she had now. She had started her own company from her home, an insurance business, and my brothers were her first employees. Years ago, I had watched as they sat at our kitchen table making cold calls from the phonebook. Later, this company would be able to afford her, and the family, some of life's luxuries.

My brother Caleb looked amazing in his black-and-white tux. He waved hello, and I went to get Alfie to introduce him to my brother and my mom.

"Alfie, come here! My mom is here, I want you to meet her!"

"Is *that* your mom?" He pointed towards the door.

She was a vision. She wore a heart-shaped, floor-length, sequined black-and-gold gown. It had loads of tulle. She looked as if she was going to the Oscars. Her hair was beautifully wrapped in a bun, and she wore impeccable makeup with large jeweled earrings that dropped from her ears. She looked like a queen.

I was in shock. How could she upstage me? How could she not think of how this would make me feel?

The moment I saw her, I ran out of the room and sat in the abandoned bleachers.

Alfie joined me and asked, "What's wrong, what's wrong?"

"How could my mom wear that? How could she dress like that? I mean, look at me!"

"You're beautiful," he said gently.

"No, Alfie, I'm not. I hate this dress, I hate these shoes, and my hair—they chopped my hair. I hate this place, I hate this crown!"

Alfie grabbed my crown and threw it in the nearby trash. "I hate that crown too." And we laughed through my tears.

"Come on, smile, we have a few hours to go and it's not like we can leave. You can't leave early as prom queen. Let's dance," he offered, holding his hand out to me.

After meeting my mom, my therapist pulled me aside to ask if I was okay. I denied that anything was wrong because any trust I ever had was chopped along with my hair.

I put on a happy face, and I danced with Alfie, my roommate, and my brother. My brother is truly one great dancer. He was such a sport to come for the night.

I respectfully acknowledged my mom, saying how beautiful she looked. She said, "Tonight is about you, honey, go and dance more; I'll take some photos!"

I said goodbye to my brother and mom, shaking my head as my mother struggled to get the length and vastness of her tulle dress into the car as she left.

Later, I would pen some lyrics about the moment in one of my songs: "Mom, sing me a lullaby, but don't wear a crown to my prom."

That night after dinner, I walked past the room of a mutual friend of Alfie's and mine. His name was Thomas. I was looking for Alfie, but I saw Thomas sitting in the corner of his bed with his head cradled in his hands. I backtracked my steps and stood at the doorway of his room.

"Hey, Thomas, everything okay? I was walking past, and you looked sad or something."

"I'm good, Holly," he said. But he wasn't.

"No, you're not. What's going on?" I softly asked.

A moment later, a man exited his bathroom. I recognized him. It was the custodian. He looked surprised to see me. *What is he doing here so late?*

"Holly, is it? I'm Jack."

Jack wore stained, olive green pants and a gray T-shirt. He had sandy hair and weathered skin, as if he had aged badly. His eyes looked tired, but his whole face morphed with his smile, and his ears moved when he spoke. I didn't like it. His teeth were stained and I figured he smoked. I had only ever seen him speaking to Thomas, and another boy we vaguely knew, Jose.

"Hello," I replied.

"Hey, so tomorrow I'll bring in Snickers, and a few other candy bars, if you want. I just dropped off Thomas's."

"You can do that?" I asked in sheer surprise.

"Sure, but let's not say anything because then I won't be able to. I know how it is in here, and sometimes you just need a candy bar, right?"

"Yeah," I replied. *That was nice of him*, I thought.

He started towards the door. "See you later, Thomas...and Holly, you should get back to your room; you're not allowed to be in here."

"Later," Thomas replied.

As soon as Jack left, I looked at Thomas and said, "Okay, Thomas, something is going on; why are you so sad?"

"It's nothing."

"I am not going until you tell me," I sternly replied.

"I can't," he said, as I noticed his jaw clench tightly.

"Not leaving."

"Fuck, Holly, get out of my room!" he demanded. "You're going to get us both in trouble."

"Okay, okay, okay, I'll go, but I'm here if you need someone to talk to, okay?"

"Okay," he said, and I left. Something wasn't right. Something was really off.

The next day, I saw Jack speaking with Jose in the cafeteria near the trash bins. After the conversation finished, I stacked my tray of food and rushed over to Jose.

"Hey Jose, I found out about the candy bars. He's bringing me some, too," I said.

"He brings them to you too?" he asked in surprise.

"Well, I found out last night...so it's my first time, I guess. Does he bring them to you all the time?" I asked.

"When he visits my room, yeah," said Jose.

"Does he also clean your room? Will he clean mine now too?" I asked.

"I dunno," he replied sharply and left without a goodbye.

A few days passed. I went to school, and after dance class, I walked to my room with permission to change my clothes. Standing in my room was Jack. He held a Snickers and a Kit Kat bar in one hand, and Skittles in the other. He was smiling and gestured for me to take them.

"Wow, thank you!" I said. "Skittles are my favorite!"

But he held onto them.

"I thought you would like these ones," he replied. He walked into my bathroom. He stood just past the doorway.

"Oh, you don't have to clean my bathroom, I just did it last night."

"Well, could you do me a favor?" he replied.

"Sure," I said.

"You can keep a secret right, just like the way we have to with the candy?"

I nodded.

He unzipped his pants and said, "Well, you could help me out, too...?"

I stood there, stunned.

"I'm going to be late for school," I replied. I ran. I ran straight to my next class. I sat at my desk and struggled to catch my breath. I was embarrassed, and I thought it was my fault. I wondered if he would be waiting in my room when I got back. I attempted to act as if nothing had happened. All the while I thought of which staff member I should go to, or if they would even believe me. Jack's needy facial expression flashed in my mind, and my stomach churned as if I had eaten something sour. Now I knew what was happening with Jose and Thomas. After school, I ran to Thomas, and I told him what had happened.

We found a spot where we couldn't be heard on the quad outside the main building.

"What the fuck, Thomas!"

He immediately knew what I meant. "You will ruin my whole life. You can't tell anyone. Holly, if you tell... My mom, my fiancé, my dad will never speak to me again." He put his head in his hands the same way he had when he was in his room that night. "I have a baby on the way... You will ruin everything. I live in the smallest fucking town, Holly."

Why wouldn't his family understand? I thought, but I remained quiet. I couldn't understand at the time, but later I would realize what coming from a small town meant. My mom had come from a small town. Once you are branded, you never live it down, no matter what the label may be. You can disgrace your entire family so easily; word spreads like wild fire, just like at the boardwalk. Thomas later said his father held a high position in the church and that he had only two weeks left before he was being discharged.

What was I to do? I held onto what I knew, and later on decided to try and talk to Thomas one last time. I didn't know Jose as well, but I had planned to speak with him, too. I had hoped we would all expose Jack together.

Later that night, I went back to Thomas' room. He was lying under his sheets.

"Thomas," I whispered.

"Go," he said.

I walked straight over to his bed and pulled the sheet back.

"We need to–" I couldn't finish speaking. His head had been shaved, and he was bleeding from his skull. Band-Aids had been placed on a few of the cuts. But there were still rows of raw, bloody skin. It terrified me. Why would he do this?

"What happened?" I gasped in a panic.

"I shaved my head." He seemed distraught. "I pushed down too hard... Look at what you are doing to me, Holly—get out of my room!"

I pushed him to *this*. I made him cut himself. I left right away.

I passed a staff member on the way and said, "You should check on Thomas." I didn't wait for a reply. I went straight to my room. I packed my backpack.

My roommate asked, "What are you doing? Are you going somewhere?"

As I shoved the clothes in my bag, I angrily muttered, "I'll tell you if you promise not to tell on me."

"I promise," she assured. "I won't say a word."

I believed her. She had a rebellious nature and didn't strike me as a rat.

"Away," I said.

She didn't ask why. Instead, she asked, "Where?"

"I don't know, anywhere but here."

"Holly, we are in the middle of the fucking mountains, and it's dark."

I interrupted, "I don't care, I'm going."

She looked at me defiantly. "I'm coming with you. I know where we can go; I know somewhere safe kind of in the area." *Kind of* was good enough for me.

Our room was the very last room before an exit door to the outside grounds. Usually, it was locked—or so we believed. I waited for my roommate to pack her bag, and we stood close to one another, ready to go. I said, "Ready? Run as fast as you can over the gate and hide if anyone comes. But we stay together."

She replied, "Yeah."

I pushed the door, and we bolted. My arms swung fast,

scissoring the sides of my body. It was dark, darker than I expected. An alarm went off, a piercing bell's ring, and I ran as fast as I could in the direction of the street gate. I had never run so fast in my life. My feet were the wind, my heart was pounding outside my chest.

We were, in fact, situated in the mountains and the road was barren of places to lie low if we needed. We slowed down our pace, walking quickly down the only road leading to and from the academy. I spotted a white school vehicle driving in the distance. The staff was trying to find us, so we dove under a single parked car to hide. We started to make our way in what we believed to be the direction of my roommate's acquaintance. We had no plan, and this seemed like the best option at the time.

We hitchhiked with a truck driver. We both thought he was high because of the way he kept talking. On and on and on. Or he was severely lonely. You would have thought he'd have wondered what we were doing in the mountains, all alone, running with backpacks, but he didn't care. Plus, he thought we would pay him for the ride.

My roommate asked him to drop us off in front of a random apartment two blocks away from where we were going. We hopped out of his truck. She told him to wait so she could grab his money from her place. He was a high idiot. We took a sharp left, shortcutting into an alleyway. She led me down two blocks to the woman's house, leaving the truck driver waiting for his money.

We arrived at a two-story, olive green apartment building. It was worn with time and negligence. We walked past a man who seemed to be guarding the door, and we went up the stairs to an apartment on the second floor. He greeted my friend with a nod, as if they knew each other, and allowed us to enter the apartment. Then, I was introduced to my host.

"You can call me Ma'am, and that's how you'll refer to me while you are here."

"Okay," I nodded, trying to discern her ethnicity. I wasn't sure if she was Indian, Ethiopian, or of some other eastern descent.

"Go, over there, to that room." She motioned sternly. I was taken aback at how bossy she was. On the way to the room, I saw eight men in the living room, sitting in a circle, watching me walk. The beige carpet was splattered with dark stains and the walls were covered with a thick layer of filth.

Ma'am had a quick conversation with my girlfriend privately, then my girlfriend came back to me and said, "I told her that you know what's up; that you know what you're supposed to be doing here."

I quickly realized that when my roommate had said she'd worked as a dancer, that this was what she meant. I had never known much more beyond that, and I had never thought to ask. I should have. I understood then that my friend had known this life, and this world, quite well.

Ma'am walked in, opened up a suitcase, and said, "You can pull from here. We need to see where you're at."

I looked inside the suitcase and saw a cheap collection of worn-out, skimpy bikini tops and underwear, as well as fishnet stockings. I realized we were going to be performing for the gentlemen in the living room very soon.

My friend got quite excited looking through the clothing, but I felt like there were jitterbugs in my stomach. I thought of the man posted up outside the front door, and those out in the living room. Would those men sitting out there try and stop me? Would they let me out of the apartment?

I wondered, *Who's worn the clothes before?* But I quickly pushed those thoughts away, the same way I pushed away the thoughts of the sleeping bag that first night on the boardwalk.

As I sifted through the garments, I decided on a green bikini top, and a pair of green underwear that looked like the scales of a mermaid.

Even though I did not know how to dance, I was required to in front of those men. Ma'am pointed at the men sitting in a circle who were looking at me as if I was a piece of meat. The look in the eyes of those men is something I will never forget. It taught me so much. I learned early in my womanhood what severely ill intentions looked like in the eyes of a hungry man.

I could never forget the song that was playing: "No Diggity" by Blackstreet. The sight of the club lighting in the room, red and green strobes bouncing off the walls, and the men sitting and watching, is etched into my mind. I was heartbroken and humiliated, having expected a place of safety, and yet there I was, sacrificing more of myself. I remember wondering how long the song would continue to play. I felt like an imposter. I just could not dance the way I was expected to dance. I felt disgusted being there, but in some weird way, I wanted my dancing to be good.

The men were laughing about which of us was the better dancer. There was this one particular man that made me deeply cringe. Beads of sweat pooled on his forehead, and he licked his thin lips as he watched me. I could see he was planning on doing something much more than watching. Finally, Ma'am turned on the lights, and I was so relieved that it didn't look like a club anymore. I glanced over at my friend and resentment washed over me, but I knew it wouldn't serve me well; I needed her in this strange world.

"Alright, now you can go to bed," Ma'am announced.

As I was washing off my makeup and taking off the skimpy clothing, I felt like I was removing the disgusting persona that I was in. With every layer that came off, I became closer to my authentic self. I couldn't wait to go to sleep and dream away what I had just done. I hoped that I wasn't going to be asked to sleep with one of those repulsive men.

I knew then that I was fully out of my element.

In the near distance, I heard Ma'am putting her children to bed. The soft voice of a child was comforting. I was closer in age to the child than Ma'am, yet there I was behaving like a much older woman.

Ma'am allowed us to spend the night at her apartment, but the next morning she wasted no time telling us that we would have to pay off the expense of the room and board by working; selling our souls.

"Hey you, come here." She pointed at me while I was eating a bowl of cereal with her children. I followed her to her room. She had an unmade bed, a pile of clothes in the corner, and mismatched curtains—maroon and dark blue.

"You will work for money. You will pay for food, rent, anything else you need. It will take a couple times before you make good money—but you will make good money, and I will take a percentage, and so will your bouncer."

"Bouncer?" I interrupted.

"Yeah, bouncer. You can't go to work without security! You don't know these strange-ass men or what they will do. Oh, and you need to tell me if I gotta worry about cops or anyone coming to look for you here."

"No," I said. "You don't have to worry."

"Go eat," she instructed. She paid me $50 for my efforts from the night before and walked off.

That morning, Ma'am commanded me to take a shower. I was so weak and out of sorts that I fell to my knees. I had never slipped in a shower before. I heard banging on the door. I stood up quickly.

The woman barged in, pulled the curtain aside, and looked at me dubiously. "Do you have a mark on your body?"

I furrowed my brows a little, wondering why she only asked about my body. "No, I'm okay."

She walked away.

Cold and wet, I exited the bathroom wrapped in a worn towel.

"Go pick a new outfit out of the suitcase," she demanded, "You've got work this afternoon."

My girlfriend was excited that we were going to make some money. We were sent out to dance at some unknown location, Ma'am driving and a bouncer in the passenger seat. While we were on the way there, I looked at my friend and noticed how relaxed she was. I couldn't even fathom her ease.

As we drove to the location, Ma'am looked at us and said, "If there is danger, the one thing you need to know is that you have to get to the door and bang on it three times. And he'll come in and rescue you. That's what you have to remember. You're timed, and if you don't come out in time, he's going to be banging on the door."

My heart fell to the bottom of my feet. We approached the door of the cheap hotel.

"Get in there," Ma'am said impatiently. I opened the door to see a man lying on the bed. My friend and I were told to stand on either side of the bed.

Ma'am asked the man, "Who do you want: her or her?"

It was the first time I realized I was being offered up as a choice, and I was both relieved and terrified when he picked me, because at least I wasn't rejected. I was wanted. But then I didn't know what to do. I had never personally danced for a guy.

"You know the rules," Ma'am said to all of us, and gestured to my friend. "She's going to stay here in case he wants another girl."

Just when I thought it couldn't get more awkward. "The bouncer is outside the door," she warned. I didn't know if he was only there for our protection or to enforce that I stay in the room to do my job, but I was frightened to find out.

Ma'am left. I shyly asked, "What would you like?"

He said, "Just dance for me. Just dance on top of me."

A few minutes later, I wondered if the sexiest thing to do was to move my hips from side to side. I didn't really know what I was doing.

The day before, I had studied my friend's moves, so I tried to copy that. *Maybe I've seen this in a movie? Is that what he wants?* I realized when I saw his face that I wasn't doing such a good job.

"How about her?" he asked and motioned for me to stop.

My friend knew just what to do. She climbed onto him like a female spider above her victim. She straddled his hips and moved her body like a snake. It was as if she heard a song in her mind that she was dancing to the rhythm of. She brushed against his groin slightly every now and again as she continued to move back and forth. She knew when to stop. She asked if he wanted further services before he physically finished.

Time was up, and Ma'am came in. She asked if we had done any further services for him.

My girlfriend said, "Yeah, he didn't really want her, so I had to jump in."

I was met with a look of disappointment. I didn't know the consequences of letting her down. I was quiet on the way back to Ma'am's. I got a quarter of my pay cut. I decided to save anything I made, because I knew I couldn't stay here.

I eyed my friend and thought, *Who are you, that you're comfortable with this?* Later, when I planned my escape, I asked her to come with me and she said she wanted to stay. I was offended by her answer.

"How can you want to stay here? Something could happen to you!"

I laid in bed that night, in tears, considering how deeply sorry I felt. For everything. For myself, and how lost I was now, how far I had veered away from my dreams. I never wanted to perform for strange men; I wanted to perform with song and art to a better world than this. I regretted my anger towards my mother, who had driven over two hours back and forth twice to bring me my dress. I should have celebrated her. Maybe I'd misunderstood how she wanted to be beautiful for me, and wanted to make me proud. Maybe she thought my dad was coming, too. Maybe she wanted to show how well off she was, how much money she had made. Had I not gotten so upset, maybe I would have better dealt with Jack. I was truly a leaf blowing in the wind at the mercy of the devil's breath. I wept quietly from the depth of my stomach.

The next morning, I took a shower, and again, I slipped and fell to my knees. It was an omen. I had hit my rock bottom. I knew that God spoke in mysterious ways. This job had brought me to my knees. I had lost my dignity, my morals, and my self-respect. I started to plan in earnest. I knew it wasn't an option to ask if I could go, so I didn't bother.

In the night, I waited until everyone was asleep. I took the money I had and put it in my pocket. I tiptoed to the front door. *Stay focused, Holly.* I unlatched the lock slowly. Now for the screen door. I slowly opened the screen, and it creaked. I froze in fear, waiting to hear if someone would come. When they didn't, I forced the screen door open and bolted down her apartment stairs. I had no idea where to go, so I listened for cars and followed the sound. I saw a line of small shops that looked vacant of customers, but the lights were still on. There was a payphone.

I called Lauren.

I gripped the payphone tightly, pushing the receiver hard against my ear to hear her. She told me, "Put the phone down, and go ask the shop for an address so I can locate you."

"Okay," I said. I did as she said, and then thought, *I'd better call her back. What if she changes her mind, and she's not coming to get me? What am I going to do?*

I called her back four or five times.

Sternly, she said to me, "Holly, I'm coming—I promise. You have to stop calling me. I'm trying to figure out where you are. You're about forty-five minutes away from me. Just sit down and relax."

They are going to come and find me, and I'll be sent to California Youth Authority, which was where everyone was sent in the state as a last resort punishment before county jail.

With every flash of headlights I ducked, face to the ground. I was afraid that one of those men from the dancing circle would come and throw me in a trunk.

I was completely terrified. Those forty-five minutes waiting for Lauren felt like a whole day. Even though she had told me to stop calling her, I called her twice more. I had fifty dollars' worth of change, and it was nothing for me to call. It was worth it. Then, at last, she picked me up, and we drove back to a warm safe haven, her home.

CHAPTER TWENTY-FIVE
ONE HIDDEN PLAN

Realizing that I needed to face the impending court case, I knew I couldn't stay at Lauren's house for very long. After weighing what little options I had, I called my mom.

I was close to eighteen years old, and if I got caught by the police again, I was going to adult jail. That really scared the hell out of me, because if staying with juveniles was dangerous, I didn't want to imagine being in a jail with possibly further experienced criminals. The probation officer said I would spend my full sentence of five years in county jail, and that fact kept ringing in my ears.

"Goddammit, Holly," Mom snapped, "How do you always get so caught up in this shit? Why can't you just play by the fucking rules?"

I winced. "Mom, you don't understand."

"And I just heard something on the radio about a serious incident that occurred at Tall Manor Academy!"

"Mom, I was involved in that."

"Goddammit, Holly, you're involved in that too? How do you always get caught up in all the drama? What are we going to do? They're going to be looking for you. What are we going to do?"

"Mom," I said, "I don't know. That's why I'm calling you."

"You need to get to my house," she said. "Get away from that girl, Lauren—and get your ass home."

"Okay."

"She going to take you home? Do I need to come pick you up or what?"

"She'll take me home, Mom."

Lauren drove me from West Los Angeles to Long Beach, racing down the 405. I couldn't smoke enough cigarettes; I couldn't get it off my mind, the heaviness of what I'd done.

My mom opened the door for me; she was in her penthouse apartment with a 360-degree view of the city of Long Beach. Things had changed for her, big things. I could sense Lauren's discomfort by her passive disposition. We said our goodbyes as my mother watched like a hawk, darting her eyes back and forth suspiciously at Lauren and I.

Mom and I sat outside on the balcony. I scanned over the city lights. I lit a cigarette, she lit a cigarette, and she said, "Holly, they're going to come looking for you here. I know why you ran. I don't want you to tell your dad you're here because they may come and arrest you again. So, we need to find a place for you to be away from all of your hoodrat friends for a little while, till it calms down. Then we need to fight this case. 'Cause right now I'm getting a lot of phone calls, and I just can't have you here."

"Mom, I don't know where I'm supposed to go. I definitely don't want to go back to the boardwalk."

She huffed at me. "Oh hell no, I'm not gonna pull you out of a tent again. You're going to go to the ranch with your brother for about three weeks, till we figure out what we're going to do."

I agreed to her demands, appreciative. This was the first time I had heard that my mother owned a ranch. I felt happy for her; I knew she'd always wanted one. My mom was a country girl at heart.

The ranch was situated in Norco, forty-five minutes east of

Long Beach. My brother Sean was living there, working as a ranch hand, and the first thing he said to me was, "You're going to get to work."

"What kind of work?"

"You're gonna pick up horseshit."

"What?" I narrowed my eyes at him in disbelief.

"Yeah, you're gonna pick up horseshit. What did you think you were gonna do? Sit on your ass out here and do nothing?"

"I'm hiding from the cops!" I exclaimed.

"Yes, I know. Make yourself useful. We have shit to take care of."

"Oh my God," I muttered under my breath.

During the first three weeks, I acquainted myself with a few horses—mainly horses from across the street at another ranch. I found them to be very peaceful creatures. They carried a quiet stoic presence which felt stable. In fact, I hardly picked up any horseshit; instead, my brother would let me sunbathe and get some rest. I think he knew I needed space. But what I really needed was to know my plan.

I called my mom.

"We are going to meet with a lawyer because you were involved with what happened at Tall Manor Academy, and that will be your defense; you ran away for good reason. We can use that so you don't get sent to county jail."

"Okay," I agreed, but I was worried.

"I've been thinking, and that's the only way we can get you out of this."

"Alright," I said. At that point, I would have agreed to almost anything. My eighteenth birthday was looming.

"Come back to Long Beach now, and we can start meeting with a few people."

I returned to Long Beach and my mother, in her take-charge manner, dictated precisely what I needed to do.

"You need to get a job, you need to get your narrow ass to school, and you need to get your GED. And we need to prove you're out here doing the right things. Which is what the lawyer has advised."

I agreed to her conditions with no complaints.

"Holly, if you fuck this up, you're going to go to county jail."

CHAPTER TWENTY-SIX
TWO SWINGING GAVELS

It was my eighteenth birthday. Judgment day.

There I stood, the future of my life in the hands of someone I had never met: the judge. All my secret deals with God were hanging upon this day. I hoped he had heard me.

Please, no county jail, I prayed. My celebration of adulthood—or mourning of—was at the mercy of a flawed court system. For a split second, I considered my sister's afternoon, at lunch with her girlfriends, while I was surrendering myself to the mercy of the judge. That day, only my mother, myself, and our attorney attended court.

I gathered all of the evidence I could to prove I was a functioning normal citizen of society. I got my GED by luck, after failing three times and begging the head of testing for one more shot. I had a clean drug test, transcripts showing that I was attending Long Beach City College, evidence I was taking music classes, and proof that I was working a part-time job as a waitress. I also brought a CD with three of my own original songs on it, showing I had a goal to be a singer. I still have that CD. "Passing Me By" was the song I was most proud of. I had written it on my mother's piano and recorded it at a local studio, which I paid for with my tip money.

Voice shaking, I asked the clerk if he could present everything I'd brought to the judge. This included the paperwork revealing the lawsuit we had filed against Tall Manor Academy.

In the courtroom, the judge looked at me suspiciously from

above his eyeglasses. And before he had another moment to analyze me, I spoke up.

"I can't let my bad past affect my future. I don't want to go to L.A. County Jail. I don't belong there. I can assure you I am a good citizen doing the right things"

As he looked over my paperwork, he mumbled, "Very good."

I responded by gifting him my demo CD.

"Thank you," he said compassionately. "I hope to see your name in lights one day."

With a hard bang of his gavel, he announced he was releasing me with one-year probation, and he added, "Do well."

And I looked back at him, confused, and asked meekly, "That's it?"

"Yes, that's it."

I repeated, "That's it?"

"Yes, that's it," he replied again, with an almost flabbergasted expression. He moved his eyes and looked beyond me. "Next we will be calling the case of…" He mentioned some name, and there I was, released.

The relief, and disbelief, I felt couldn't be explained with a thousand words.

We headed back to my mom's apartment, and she left me there because she had to go to work the rest of the day. I sat in her penthouse that overlooked all of the city. I took in the view, and I thought, *Oh my god, I can't believe I'm free.*

I wasn't being hunted anymore. It had been years of worry. I could go between rooms or down the hall without feeling like I was on borrowed time. I could brush my hair the way I wanted to, wear makeup like other girls my age without the worry of being noticed too much. I could take a bus, go meet with friends—who actually didn't know me anymore, because I had lost contact with all of them. Their lives had moved on.

There was no heavy weight behind my choices. I was fully

free, and no one was going to find me and take me back to an institution. It was a whole new chapter.

My mom let me sleep in for the next several days. She just allowed me to *be*. I tried to figure out how to be a normal girl again.

When I went into the bathroom, no one was ever going to time me again, and I didn't have to worry about the amount of toilet paper I used, like I did in juvie, ever again. And I just sat there about five minutes. I washed my hands, looking at myself in the mirror, and thought, *Wow, it's so nice to be here. It's so nice to be in the bathroom. The lighting is warm. The walls are freshly painted.* I took it all in, because for the first time in ages, I was now willing to be in the present. It was at that moment I thought, *Wow, I'm really out. Things are going to get better; you know?* I was so appreciative to be in that small bathroom. To me, it was everything.

I opened the drawer in the bathroom, and there was a hairbrush. I recognized the brush from years ago. It had been a staple on Mom's countertop at our childhood beach house. I recalled the paycheck taped to her mirror addressed "From Love." I remembered her ballet slippers which had hung from the ceiling. I could almost smell her Lancôme lipstick in that moment. My mom had kept it, and even though it was just a brush, it was a tiny bit of family history that I could recognize, that I could share, that I could remember.

Resurrection can happen anywhere—even teary-eyed and in a bathroom.

And as the evening went on, my mom came home and we had dinner.

"I'm going to my room now," I announced.

She replied, "Honey, you don't need to tell me every time you're going to your room, or to the bathroom."

She wasn't kidding, but I always told her so she didn't think I was escaping. I no longer needed to escape.

It wasn't perfect. For everyday normalcy, I was an outsider trying to get in. It had been three years; that's a long time when you're in your teens. And while Heather was having her first kiss, I was giving my first lap dance. While she drove her first car, I was escaping on a bus. While she was studying for her SATs, I was running from a molesting janitor. I was never going to share the same experiences as many of my peers. It was just something I had to get used to. It was what I had done to myself.

Interestingly enough, over the years, the feeling of being an outsider became an asset. I eventually became proud of my unique worldview because of what I had been through.

There was no program, no therapy to help me acclimate back into normal life. I relied on the support of my family, and on the support of my friends. And frankly, as much as my mom loved me, she was a very busy woman, an entrepreneur, and she had other children to look after. Nervously, I made the call to Lauren and admitted to her how I really felt—that I wasn't gay. She was angry, as I suspected she would be, but I thought I would reach back out as a friend when the time was right. I stayed in touch with Alfie. And other than getting in contact with a few old friends, I was left to do my routine: go to my school, and go to work. My mom had set up a meeting with the lawyers, and a court date was scheduled to sue the rehab center.

I met with lawyers, detectives, and police officers a few times. And I went to court for my cross-examination. My mom had to work, so I reached out to Alfie, and he gave me rides to and from court. I preferred it this way. It was easier than riding with my mom, and more enjoyable. We became a couple, just as I had planned.

The court date came. I sat down in the chair beside the judge and he swore me in. I felt my heart beat just as strongly as the last time I had been in court. I scanned the room for Thomas, but he was nowhere in sight. They asked me questions about time frames and clothing, what I had seen and when. After answering, I was excused to a waiting room. I asked my lawyer about Thomas. He had said he wanted nothing to do with the case, but he was subpoenaed for information. I wondered if he was okay. Jose was there; I could see his shame by his caved-in posture. He was always thin, but now he looked tiny. He said nothing more than "hello" and "goodbye" to me; his mother, grandmother, and father were surrounding him. I was called back into the courtroom the following day. I went to the waiting room and there was Thomas, his fiancé, carrying a young baby, and his mother. I ran to him. His fiancé blocked me before I could say hello.

"He is unwell from the entire situation and needs to rest," she said sternly, as if she was his mother. I peeked behind her at Thomas; he looked vexed and nervous. It saddened me, but I respected his fiancé's request. I knew it was a lot for him, but we couldn't allow Jack to get away with it. And I couldn't live with the thought of him molesting other young people who were recovering from addiction.

There were five more court dates, and on my last day on the stand, Jack was brought in. He sat directly across from me. He was wearing an oddly large cross around his neck, and the people sitting behind him appeared to be his parents. *That cross won't save you from what you did, Jack*, I thought.

I didn't fear him the way I thought I might. I almost felt sorry for him. The judge turned to me and asked, "If it were up to you, what would you like to see happen to Jack as a consequence for his unlawful behavior? Please address your answer to the court." I gaped at him. He was asking for my opinion? The court wanted my thoughts on what justice should be?

I took a moment, and then I looked directly at Jack as I spoke. "I think he should never be allowed to work near any children, teens, or recovering people ever again." I felt good about my answer.

"Then this is what will be," said the judge, and he asked that I step down.

I haven't stepped back into a courtroom since. I left that world on a high note, having served for justice rather than against it, and I would like to keep it that way. I felt a moral high that I hadn't experienced since defending Heather against bullies in school. I wondered if this was the feeling Heather got to experience daily.

I was on good behavior for a year, and I completed my probation.

After, I was expected to know how to live a completely normal life, and have all the right tools. I didn't feel reformed. The only semblance of consistency in my life was my prescription bottle.

CHAPTER TWENTY-SEVEN
THE MYSTIC MOON ON ELM STREET

I worked as a waitress in a tiny little house converted into an Italian restaurant. It was quaint.

My brother Jeremy's girlfriend, Melody, was an employee there and got me the job. I had so much anxiety; the only reason I accepted the job was because she would train me. I never accepted a shift unless she was there because I knew she would look after me. I was that out of touch with average life, and I still had emotional hang-ups over my last real job at the Deli.

I made friends with co-workers and started to feel comfortable. I enjoyed the various personalities of the people I waited on, and it was fun to socialize. I started to feel like a part of something.

The owner was a short, fat, white-haired man named Antonio. He was the son of the woman who started Roma's Pizza House. He was always complaining about someone not doing their job properly. He spat saliva when he spoke, and all of the waitresses used to make fun of him the moment he walked away.

He had a deaf brother, Lorenzo. He was the cook, and any time we had a change in one of our orders, we had to move our lips dramatically so he could understand us. He refused to learn sign language because he refused to admit that he was deaf. He was a nightmare to work with. His face would beam red with anger any time we returned an order, and he would bang the order bell profusely when food was ready to be served, alarming the entire restaurant.

The two brothers would fight in front of customers. Watching a deaf man yell was something I had never seen, not even in a movie. Lorenzo would brandish his chopping knife in the air, using his muffled, gasping voice—which you could hardly understand—to tell Antonio he was going to kill him in the middle of rush hour when people would be coming in for dinner on a weekend night. For the first time in a long time, I was watching two adults that were crazier than myself, and I felt somewhat normal. I can guarantee their dead mother would have turned over in her grave had she seen them. Meanwhile, among the fighting, the waiters would try to keep the customers happy.

If an order was wrong, we'd all point at each other. "You tell him!"

"No, you tell him! You need to change the order!"

Then we would begin figuring out which one of us would ignite the least wrath.

"Is he mad at you today? He's not mad at you today!"

And if the order was under the heating lamp for too long, he would tap the bell compulsively.

Six months into the job, I was doing my cleanup during a slow evening. Antonio came to me and said, "I'm sorry you didn't make much money tonight."

"Yeah." I shrugged. "I know, it was really slow tonight. I think I made only thirty. Oh well, it will be better tomorrow at lunch."

His eyes widened, and he presented an offer. "You can always come to my house and wash my dishes."

For a moment, I considered making the extra money, until he continued to talk.

"You can make even more money if you did it topless."

I just laughed at him, and I thought, *Man, if you knew some of the things I have done for money...but this won't be one of them.*

He lived across the street from the restaurant and had a penchant for using binoculars to peep at clients coming in. He thought we didn't know, but everyone did.

I turned him down enough that eventually he stopped asking. He would walk away disgruntled.

During any inappropriate flirtatiousness I experienced at Roma's, I counteracted the negativity by thinking of Alfie. My mind would revisit the experience, three months earlier, when I had become pregnant, but then lost the baby. It was a crushing ordeal for both of us. Only a week later, we were in his van when he pulled out a box from the pocket of his pants. I gasped. I knew what it was. I opened the box, and there, perched in a velvet cushion, was a diamond ring. He placed it on my finger and we embraced. He called it our promise ring, and he openly stated that we were to be married soon. It was one of my happiest moments since being released from court on my eighteenth birthday.

I would gaze upon the ring with love, and it covered up the sadness of a lost child, and the long days with an inappropriate boss.

On a slow night shift, a group of four women came in. They asked to be seated outside on the patio. I served them like I served anybody else: cheerfully and meticulously.

One of the women, with cat eyes and Aztec-like features, noticed the shiny promise ring on my finger.

"Don't marry that boy. I know he's coming to pick you up

tonight, but don't marry him."

I stopped dead in my tracks, almost dropping the pizza. How could she know who was coming to pick me up?

I was awestruck.

There was a mystical, knowing energy amongst these four women. I could feel it deep in my soul, as if they kept a hidden passageway to somewhere far and magical.

She continued, "You have no idea you're clairvoyant, do you?"

"What does clairvoyant mean?"

"Clairvoyant means that you can see things."

"You have no idea yet, do you?" another woman repeated.

It spoke to my intuition with the old woman from my childhood, Whinnie, it spoke to my brother's crystals, it spoke to the nurse in the juvenile hall, and it even spoke to the homeless man on Venice Beach, screaming at the ocean.

Even though I didn't truly understand the word "clairvoyant," I knew exactly what she meant. Was I serving them or were they serving me?

The four of them continued chattering amongst themselves. They sat in the center of the busy patio, lit by the subtle glow of the moon. The woman with the cat eyes and shoulder-length black hair with ancient, tribal-looking features was Maria. She sat beside a woman with piercing hazel eyes and fire engine-red hair. Across from her sat an angelic-looking blonde. To her left was a dark-skinned, long haired brunette vamp, sultry and sexy, perched on the edge of her seat and leaning into the conversation.

Then, they turned and stared back at me. I was balancing two large cheese pizzas before a table of witches. I was hooked; fascinated.

Maria said to me, "I have this psychic store where I sell books, if ever you're interested. You can always come and check it out. It's called Mystic Moon on Elm Street."

I silently took note of this and thanked her for her invitation.

"When you are about thirty years old, you will be a full-blown psychic. Listen, we can see it in you right now. You can SEE, and you're incredibly perceptive, but the clairvoyancy will remain dormant unless you *go there* with it," Maria spoke, as if for all of them. Her prediction prompted me to remember a time my mother admitted her own mother was psychic, and she had said it passes through the generations.

She continued, "Whatever you do, don't marry this boy. It's the wrong path. Whatever you do, don't marry him."

I said okay.

That night, I took the ring off. I had to end my relationship with Alfie. If that wasn't enough of a sign, then what was? The table of four women impacted me deeply. There was no easy way to say it.

I sat in his car and said, "We have to break up. We can't get married I love you, I always will, but it isn't right and we are too young." I took off the ring and gave it back to him. He was heartbroken and argued with me, but I held my position and we parted ways.

I cried...but alone. I had lost the baby and I believe he had been trying to make me feel better with the ring, but it was never right; being married. I had a lingering thought that it was all too soon, and I hadn't had enough time to heal from all I had been through. And Alfie had started drinking again, which I felt derived from the sadness of our lost child. What was right was our care for one another. I knew I still had a lot that needed fixing; I just couldn't admit it until then.

Every day after class, I'd get off the bus and pass Maria's store on Elm Street. And one day, I went inside.

As I was skimming over all of the crystals for sale, Maria looked up at me and, with ownership, mentioned, "So you decided to come in."

I casually perused the shop full of spiritual books on channeling, reiki, mediumship, clairvoyance, and audio-clairvoyance. An entire corner of the shop was exclusively dedicated towards essential oil therapy. Shelves upon shelves of crystals, rose quartz, amethyst, tigers eye, and pendulums. Stacks of tarot-cards, Ouija boards, incense. You name it, she sold it. So I started to delve into what some of these things meant.

For a moment, as I stood amid these spiritual items, my mind wandered back to when I was a young girl at my parents' home. I had seen my grandmother recite an ancient Jewish prayer while standing over the lit Menorah. She waved her hands, coaxing the flame to cast a glow upon her face. I knew it meant more than the meaning of the words she was reciting. She was inviting the light into her soul. Her belief and mysticism were deep within her roots. And therefore, deep within mine.

My memory was interrupted by a cascade of cards falling. A blonde lady had knocked them over. A different blonde than the one from the unforgettable dinner. She was delightfully bubbly and cheerful with a personality larger than the room she was standing in.

"Hi, who are you?" she said with a smile and raised eyebrows. I answered, "My name is Holly."

She said, "Well, hello. Gosh, aren't you pretty. My name is Cynthia. You should come over to my place, and we can make cupcakes." She giggled and continued, "Oh, Maria! We can use that new Hello Kitty cupcake mixer I bought!"

These women were different to what I was used to or anything I had come to know. Cynthia had me smiling at Hello Kitty.

Maria came over to me and said, "I can see you are really

interested in everything. If you ever want me to discuss what some of these things mean and help teach you, I am happy to do that. Then you can become a part of our little group—with me and my sister, Cynthia, if you want."

Wow, this is really out there. These two mysterious sisters want me to hang with them. My mind went straight back to Whinnie. Maybe these were her people.

So I thanked her and said, "Maybe some time I'll come over for cupcakes. I'd better get going." And I went home.

That night, I thought of my dad. I wanted to call him but I thought he must be angry with me for running away. I thought he wouldn't believe me if I told him why. I figured I would reach out to him and Susan after the whole trial for suing the rehab center was completely settled.

A few days later, I was in the shop again.

"Oh, you're back. You must be curious," Maria said.

I replied, "I am curious."

She said, "Let me give you a reading." She walked me to a back room and pulled open two large floor-length curtains. They were made of purple crushed velvet, embroidered with tiny silver stars. It was a small simple space with only a table, two seats, and four walls; dark, enclosed, and private. She motioned for me to sit down. She took in a deep breath and asked me to do the same simultaneously with her. We both let it out. She took her hand and placed it over my heart, and took my hand and placed it over hers. I quietly wondered what we were doing, but I didn't want to speak and disrupt the ceremony she had begun. With power, she said, "We are in sync".

She shuffled the cards gently as if she was shuffling my future. She split the deck and asked me to pick a few cards from each pile, channeling the intention of getting answers to any question I had, but to not tell her what my questions were yet. She turned the cards over in the design of a cross and started to foretell my future.

"You love music," she said.

I said, "Yes, I do."

And she said, "Well, I can see that. I can see how creative you are. Looks like you've got some bad people in your energy field. Who would those people be?"

I answered, "Well, maybe some of my old friends from the places I've been."

"Yes, that would be it. Make sure that you stay away from them." She picked another card, and it was The Hermit. "It looks like you need to spend some time alone and figure things out for yourself. It looks like you've been through a lot more than what would be considered normal for a girl your age. I see a cage of sorts."

"I have." I nodded.

"But it's good, it's good for you. Don't worry, nothing will be a waste," she comforted.

I just smiled. She had picked up on something I had known for myself.

"If you ever need someone, I'll be here. It's not a problem. I've felt so connected to you since the day I saw you; just know I'll always be here for you."

Over time, I ended up helping Cynthia out as an assistant in her photography shop. I held her lights, her camera, her second camera, her camera batteries, and I had the perk of going with her to the weddings she photographed. It was healing for me to see love ceremonies–and the support of friends and the glimpse of a future these couples had lovingly committed to, and I enjoyed playing a small role. My jaw would be sore from smiling all day, and my feet from dancing. I'd go to sleep exhausted, but happy.

Cynthia would ask me to model. I always declined. I never felt I was model material, especially after all I'd done and been through. But one evening she tricked me, asking me to meet her at the beach to watch the sunset. We often did this, so for me it wasn't anything out of the ordinary. I arrived and there she stood with her camera, ready to shoot. She flashed me the sweetest smile, almost begging. There was nowhere for me to run; I couldn't, not when she looked that enchanting. I uncomfortably went for it, posing through gritted teeth.

With each snap of her camera, she would say, "Oh wow, there she is, that was beautiful—give that smile again!" or "Oh my goodness, Kwanch, where have you been? Look at you now, coming out of your shell!"

"Kwanch" was a funny little nickname she'd made up for me.

I have to admit, after a couple takes, I started to get into it. A few days later I came home to a present and card placed on my bed. I tore open the card and it read, *Here is something to keep to always remind you of how beautiful you really are.* Touched and teary-eyed, I opened the gift. I could hardly believe that someone took the time to do something so selfless and kind. It was a silver-framed professional print of me, looking like a glowing model with the sunset as my backdrop. I had never seen myself smile like that. So big.

But there was darkness lingering in the background. David Walker had been coming over to my mom's house to say hello to me. David was a very close friend to my mom. He was the CEO of the company Mom had first worked for. She still had business dealings with him, and he had ties to the music industry. He offered to help me, inviting me to a meeting with him to discuss my goals. Before I knew it, there was a car. David had it delivered to my mom's house—a Volvo. David planned his arrival simultaneously with the delivery of the car.

"Here's a car for you, so you have independence," he said warmly. I felt my world was finally coming together for good, and that, like Maria and Cynthia, he was a support system.

I now had reason to study for my driver's license. I did the best I could and barely passed the written test. But I knew the driving part from when Susan allowed me to take her car for a spin or two, just around the block, when I was fourteen, monitored of course.

In my mother's eyes, he was a loyal family friend. She was pleased to see me receive such a gift.

I proudly drove myself to Maria and Cynthia's house. I showed them my new ride. They *oooh*ed and *ahhh*ed at my 1989 white Volvo. My mother said it would be like driving a refrigerator, and therefore would keep me safe in case of an accident.

Within a few weeks' time, my check arrived in the mail from the settlement. I opened the envelope and pulled out the paper, and it read, "Fifty thousand dollars to Holly Cohen."

I darted into the house.

"Mom! Look!!" She took the paper and had a look for herself. She smiled.

"See, baby, I knew this would turn out alright. Put it somewhere safe so we can figure out what we will do with it later," she replied.

What does she mean by "*we?*" I left that thought and I quickly placed the check in my desk, tucking it away in the far back corner where it couldn't be seen.

I moseyed into the kitchen for my morning coffee. I heard the tapping of fingernails on the counter, and I turned around to see my mom.

"Good morning, baby," she said in a much sweeter tone than normal.

"Hi, Mom."

"Baby, I need that check." Her tone worried me, and I wondered if something was wrong.

"Why?" I asked.

"I just do. I need it in my account to show I have the money there…"

"Money for what?"

"I just need it in there, honey, so you just have to sign it over to me."

"When will I get the money back?"

"I just need it in the account, and we can work that out later. We can do ten percent at a time."

I was so confused, and the more I asked, the more muddled her responses became.

"What are you going to buy?"

She paused and said, "Baby, I just need it to show in my account."

I never got a straight answer.

As the days passed my mother's tone towards me continued to morph, as if I was becoming the enemy. Her answers to my questions were short, and at times she wouldn't acknowledge me at all. I felt as though she began to dislike me, and the more questions I asked about the money, the stronger the resentment felt. I began to hate the money. I would walk past my desk and feel detest for the check sitting within it—like if I were to open the dresser, I would be unleashing evil. The last remark I remember from my mother about the check was, "Holly, you wouldn't have that money if it weren't for me," and she was right.

But, hadn't I deserved to keep it? Or at the least know fully what the plan was if I gave it away to her?

Within another week, my mother's resentment had grown to an intolerable amount. It began to dawn on me that I was eighteen years old and technically I was an adult. I felt provoked to take ownership of my autonomy, and I drove to Maria and Cynthia's.

"Maria, how much would you charge me to rent a room in your apartment?"

From upstairs, Cynthia chimed in, "I will rent you a room for $330 a month for the next six months if you want, and we can make cupcakes every night!."

"Done! I will pay you six months in advance!" I put everything in my car and within two hours, I was gone. I left my mom a note telling her where I would be, the address, and with whom, and that I made the decision to keep the money. As I write this now it sounds brutal, the way I left, but her unresolvable, unreasonable anger drove me out. She was probably preventing me from wasting it away, but the fact that she couldn't be straightforward concerned me.

I drove to my new apartment, letting the wind blow through my hair, turning up the volume to Radiohead, and smoking my cigarette extra slowly. I moved all my belongings into Cynthia's house that evening. She had an extra bed, and I bought the bed off her. I decorated the room. I had taken all my clothes with me, and of course, my psych medication. I went out that day and went furniture shopping for myself; I found a dresser at a really shitty corner shop. It was made to break, but it was mine. I was organizing my life the way I wanted for the very first time.

That night, before bed, I fantasized about dreams I had left behind. Singing to people. Creating art. Leaving something to this world that mattered. It now felt attainable all over again. And this is how Cynthia and Maria entered my life, and became my little family.

We cooked dinners together, we listened to music, we ran errands. Maria had a dog named Lucy that I loved as my own. I got card readings, psychic readings, Reiki sessions, and energy-healing sessions all the time.

Maria introduced me to her friend who worked in an investment firm, and she helped me set up a portfolio. I didn't understand what this meant and what my money was being invested in. I asked a few questions, but I became embarrassed because I apparently kept asking the same ones over and over, and she started to look a bit frustrated with me. It was pushing some of my older and unforgettable school buttons. Maria sat beside me and said I should trust her, that she knew what she was doing, and so I listened. I knew the money was safer invested than sitting in an account. I was told I shouldn't touch it.

David continued calling to ask me if I wanted him to set up meetings with vocal coaches, producers, and all sorts of known music industry professionals. He dangled the carrot of success in front of me and I chased it.

"While you're spending all this time going to school and working," he said, painting a lavish picture, "you could be becoming a star. I'll cover your expenses."

I thought, *When will I ever get another opportunity like this? This is my shot.*

I quit my job. I quit school.

CHAPTER TWENTY-EIGHT
A SOUTHBOUND TICKET

At not-quite nineteen years old, I was still basking in my freedom, getting used to a life without restrictions. David casually asked me if I would have coffee with him. He was warm in his demeanor, but quite powerful—a self-made businessman. He always smiled; he had straight white teeth and flashed a wide-toothed Hollywood-star grin. He had the air that anything he wanted could be bought. He spoke lightly about previously being a pastor or a pastor's son, as if he had a direct line to God. On his visits to us, he would bring expensive champagne. He would ask my siblings what they wanted to do with their lives. One by one, they would all speak, uninterrupted. I remember once he took off his Rolex watch and tossed it to my brother Jeremy as a gift, just for kicks.

He wanted to meet at the Westin Hotel, and I realized only halfway through the lunch there were indicators of some secret sensuality. But I shoved the idea away.

"What do you need?" he blatantly asked.

I didn't know exactly how to answer him. I reemphasized to him that I was a serious aspiring singer; that I was an artist. My first need was to meet with someone of value in the industry.

David added, "You need money too."

We shared a meal. He ordered for me. He asked if I would like a glass of wine. I was taken aback; I wasn't twenty-one yet. I reminded him of this, and he didn't seem to care.

We shared small talk about my siblings and his hobbies as

we picked at our food.

I didn't understand the seriousness of what was about to happen, but he did.

David asked me to sing for him.

"Where? Here, right now?" I asked.

"No. Upstairs. I have a room."

On the way to the elevator, we both gauged each other silently. I was attempting to pick up signals of anything inappropriate, yet he behaved so casually that I assumed he was being thoughtful and wanted to hear me sing privately instead of in a public performance at the restaurant.

Walking towards the room, there was small talk about people he knew, and he rattled off names and scenarios in which he could set me up.

We sat on two opposite ends of the same couch, and he looked at me and studied my face.

He said simply, "My God, you are so beautiful." I felt, at that moment, so appreciative that I was being admired, but also wary.

He placed his hand on my knee and asked if I could scoot a bit closer. Then he took his hand and placed my hair behind my ear.

"How is the car treating you?" he asked, while studying my face.

"I love it, thank you so much for the car. I never expected a present like that. It pushed me to get my license and now I can go anywhere."

"It was my pleasure to help. There are so many ways I plan to help you, Holly. You will see," he said, flashing those white teeth.

"Okay," was all I said.

He moved closer to me.

I felt frozen, like I couldn't—and wasn't supposed to—move.

The same way I did in the cell with Rodriguez. *What is right or wrong? Who else is going to help me, and when is this opportunity ever going to come again? Is this my shot?* Had my moral compass been shaped properly, there would've been a phone call straight away to my mom about what had just happened. Instead, he called room service to order a bottle of champagne.

"You cannot tell anyone about us meeting here like this," he said.

"I hate to tell you this," he continued, "but I can see why your mom would be so jealous of you." He paused, and my mind ran wild with just how he would know how my mom felt about me. He interrupted my thoughts, asking me to sing.

"Pick any song, something you know."

"Wishing on a Star" by Rose Royce came to mind, and I began to perform.

He watched me and I felt uncomfortable with his stare; it was penetrating.

Maybe this is what they do in this industry, I thought to myself. What the hell did I know?

"Wow, you're like Madonna! You're what we call a little starlet. You've got the hair, you've got the eyes... Look at your figure!" He paused, admiring me as though I were a newly discovered diamond in the rough.

I thought, *This is so different from what I have experienced.* I liked it. It felt amazing to be believed in.

"My God, you're so beautiful." He leaned in without the slightest hesitation and kissed me.

After the kiss, he seemed as though he was in awe of how he felt.

I felt violated, much like how I felt underneath Rodriquez. The dichotomy of him igniting the flame of my dreams yet simultaneously smothering it with his control took away my self-determinism.

He was a mental predator. David started to supplement me by depositing sums of money directly into my bank account. His offer to help me in music meant meeting more often to discuss developments. He inched his way into bending my ethics by dangling my dreams in front of me, and it turned the affair into necessity. It didn't even become a decision of right or wrong; it became a decision of survival or failure. Flat out.

I was, in a way, jailed again; I became beholden to the opportunity. And I paid the price for it, because I couldn't give him what he wanted—sex—sober.

So back down the rabbit hole I went, and my daily dose of psych meds was far from enough to escape the horror of my actions.

One hotel visit became many. One deposit of sums became many. One phone call to a drug dealer became many. But I had my vocal lessons, and David set up meetings from time to time—finally fulfilling the promise he had made to me.

Maria and Cynthia would often ask me if I was okay. They were both concerned, watching my decline. I would assure them everything was alright, even though I stopped coming home most nights. I made excuses for where I was and who I was with, never revealing the whole truth. I hid from them. In a funny way, I felt I was saving them by not having me around as a liability.

I still hadn't heard from my mother, or my father, or Susan, or even Heather. I assumed they must have known I went back down the rabbit hole and wanted little to do with it. I called my brothers every now and again to check in. I had heard Heather had moved into a furnished apartment in Beverly Hills. My mom was staying with her, and paid her rent, because her new home she had bought was being renovated. Heather was attending college now—an expensive college, twenty minutes or so from her new apartment. I had heard stories of her and my mom going shopping together in Beverly Hills regularly. I somehow felt it was unfair, but I wasn't sure why. Why would I have deserved that type of treatment? I never did as anyone asked.

CHAPTER TWENTY-NINE
A STARLET'S EMBER

I was withholding truths from basically everyone who knew me. All of a sudden there were secrets upon secrets upon secrets. They were piling up and taking on a life of their own, a monster of sorts, and all I could do was run from them. And the more secrets I had, the more drugs I wanted to do. I spent the fifty grand on nothing of value. I carelessly gave money to friends who were never really my friends while high. I went on silly shopping sprees for clothes of no real value. I paid for some guy's expensive camera he wanted; I didn't even know him. I believed him when he said he would pay me back, because I was on drugs. I bought dresses for girls I had only met that day, just for fun, but I never really felt like I was having fun while doing it. It was a desperate attempt to distract myself. It never truly worked. All it did was leave me broke and furthered the emptiness within my soul.

I could hear David's words on repeat in my mind: "You know what? I really do care about you, and I care about your dreams. And I truly adore you and think you're quite talented." Those words strung me along like the lights to a Christmas tree, yet each one was starting to burn out.

David was coming to get me in five minutes. I tried on fifteen different outfits, my decision-making castrated by a thick fog from three days of partying. During this haze, I had dyed my hair, thinking black would suit me. I settled on tight maroon corduroy pants and a form-fitting black T-shirt. I crayoned makeup over my face to conceal my exhaustion and pain. I put my cigarette out, and walked downstairs.

His Porsche pulled up to my apartment. I hopped in and we jetted off to Beverly Hills.

He pulled up to the Four Seasons hotel, and I was immediately reminded of Susan's etiquette lessons. My wild black hair was untamable, falling over my shoulders. I felt like an impostor.

As we walked through the corridor of the hotel, the sound of my cheap costume jewelry pieces clanking against each other rattled in my ears, making me more and more self-conscious of my appearance.

David told the host we were meeting with a man named Alex Hurst, a producer and artist manager, and we were escorted over to a table.

Alex stood up and put out his hand to shake mine. He had deep brown eyes, and he was 5'9, but stood tall as if he was 6'4. We sat down and began talking. Alex's voice was deep and he spoke with certainty, but I couldn't shake my discomfort. Here I was, at a meeting that could be the start of my career, yet I couldn't enjoy it, and I didn't feel like I truly owned it because it came from such destruction of my integrity. David put his hand on my knee as Alex spoke, as if to say, *Don't forget me*. One man had my body and the other, my dreams.

We talked about what type of music I liked and what type of genre I saw myself in. He asked me what my past experience was as a singer and how I saw myself in the future. What impact did I want to make on the planet? What did I want to tell the world?

I answered as best as I could, knowing that I wanted it to be about people believing in themselves. I knew I wanted to leave the world a better place than when I had gotten there. And I knew that I had a story to be told.

Alex smiled in response to my answers, and I felt like I had done something right. David drove me home. I made excuses as to why I couldn't be with him that night. I needed to sleep. Three hours later, Alex called me.

"It was great to meet you today," he said. "We should set up a time to meet again."

He then asked me directly what my relationship was with David, saying that he didn't know me well, but he could see how uncomfortable I was at the Four Seasons. We stayed on the phone for four hours. I remember hanging up the phone, worrying about the cost of the call. I told Alex everything regarding David. I don't know why, but I did; I felt he already may have suspected something between him and I. He told me David was a predator, and that I didn't need him to prove anything to anyone. He sympathized with me by gently apologizing for all that had transpired. He felt angry and sad for me.

The next day, I woke up to a message saying, *Call me -Alex*. I hoped I hadn't scared him away. I prepared myself for the worst, wondering what was so urgent.

Alex said, "I am going to take you completely out of Los Angeles, and you need to get away from that man." I knew if I didn't leave the state, an idea that I never would have thought of myself, I would have stayed in that vicious cycle. I was surprised yet oddly relieved.

After my coffee, my meds, and my cigarette, I began organizing my move. I told Maria and Cynthia what had taken place and they supported my move. I needed to go. This was probably the only way out of my tangled mess.

Within three weeks, Alex moved me to Atlanta, where he was from. He was openly disgusted by the predatory relationship with David, but at the same time not surprised at all, and never once did he blame me.

As we boarded the plane, Alex looked over his shoulder and asked, "Are you ready for a new journey?" It was less of a question and more of a statement. It was as if he looked at me like I was an angel he was divinely assigned to protect, and he would do so without asking for anything in return. It had been a long time since someone saw me in that light.

It took me years to realize I had been facing emergencies for so long that I had post-traumatic stress.

We arrived at Alex's home; he lived in a luxurious apartment in the city; I was told it was on one of the most expensive streets. He had leopard-print upholstered chairs and marble floors. His floor-to-ceiling windows looked out across the skyline of the entire city. I could see miles and miles of trees. If I ever wanted to be a weather reporter, I could just look out the window and see what weather was sweeping over the city. I'd never seen a view like that.

The ceiling was painted with gold-traced clouds. He had black leather couches, white-carpeted rooms, a walk-in closet, and a large bed. His bathroom walls were marbled. His TVs were larger than the window in my last apartment, and they were in every room. The art on his walls was all modern; Alex stood beside me explaining what each piece meant to him. This was my favorite part of his apartment.

He showed me to my room, where I unpacked my clothes. "This is your own room. You can sleep here. Just know you're safe here. Why don't you show me the clothes you have?" he asked.

I thought it was a little strange, but I went with it. I pulled out a pair of pants, and I said, "Here's these pants, and I love them."

"Why do you love them?" he asked.

And I told him these were special, because they had stars and my name along the sides. They had been handmade by a guitar player/fashion designer in downtown L.A. He smiled about the story I told him.

He looked at me and he said, "You know, all the clothes that you pick, you dress like a star." I hadn't had anyone call me an actual star before...and the person who had suggested it was David Walker.

I was surprised. "I do?"

"Yeah, all the clothes that you pick, you dress like a star... You're a star."

I got teary-eyed when he said it. And he got teary-eyed, too. "You've had a really hard life. I can see that. But that ends here." He gave me a hug, not in a possessive way—just a hug from one person to another.

"Alright, when you've finished unpacking, let's get something to eat. You must be hungry." This was the way it was with Alex. He was gentle, sensitive; aware and slow.

Alex truly saw me the way I wanted to see myself. And later he would change the course of my whole life.

One night, Alex came to me, concerned. "You've been quiet all day. Do you want to talk?'

I was processing my situation, and my body was detoxing. I could feel the imbalance in my brain. My Prozac had been switched to Lexapro on the advice of my doctor; I felt quite exhausted from it, both physically and emotionally. I felt like I could sleep all day.

"Not really, I'm just getting used to everything," I replied. The truth was that I felt alone; all I had was Alex. I had no friends, no car, no identity outside of him and his apartment.

Alex had events he would get dressed up for, and he would ask, "Why don't you put on a pretty dress, and come out and be with me?"

My social anxiety would scream to the heavens, and I would always decline. There was no way I could face a stranger and answer questions about my past. Alex had college-educated friends. I had little in common with those people. He would have been better off going with Heather. Although it was wearing on me, I felt safe in Alex's cave. The world outside of Alex's cave frightened me, and at some point that would have to be addressed.

We found ourselves sharing smiles and looks of admiration that filled the room with electricity. It was more than friendship; we were becoming a couple, and it was natural. There was no other way to be. He seemed, at that young age, like a life partner. He felt like a staple in my life; I was protective of him. There was no effort in having that happen. It just happened.

We ended up making love, and afterward I curled up, and he held me, spooning me. It was the most romantic moment, as he stroked my hair.

I was almost in a fetal position, and he asked, "Do you feel like you just gave something away that you didn't want to?"

And I said, "The opposite. I feel like I just did something with another version of myself." He and I were profoundly connected.

I started to cry, and he asked, "Why are you crying?"

"I don't know, I just feel so emotional. I'm afraid to tell you everything. I'm afraid you'll judge me, and not want to believe in me as the star...that you think I am."

He gently stopped me from continuing. "There is no not believing in you! You are!" There was a command in his voice that made his words feel true.

I started to cry again.

"Why are you crying, Holly?" He held me tighter. "Tell me what's going on, tell me what's happening."

I kept sobbing, and he said, "Okay, let it out, then just let it all out." I was *feeling something* for the first time in what felt like such a long time. It was the lovemaking, it was the connection, it was his friendship, it was his intimacy, it was his protection, it was financial support without something feeling odd or owed. It was someone believing in me, and someone making me important. It was all mixed with my past, and my hiding and medicating. And he made me feel vulnerable, and I cried. I think the vortex that's opened when you love someone else becomes a pathway to your own vulnerability, or lack thereof. I was actually deeply loving someone else, and it scared the hell out of me. It was the love, the shared love, that dented my steel perimeter, making me change, making me softer.

Alex held me in that same position. He did not let go once. He didn't get up to go to the bathroom; he didn't even get up to get me a tissue.

Afterwards he kissed my forehead, and said, "You must be exhausted. Are you hungry? Do you want to watch TV to get your mind off things? What would you like to do?"

I said, "I just want to go to sleep." We woke up in that same position.

I had experienced a kind of rebirth. I emerged again, and this time I was holding something I thought I had lost at the bottom of the sea—when I had first drowned. A piece of myself.

For several months I stayed in Atlanta, and I lived in Alex's world. I lived within him and through him. I had no friends. I spent time with his sister. I got to know his mother who has become a huge pinnacle in my life, a really beautiful, gentle woman. Alex gave me a place to heal. We talked about our goals, and it gave me a future to look toward.

There would be nights when I was left alone while Alex attended events in the industry. Just like at Lauren's, I would put on music and dance—I was dancing above the sky, overlooking the dazzling city lights below.

But like a wounded bird, once my wings felt healed, I wanted to fly. I wanted my car and my city back. I wanted to take Alex with me, yet he wasn't quite ready to go. There were numerous unfinished business cycles needing to be wrapped up before he could take the leap.

Alex had planned on coming to L.A. anyway. The music scene there was much more active. We settled in a one-bedroom apartment in Beverly Hills. While he was away, I got myself a little puppy. I wanted to look after something. This way I wouldn't let myself slip. I named him Camper, short for Happy Camper. Alex and I happily merged our lives together with no restraint. He knew I still smoked weed, and I had added an unexpected furry addition to our household, but it never seemed to bother him. We sketched out our master plan, setting out on our dream of creating original music; music with a message, music with a story, music with truth. We watched MTV everyday, poking fun at the pop singers.

Some of my time was filled with working a part-time job at a pet store on Pico boulevard. I spent a lot of time writing music at a desk dimly lit by my *Alice in Wonderland* candle. Other than music, I focused on Alex. Alex had contracts drafted and it became official that he would represent me, becoming my manager and sole investor of our project. I went almost everywhere with Alex, and he with me. We were inseparable. At times I would feel a psychic connection with Alex, the way I used to with Heather when we were young.

I entered into my own professional recording studio, mingling with studio musicians, fellow songwriters, and world-seasoned producers. The ones that harnessed a depth of awareness and saw the world from a different place. We spoke the same language of artistic expression, and I felt I had at last found my group.

I would step into the soundproofed studio and be taken aback that I, the juvie girl, was standing inside of a place where stars created their magic. Vocal take after vocal take after vocal take, I would still pause in disbelief that all I had ever dreamed of was coming true, and that it couldn't be more perfect. Sober or high, it was everything I had imagined, playing out right before my eyes. I breathed the enchantment in from a place that had long since been shut down. I found a space within my lungs that opened up, allowing for more life to come in.

A year and a half later, Alex and I made a whole record. It came time to "shop a deal." He would try to explain the business aspects of the industry to me, but it fell upon deaf ears. I was only the artist. He giggled at the fact that I left all business dealings to him; I believe he was flattered that I trusted him so much. But, how could I not? He was my everything, and no one could ever take his place. Without him, there was no music or art, and without music or art, there was no life. So I guess one could say, he was my whole life.

Alex made calls booking my shows and arranging the backup band. Within a few weeks I met my backing musicians for rehearsal. After a few sessions we were ready for shows, and off I went. There my name was, up in lights in Melrose, Sunset, and all the places I had dreamed of performing. I replaced my "damaged girl" inner narrative with Alex's love, and gave it my all.

I sat down at my vanity to get ready for my show. I intricately glued small, gem-colored rhinestones to my cheekbones, doused my eyelids with glittery eyeshadow, and tied multicolored ribbons throughout my hair. I never went on stage without shaking gold metallic powder into my curly mane, as a tribute to the gold dress that Tina shimmied in that poignant day. The TV was playing in the background. "Live at Five" echoed from my television. My ears perked up at the teaser being announced: David Walker, CEO of Corner Investments, was arrested today at his home for tax fraud. The staffing and insurance mogul owed over 5.1 million in taxes. My eyes grew wide, and my makeup brush fell from my hands. I stood in disbelief and walked to the TV—I had to see it to believe it—and there he stood, cuffed.

I drove myself to Venice for my gig. I tossed my cigarette out the window and made my way into the club. My band was setting up; I could hear the scattered sounds of strumming basses and guitars. I strutted to the bar and ordered a shot of tequila.

"Bottoms up," I muttered, and downed it. I chased the liquid courage with a honey stick to coat my throat. I heard my name on the loudspeaker and walked onstage. The bright light made it impossible to see the crowd; it was as if I was the only person in the room.

"Thank you all for being here tonight," I said, "My name is Holly, and I hope you enjoy the show."

With a cue from my drummer, I started the show. I felt the nerves jolt throughout my body, but I pushed through and began to visualize painting the room with sound—my music, all rock 'n' roll and honesty. I had been told my voice resembled a combination of Alanis Morissette and Bjork.

I took it as a great compliment. I belted the sounds out so forcefully I thought I might leave my lungs right there on the stage itself. My songs were about my journey; "Lullaby," "Justify Why I Cry," and eleven others cathartically spilled out moments from my past. I stood tall, jeweled, brightly lit, and *seen*. It was just as I had imagined. I twirled and jumped with the beat. I offered the rawest version of myself, trying to sweep them all away to a world I wished to feel connected through.

And as the show came to an end, I lowered myself back into my body, sinking down towards the stage, being reminded of my corporeal self. I felt, for a flicker of a moment, that I had never been in the body that had once drowned.

"Thank you so much for being here, and have a great night." With a wave, I exited the stage, allowing a piece of myself to remain there.

"Great show!" echoed from friends and co-workers, past and present, as I made my way to the bar. I ordered another shot of tequila, and my band joined me. Alex made it a point to be last to congratulate me. He walked over to me, cutting through the crowd, wrapped his arms around me, and kissed my forehead.

Within a month of that performance, I got a call from Maria. She urged me to come and visit Cynthia, and I wondered why she was so insistent. I drove to Long Beach and arrived at the apartment by the afternoon. The moment I entered, I was shocked by how dark it was; the curtains were closed and the lights were dim. This was way out of character. Cynthia always welcomed the sunlight.

"Is that you, little Kwanch?" Maria's voice called from upstairs.

"Yes, it's me. Should I come up?" I asked.

"Yes, but quietly. Cynthia is sleeping," she said.

This was out of the ordinary, too.

I found Cynthia in her bed, dozing with her mouth open.

Her yellow skin and dry, chapped lips caught my attention.

She blinked her eyes open and feebly mumbled, "Kwanch, is that you?"

"Yes, it's me, Cynthia. What's happened?" I said.

Before Cynthia answered me, she watched Maria enter the room and said, "She's too young, Maria, she shouldn't be here."

"No, I'm not," I sternly said. "Tell me, what's going on?"

Cynthia had cancer. Vicious ovarian cancer.

I climbed into bed and nestled against her skeletal, waif-like body, and as selfish as this may sound, I began to cry.

"Will it go away?" I asked through my tears.

"I don't know, but I promise you, I will fight," she said as she gazed towards the ceiling; as if she was talking to herself and God. She continued, "Kwanch?"

"Yes?" I replied in a respectful whisper.

"Would you open the window to let the breeze in?"

"Of course." I walked to the window and the wind gently entered into the room.

"Oh, that feels so good," she said as she closed her eyes and drifted back to sleep, and I quietly left.

I was so young. I had never known anyone with a disease before, and out of all people, it had to be beautiful Cynthia. She was thirty-seven. How was this fair? On the drive back to my apartment, I prayed to God to not take her. I promised God I would do all the right things if He made her better. I made deal after deal in hopes, somehow, I could make her better.

I went back to Alex, but my worry followed me. Days turned into weeks, and I visited regularly. I helped Maria when I could, taking Cynthia to medical appointments and at times, taking care of the grocery shopping.

On a Tuesday afternoon while on my lunch break at the pet store, I received a call from Alex.

Alex's back was numb, and even though he hadn't mentioned it, it had been going on for a few days. After seeing a doctor who did a few tests, he was immediately sent to the emergency room, where they scanned him.

Alex had cavernous angioma which had grown larger than the size of a lemon. He had suffered a series of strokes. He was admitted into the ICU where various tests and medical solutions were discussed.

I arrived at the hospital and bolted through the door to his room. I found him on the bed, sitting up.

"It's in a part of my brain that is complicated to get into," he said without first saying hello.

"How did this happen?" I asked.

"It just does. They don't really know why." He teared up, "The worst part is that I have to wait for it to bleed more, because they need a passageway into my brain that the blood creates; then they can remove it."

"How long?" I asked.

"They don't know." The tears began to fall from his eyes and onto his hospital gown. I had never seen this stoic, masculine man who had the answers to everything cry so hard. It made me cry to see him weakened and fearful and in pain. I was scared. He was only thirty years old. I couldn't understand it.

I hugged him. "I'm so sorry," I said. I hugged him tighter and whispered into his ear, "I will be here every step of the way. You won't go through one thing alone, I promise you."

My days were filled with searching for answers for Alex and going to my Cynthia. I took Alex to the hospital every week. They needed these weekly scans to see how much his brain had bled. Weeks turned into months. With every scan, we hoped it would be time to perform the surgery, and yet we were terrified of the thought. Because there was no guaranteed outcome–as was the same for Cynthia–there were no more shows, no more meetings, no more writing, and no more singing. My time and loyalty were stretched between them, praying and helping where I could. I never stayed away from Alex too long; I didn't want his mind to go down dark paths without me there to uplift him.

Pep-talking a Type-A, entrepreneurial mind who was in his element creating and controlling the future, was beyond difficult, for him and for me. At times, the anger was misplaced from the both of us, as I wasn't prepared for this type of responsibility, and he wasn't used to leaning on anyone. Together, we forged a way. And as he deteriorated, he lost mobility and most of the sensation on the left side of his body.

In late November, I received a call from my mom. "Holly, I bought us all first-class tickets to go to Europe as a family for Christmas." Her voice was shaking with excitement. "I have suitcases, and you will have to come and pick them up because I am too busy to chauffeur them to you."

I was thunderstruck, as Mom could never have afforded to do this before—to pay for every child, and grandchild, which now she had two of. None of us had traveled and it would be the experience of a lifetime.

"I can't go, Mom."

"Why not, Holly?! When will we ever be able to do anything like this again? All of us traveling at the same time?"

"I'm sorry Mom, I can't leave him. I won't," I said.

"Who, Alex?" she said with irritation. "Doesn't he have his own damn family to come and help?"

"I'm his family, Mom, it's just us, and I have to stay," I replied.

My mom didn't understand that to me, this was my duty. It

wasn't even a question. Alex and I spent Christmas alone, eating our favorite meal: tikka masala, garlic naan, and papadums, while watching movies.

I quit my job to be his full-time caretaker, and it was my pleasure and my duty to do so. He was more frustrated than I was. I stayed to watch over him while he showered and helped put his clothes on. I sorted out his daily meds, keeping a calendar to ensure I never lost track. I did the shopping for us both, all the driving, the washing, doctor appointments after doctor appointments making sure to listen intently and write down all the details. I baked chocolate chip cookies every night. In my young mind, I guess I hoped it would cheer him up. There were very, very, dark days in which I had to lift a crumbling physical body and alpha male personality—which I knew he felt emasculated him.

Every night before bed, Alex would contradict all his doubtful statements he had made throughout the day.

He would turn to me and say, "I know I will be okay." It was as if he needed to proclaim it to the universe. I believed him. I always believed him.

We listened to Mazzy Star and Sigur Rós, side by side in the dark with only a lit candle between us.

We had our own special light show, and we would hold deep discussions on life, which was now so fragile.

Ten months later, Alex went into brain surgery. During the ten hours waiting for him, I locked myself in the bathroom stall when I needed to cry out the fear. Ten painful hours later, the doctor entered the waiting room, letting me, his mother, and his sister know he did well and he was in recovery. I bypassed the usual handshake, and instead I hugged him and profusely thanked him.

I walked in and saw Alex's head wrapped in turban-like bandages, and underneath them, thirty large staples keeping his skin together. He was in a white hospital gown with wires spurting out in all directions, but nonetheless, he sat upright with a smile.

"I told you I would be alright. Come here," he said, opening his arms, and we embraced. "You wanna know the first thing I heard when I opened my eyes?" he asked.

"What's that?"

"Your song, Holly. Your song 'Justify' playing loudly in my head."

Alex and I had spent months recording "Justify." He had sat beside me in the darkly lit studio as we played "Justify" back at least one hundred times, making tiny, but important, tweaks to the song. It was the last piece we had worked on before the project had come to an end.

A few weeks later, I was in the pharmacy, filling Alex's prescription. It was there I got the call that Cynthia had died. Life on earth is so fragile. She had fought hard, but the cancer fought harder and took an angel from us. As I mourned losing her, I sifted through photos of us together, promising her that I would never forget her. I convinced myself that she was now a zephyr in the trees, or the subtle gust of wind that would cool me on a hot summer's day, or the sunset God painted across the skies. But nothing could replace the emptiness. No one else would ever call me "Kwanch" again. She'd told me that she called me that because I quenched her thirst from her drought of friendships. Her drought had matched mine, and we'd flooded our companionship into each other.

Alex's recovery was slow and rough. It made it hard for us to get along. His mother was now staying with us and at times, I sat on the toilet seat alone in the bathroom, feeling utterly worn out from it all. Alex's parents were in the middle of a horrendous divorce, which didn't make things easier. Weed did not manage the degree of pressure I wanted to be relieved from. Nothing could. Only time would heal the sadness from Cynthia's death.

Everywhere I went I carried a new type of exhaustion and pressure I had never known before. I had given so much away; I was depleted and empty. I needed solitude. I needed to recharge. I knew his mother was now there to help, and I was desperate for some type of respite. I needed rest.

Six weeks post-operation, I was still not prepared for his traumatic recovery; it was more difficult than waiting for his brain to bleed. It became time for me to go. I felt, without a doubt, that all I could do for Alex while he needed me had been done. His mother would be the one to take it from there. I felt in my heart I had returned the care and companionship that he once gave me. Waiting for the brain to bleed took from our intimacy, leaving a gaping hole in our love life, and the aftermath, even more so; but more importantly, I was emotionally depleted.

I walked away knowing I did for him what he would have done for me, and in one way or another I had repaid him. I was proud I was able to handle what I did, but I needed rest from it all—and the relationship too—and Alex agreed. Our arms reached for each other, we embraced, and he kissed my forehead, leaving his lips planted on me for a few extra seconds.

"You will always be my Holly," he said.

"I know," I replied. We let go and I stepped out of our room. I passed his mother seated on the sofa as I walked towards the door. She knew I was leaving.

"Please know, Holly, you are a part of this family and you can always call me."

"Thank you," I replied. I cracked a little smile, she matched it, and I left.

I moved to the one place I made fun of, Hollywood. But it was all I could afford. I scored a job at a 1950's diner where I wore a red retro uniform and white converse sneakers. I popped quarters in the jukebox and sang along with all the songs I had once memorized to impress my father. My father and Susan visited the cafe. They loved the sweet potato fries dipped in blue cheese dressing. When Mom visited, she ordered the country-fried steak with gravy. "Wishing on a Star" would play, and oftentimes I wondered whatever happened to Maria. I started every morning with a cigarette, a cup of coffee, and a Lexapro pill from my prescription bottle, and I ended everyday feeling unfulfilled. This couldn't possibly be it for me.

CHAPTER THIRTY
A CAST GLOW

With time alone came self-evaluation. I would shuffle my tarot cards in search of answers to my future. I became aggravated and annoyed with the conflicting answers; was this some kind of trickery? I was fed up giving my power away to outside sources. It was a dichotomy, as Maria had introduced me to such a beautiful world of mystery and enlightenment; a world that opened up my curiosity and allowed the search for myself to thrive. But the other side of that world meant subjugating myself to evaluation and relinquising my ability to garner outside validation. Who was behind me? Who was in front of me? What did my future hold? Who was I?

From that annoyance I realized no one else, and no other thing, could tell me who I was or where I was going.

I needed to be free from the ball and chain that kept me beneath the surface. I needed to release the skeletons in my closet. The burden of the secrets weighed heavily on me. It was eating me up. I had to tell my mom. She needed to know about David.

I knew Mom was at work. I gave her a call and nervously said, "Mom, I know you're working, but I have to come and tell you something important."

She said, "Fine. Drop by."

She worked in this vast, glass professional building in downtown Long Beach, on Main Street. I parked the car and walked inside. I realized that I wasn't dressed properly to go into such a place. I greeted my sister as I walked in, she was working as the secretary there. She looked beautiful. She answered the incoming business calls professionally. *I would never be able to figure out how to use a phone like that*, I thought. I entered Mom's office, sat down, and looked at her apprehensively.

There were phone lines ringing and papers everywhere. As she hung up her personal phone, she looked at me and said, "Okay, Holly, what is it?"

"Listen, Mom," I said, mustering up the courage to continue. "You should have never had David Walker lingering around."

"Why? What? Why are you talking about David Walker?"

"Mom, I'm just gonna come out and tell you. I had a relationship with David Walker."

Shocked, she gawked at me. "For how long?"

"I don't know; on and off before he was arrested."

Her eyes were wide and her mouth dropped open. I could see her mind registering the information.

"Well, we should have never had a man like that around us, you know. He's not a good man; he's manipulative, and you and I both should have known that," I said

She looked at me with blazing eyes. "I'm going to kill him. I'm going to kill him. I'm going to call him right now. I'm going to kill him."

She picked up the phone to call him, and I said, "I'm not going to be here for this conversation."

I assumed David had been released from jail on bail.

She pointed at me like she always did when I was growing up, with such authority and weight in a single finger, and she said, "You sit down right now."

I thought to myself, *She's not my boss. I don't have to sit down. I've gotten it off my chest. I'm gonna go.* And I exited the building, but I exited with fury. My mother's act of ownership over me felt like a challenge. I had not come to get further punished. I slammed the glass doors. People near the elevators stopped and stared. I had to mask my embarrassment and remind myself I had every right to be upset. I had to hold onto that so I could get to my car. I stabbed at the elevator button relentlessly. Then, impatient, I turned and went the other way, around the main desk and towards the back doors. Once in my car I cried. I feared I had put so much of what my mom had worked for—her business and her connections through David—at some form of risk. And the funny thing was, as shitty as it was, and as horrible as I felt, in that moment having to openly face what I had been hiding, that didn't measure up to the relief I experienced.

I had to hide myself to heal. I feared being judged by my family and they would be right to do so, but it was time to shut the world out to move forward.

My cigarette sat in my kitchen ashtray, the smoke gently wafting up towards my face as I dialed the number to my health insurance company. They gave me a list of names to choose from. I came across the name Trisha Love. Love seemed like a wonderful name for a therapist.

Within a week, I went to her. Trisha Love had the warmest face. Her presence was soft. The light from a lamp cast a golden glow behind her, outlining her like a backlit painting. I sat on her comfortable couch, and she asked me if I would like a cup of hot tea.

"I specialize in helping young women find themselves." I said that was exactly what I needed. I had been through so much, and barely knew who I was.

"Tell me about it," she replied, and I had to get used to someone being quiet and ready to listen to me. It was just her and me. We were just working things out together.

I would go and see her on my days off. I was paying her with my own money. Over a series of months she helped me understand my relationships better—and she helped me overcome the shame I felt over David Walker. She enabled me to admit I had messed up, and she assured me it was okay. Trisha also helped me navigate my emotions I felt about my father, Susan, and my mother, and forgiveness started to set in. I spoke of Alex, Cynthia, and even Heather sometimes. I should have been a better sister to Heather.

I learned to deal with my anxiety when meeting new people. Most importantly, she validated that I wasn't an evil person.

My sessions went from once a week, to once every two weeks, then to once a month. As time went on, I began to dream of a future again. A future with that child dancing at the edge of the sea. My healing breathed life back into my imagination, my fantasies, my dreams, and I again emerged in rebirth. I began to wonder about being that mother I had dreamed of when Susan had sat beside me before bed. I felt the strength I had once borrowed from my mother surge within me, but there still was a deadened space that I couldn't find the words for. My sessions with Trisha ended with the knowledge that I had come for what I received, and much more.

CHAPTER THIRTY-ONE
A SEED IN MURKY WATER

My girlfriend from work often spoke of Buddhism. She invited me along to an introductory meet-and-greet. I jumped into the practice without much thought, which led to a dedicated year filled with chanting twice a day, once at six a.m. before my shift began, and once again before bed. "Nam Myōhō Renge Kyō," I repeated, "I devote myself to the mystic law of the Lotus Sūtra, holding my mala and ringing the golden bowl at the start of the ceremony each day." This meant that we carried the ability within to transform any difficulty to overcome suffering. I was taught that the lotus flower grew from muddy waters, blossoming untouched by the murkiness in which it sprouted from. This connected me to something intangible that was bigger than myself. I fell to my knees daily in reverence of spiritual rite. I fell to my knees by choice to chant for enlightenment. I fell to my knees chanting to turn poison into medicine.

The Buddhist philosophy provided a depth of purpose to my journey, and what I gained from it was priceless. I began to notice a shift in my viewpoints, looking for the light amid the darkness, and transforming my inner narrative to see beyond my shame. I was able to ascend to the surface and float above all I had overcome. I now had the *choice* to look over my past and realize that it was not merely wasted time; it was my actual education.

My past now meant something.

Just as the Japanese fill the broken stones with gold, making the mended piece more valuable and stronger than before, as did I, filling the broken parts of myself with something better, wiser and more compassionate.

A year had passed by the time I was sitting among a group of Buddhists for our weekly meetup. No matter the amount of chanting or prayer or reading the philosophy, nothing was easing any of my debilitating headaches, my slowed responses, the heavy amounts of marijuana still in my daily routine, or pill-taking along with all of my broken relationships. So many questions still remained unanswered about the soul, my journey, why things happened to me the way they did; it seemed there was more for me to know. I couldn't quite touch whatever *it* was, or put *it* into words, but I knew that *it* meant I needed more; more than chanting. I knew it in a way one knows something is going to happen before it does. Something always felt as if it was gnawing me; a heaviness that I couldn't seem to shake. In Nichiren Buddhism, you are supposed to study, and due to my lack of understanding for words, I often avoided it. I continued seeking answers.

Maybe retribution would further cleanse me, I pondered. I laughed at my ignorance, thinking I hadn't taken anything from AA, but I was wrong; I heard the word "amends" ringing in my ears, and the need to make things right rung as loudly in my soul. This led me back to face a few old friends...

I picked up my phone and dialed; I hoped Lauren's number had remained the same. I had always planned on reaching out again at the right time, and I wanted to pay back the money I had taken from her. She answered. I could hear the surprise in her voice. We made plans for the following night. I went to the ATM and cleared my measly savings of four hundred dollars.

There she was, sitting in that same apartment seven years later. She opened the door and I said, "I have this money, it belongs to you, and I'm sorry I took it; it was wrong. And it's been years–I hope it's okay that I'm here."

"It's fine. Please sit and stay for a minute." There were dishes piled up in the sink, the way that they always used to be. The furniture was outdated. At one time, it looked safe, new, and clean. Now it was faded and dusty, and everything looked old.

I could feel the years of distance between us. Maybe she felt my judgment; I didn't want her to.

"You're so different," she said, not fully meeting my eyes.

And I said, "I am different."

We sat on the couch, looking at each other, and I think what she expected was the girl on drugs, willing to do more than what a friend would.

"May I cuddle you?" she asked outright.

"No, I can't. I'm not here for that," I gently reminded her.

"What did you come here for?" she snapped.

I replied, "To pay you back; to make things right."

She huffed. "Thank you, but I really don't need your money—this was a waste of time for the both of us." *It's not my money, it's yours,* I immediately thought, but I bit my tongue.

I cautiously said, "I'm really sorry. I think I'm just gonna go."

She replied, "Be my guest, and don't come back."

I placed the money on her counter, and I left. And that was it. That was the end of Lauren.

I was gobsmacked. I sat in my car staring off into space, realizing that between the two of us, I was the one who had become the adult.

It was Sunday, my day off from work. The spring alerted the

flowers that it was time to showcase their bold colors of magenta, lavender, and yellow. As scarce as they were around Hollywood Boulevard, I often took notice of the stragglers strong enough to grow amongst the filth. I hopped in my ride and drove down the 10 west, towards Venice Boulevard. I entered below the Venice Beach garland wire sign, which hung in its same place. I drove past the restaurant I had been arrested in. That was all so far from me now, and I smiled in remembrance. I parked my car and walked towards the boardwalk, eyeing each homeless person along the way in search of Jesse. I walked through the crowd, passing the areas I had slept, and noticed the man who made mermaids out of sand was still there, with crowds still gathering to his see his art. I smiled again. I knew he wouldn't remember me so I walked past him. The man performing tricks on the skateboard with no arms or legs was being applauded. The turbanned rollerblader zipped past me with his boombox.

"Holly!" My sister called my name from a distance.

Heather met me at the boardwalk to browse trinkets, cheap sunglasses, and clothes.

We perused the stalls filled with art, feathered decor, and pottery. I bought a dress from the same stall I had once stolen from, on the day I danced with Jesse at sunset. The same owner was there, looking even more weathered than before. I left an extra twenty dollars on the counter.

Heather and I grabbed Chinese and sat on the wall, looking towards the crowd. In the corner of my eye, I spotted a group on a grassy hill. They looked like the squatters I once was a part of, and when I saw a white shirt and torn blue jeans resting low on a man's hips, I knew it was him. There he was, leaning up against a palm tree, smoking. I took in a deep breath in disbelief. Both joy and sadness washed over me simultaneously to see him still on the boardwalk.

"Heather, I'll be right back," I briskly said, and I dashed off.

"Uhhh, okay, where to–?" Before she could finish her sentence, I had fled towards Jesse.

As I approached, I slowed.

"Hey," I said, catching my breath.

"Hey," he replied. He inspected me. I wondered if I was unrecognizable to him.

He looked worn, older, with thinner hair, and the lines around his eyes were more deeply engraved into his face. His skin was damaged and he looked tired. The elements had been unkind to him.

"Do you remember me?" I asked.

He let out a breath. "Of course I do."

He looked down at the ground; I did too, noticing his dirty shoes.

"How are you? I'm so surprised—and happy—to see you."

"Yeah?" he replied, carelessly flicking his cigarette. "Why?"

"Because, Jesse, you meant something to me! I'm sorry I haven't come back here sooner."

"Don't be sorry. You shouldn't have. I wouldn't have."

Why would he say that? He looked around, feigning distraction, but I knew he couldn't look me straight in the eye.

"Whoever you came with is looking at you." I glanced back over my shoulder and saw Heather's worried expression. I waved to show I was okay. I signaled to her with my outstretched palm that I would be five minutes.

"Here," I said, fishing in my purse and pulling out a pack of cigarettes. "Take these."

He took only one, with his body language revealing it pained him to do so, and gave me the pack back.

"And this," I said, holding a wad of my waitressing tip dollars.

"I don't want that."

"Take it, Jesse."

He casually shook his head, with a carelessness I hadn't ever seen in him before. Like he had nothing left to give within him, and wanted nothing from anyone else.

"Then how about my friendship? Please don't say no to that." I didn't wait for him to answer. I wrote my number down on the cigarette pack and left it on the ground near his shoes.

"I'm not going to call you, Holly. I don't want you anywhere near me anymore, and don't you come back here looking for me," he snapped.

I knew it was the same boy who told me to go to my mother.

"Well, thank you, Jesse, for all you did for me. Please know I'll never forget it." I walked away shattered, my heart broken over what he looked like, and how he felt, and his choice to remain at the mercy of the boardwalk.

"Who was that?" my sister said, with the expression of just having eaten something rotten.

"Jesse," I said. Seeing him again wasn't how I imagined it would be. It all came crashing down, my childlike fantasy. I used to wonder if he would have taken shelter under my roof, where I could help him get a job and get clean. We could have done it together.

"You actually know him, Holly?" she asked, as if she'd seen a ghost.

"Yeah, I didn't just know him. I loved him." I choked up and quickly caught myself, knowing Heather wouldn't understand.

"Ew, Holly, isn't he homeless? He looks gross. Wait—loved him? Was he your boyfriend?" Her eyes grew wider.

"Yeah," I said. I turned back for one last look, but Jesse had vanished.

"Holly! You shouldn't tell anyone about that, that's—I dunno! I don't know what to say about it, but I wouldn't share that information with people…" she lovingly advised.

"Yeah, I know, it's hard to understand," I softly replied, and

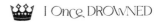

I took a handful of my rice and sprinkled it on the ground to feed the pigeons.

CHAPTER THIRTY-TWO
DIAMOND SKY

I started my day with my little pill, and a cup of coffee.

I shared a cigarette outside in the courtyard with my neighbor Meredith. Our dogs played together as she described her goals of being an actress. I told her I too once had dreams of being a singer. I left her there when it was time to get to the cafe.

Six hours later I departed work, my feet sore. I dodged broken glass as I briskly walked from my car to my apartment. I saw the flashing lights of an ambulance outside the Motel 6 across the street from my building. The neighbors were standing outside, whispering between each other. My weariness and exhaustion left my body and was replaced with curiosity. There was a stretcher being wheeled into our building, while the building manager cleared the way with outstretched arms.

I looked for my neighbor Meredith; I didn't really know anyone else in my building. But they were there for Meredith. She had killed herself. I had just seen her that morning. She was only twenty-one years old. And now she was gone. I should have known; I had seen the look in her eyes, that held the emptiness of Claire's, and now her body was being wheeled out like Nathan's.

I tried to fall asleep, but the stench of a dead rat rotting in the wall nauseated me, keeping me awake. I tossed around in my sheets, wondering what made her do it. I went to wash my face. I looked at myself in the mirror and I didn't recognize the girl staring back at me. My own eyes held the same lifelessness as Claire's. I tried to push the thought away; death, hidden within and behind the eyes of Claire and Meredith, and now in my own. My medication bottle caught my eye and a sapient contempt for it washed over me.

I inhaled a deep breath and coughed at the stench of the dead rat. I looked back at the wall I thought it was coming from. The stares from the portraits of my long-dead relatives seared through me, as if they had something to say.

With their ghostly eyes observing me, I started to question what my legacy would be. Who was I without the drugs?

What would they think of me? And it dawned on me: *I don't even know what my favorite fucking color is*. I did not know who I was without being medicated in one way or another. I paused, then again realized I hadn't ever felt the option to consider any of this before.

My chest rose and fell jaggedly. I couldn't catch my breath; it angrily avoided my lungs. There seemed to be death all around me, within me.

I walked into my bathroom and I snatched the pill bottle, hastily walked them to the kitchen counter, and poured them out; all the little white circular pills. I began to chop them, all of them, into little quarters. That morning was unlike any other moment. At this point, I knew my life was only in my hands and I needed to fight. I needed to fight for myself, by myself. I put the pills back in the bottle and decided I would wean myself.

I continued my routine as best I could. I waited to feel a difference, but it didn't come at first. I took three quarters of a pill for two weeks, then half a pill, and in two weeks' time, I took one quarter. I was tapering myself off the medication. I began to wake up as a different version of myself as the weeks went by. My dreams vividly tormented me. The questionable looks from my co-workers signaled the withdrawal was showing, or maybe it was just my frequent stops to the bathroom from diarrhea. And as any child would do when they are sinking, I called my mother.

"Hey, Mom," I said, the knot in my throat holding tightly.

"Hi, baby, what's up?"

"Mom, I can't take it anymore," I said.

"Take what?"

"Take these pills." I started to weep. "Actually, Mom, I'm trying my best to get off them. I don't know what to do from here. I've been cutting them into quarters for so long now, and I'm still not well." I should have seen a doctor.

"You mean those damn psych meds? I told you to get off that shit years ago. You know I hate pills."

"Yes, Mom, I know that." In that moment, I could have cared less about her being right. "What do I do, Mom?"

"Well, honey, like I told you before, there's always that detoxification program Jeremy did. They don't give you meds for it, and Jeremy's clean," she proudly said.

I silently pondered the idea. If something could help Jeremy, who had also seemingly been a lost cause, it could definitely help me; the last time I saw him he had looked like a completely different person.

"How much is it?" I nervously asked, knowing I had just cleared my savings to pay Lauren back.

"It doesn't matter. I'll cover it," she replied without thought.

There seems to come a time when a voice speaks to you, an urge, a quiet whisper. I heard it and it said something to me, to be me, truly me, the little bright-eyed, big-kid dreams that I once was. I encourage anyone who hears it to listen to this voice. It was the same voice that I had never questioned until someone else came along and instructed me to... And I knew I could get myself back before it was too late.

I was determined in a new way, one I hadn't known before; I wanted to know *who I was*.

Because my pride couldn't accept the handout, I instead cleaned my mom's office and the toilets to earn the money to pay for the detox.

I'll never forget the day I walked myself into the detoxification program. Upon entering I was greeted with a warm smile. No blotchy flashcards to look at, no intense therapy session, no yelling circles; there was only a sauna and stacks of vitamins. I was introduced to a supervisor. Each person doing the program was assigned a twin and that very day, I met my twin. His name was Danny. We were to meet daily at the same time, and after taking our vitamins, we were to sit together in the sauna to look out for each other.

Thirteen years of psych meds slowly poured out from my pores. Nightly doses of lab-grown weed seeped from my skin. It was one foot in front of the other each hot, wet, and grueling day, not knowing what the future would bring, but knowing that at least it would be better than what it was before and it would be mine. It was my "Fuck you" to anyone who wanted to cloud who I was. Maybe even to myself. The rebel still lived; now I made that worn, dreary, rebellious girl work for me. My body needed to be the blank canvas I had started with, and the only way I knew how to get back to that was to sweat for it, literally, erasing the foreign imprint it had been tainted by.

One evening, I finished my time in the sauna, showered, got dressed, and said goodbye to my twin. I decided to take the long way home and I traveled up the winding hills of Hollywood to the top of Mulholland Drive. I parked the car. I scanned over the flashing city lights blinking like Christmas lights. It was still and quiet. I stared beyond the stars into the blackness of the sky. Oddly, for a moment, I felt cradled within a small tunnel, on the way to something bigger than myself; my body light like a feather. I began to speak to the sky as if she were my long-lost friend, a mother within myself that I never knew. I was a small child.

"Whoever you are, wherever you are, somewhere out there—know you can hear me. It's been a while. I'm sorry we haven't spoken in so long, but it's been rough. I'm doing pretty well, though; I'm actually doing better than I have in a long time. I wanted to tell you that I'm going to show up, I'm going to really try, and it's gonna be different. I need this clean slate because there's more... I know there's more, I feel it. I'm ready for it, okay? Just so you know, I'm ready now. So please, if you really hear me—I mean, I know you do, but now so do I—I love you, and I won't lose touch again. I better go; I need all the sleep I can get."

I turned the ignition key, turned up the music, and rolled down the window to let the night air press against my face.

I was into my third week of detox. I sat inside the sauna sweating with my towel wrapped around my waist; my expression of dread and exhaustion had now been replaced with a grin. I looked around for my twin, but he was a no-show. I stepped out of the sauna and stopped off at the supervisor's window.

"Hey Mika, where's Danny?" I asked. While waiting for an answer, I noticed a man sitting in a chair behind me in the corner. "Hello," I said to the lonesome man.

"Hello," he replied. I heard an accent. I wasn't sure from where; maybe British.

"Hey, Holly," said Mika, "I'm not sure where Danny is yet. We are trying to reach him, but his twin—" she pointed to the man in the corner "—also didn't show, so I will pair you both today."

"Uhhh... Okay..." I replied hesitantly. I had grown close to Danny and we had become comfortable. I wasn't hot on the idea of being with someone new. Plus, it was rare to have a twin not show, let alone two twins not show.

The lonesome man stood up from his chair, walked towards me with his hand extended and said, "Hey, again—what is your name?"

"I'm Holly, and you?"

"Lachlan." He gestured with his hand. "Shall we go in?"

Gosh, he sounds so sophisticated, I quietly thought, *so prim and proper.*

With a nod, I walked ahead.

An hour passed while he laid quietly in the sauna. Every now and again I would catch him staring at me in the corner of my eye. I stood up and walked outside, and he followed right behind me. I sat myself down on the bench for my cigarette break, and he sat next to me.

"You know, Lachlan, you don't have to follow me outside to smoke. I mean, if you want to, that's okay, too, but it's not required."

"I want to," he said with certainty. Lachlan was tall, with dark, straight hair, smooth, tan skin, and dark blue eyes. He was good-looking and masculine, with broad shoulders and thick, football-player thighs. He was handsome, but the kind of handsome that mothers gawk over: regal and confident. He had come from across the world, from what he called the lucky country—Australia.

"So why are you here?" I curiously asked. We hadn't spoken much in the last hour in the sauna, so I broke the ice.

"I was on a holiday with my mate, and I don't really know, I wasn't quite ready to go home. I felt like there was something left for me here. So, I called my travel agent and changed my plans. I turned my taxi around on the 405 on the way to the airport, and I stayed. Then I decided to come here and do this again... Really, it's good to do it every decade or so!"

Wait, did he say another cleanse? He does them for fun?

He interrupted my thought. "No, I do them for health, you know? This is also for people who are just cleansing environmental toxins."

Did I say that out loud or did he hear me?

"Oh, okay," I simply replied.

"How about you?" I could see he was studying my face.

"Well, that's a long story," I replied with a chuckle.

"I have time, really. All I have is time."

Is he flirting with me?

"Do you have a mate?" he asked.

Did he just ask me if I have a mate? Who says mate?

"A mate?"

"Yeah," he chuckled, "like a boyfriend of sorts."

"Um, no," I laughed, "No, I don't, definitely no." My life was in no way ready for that. He started laughing too. "Why are you laughing...?"

His face was so puzzled. "*You*, single? Now that's a surprise..."

Did he just call me pretty? I was before him with no makeup, frizzy, unruly hair, and sweaty. Normally, if I were to want to show my best self...this wouldn't be it.

"Yeah, well, I don't know—I mean, I don't really know if I'll ever get married. It's just a paper contract anyway," I replied in honesty.

"You? No, oh no, you will definitely be getting married." He stood up, flicked his smoke, and strode back inside.

I sat bewildered. *I've seen stranger things*, I thought. I put my smoke out and walked back in.

The following day, Danny was back, explaining he had to switch his work shift and that's why we had missed each other. I was glad to know he was okay. After our night in the sauna came to an end, I showered and made my way outside to my car. There was Lachlan, sitting on the stairs.

"Hello," he said, standing.

"Hey... What are you doing here?" I asked.

"Waiting for you, of course."

"Oh, okay. Everything alright?"

"Yes." He paused, looking right at me. "I wanted to ask you something." He nervously sidestepped back and forth a few times.

"Okay, what is it?" I truly wondered.

"I would like to invite you to a lovely dinner somewhere nice and to a movie after, if you wish?"

"Um… Wow, uhhh... Lachlan, I really am so flattered, but I don't know; I'm just getting my life together, and right now, it's probably the worst time to jump into anything," I nervously replied.

Something about him felt overwhelming. I couldn't quite explain it.

He blinked many times in disbelief; I got the idea he wasn't used to being told no. I kind of relished in my power for a moment, then continued, "I mean, I'm happy to show you around L.A. if you want. Have you seen the city?" He blankly stared at me in silence. "Well, how about I take your number, and if I get some free time, I'll call you and I can tour you around?"

"Sure," he replied defeatedly. I took his number and made my way home. I was exhausted.

Within another week, I completed my time in the cleansing program. The girl I saw in the mirror looked like me, and my inner voice began to speak kindly to me. The colors of the world looked brighter. I walked with a pep in my step and I cheerfully said, "Hello" to all those I passed by. My parents, all three of them, were proud, and it felt great to do something right. I took a course on *how to learn* and how to study, so I could retain what I was trying to absorb. I rehabilitated myself, my education, and my soul, and I was free. I took bits of every broken piece of myself and filled them with gold. I read as much as I could, and then I read more. I reached heights of understanding I never thought were possible.

And I once again was the lucky receiver of some divine intervention in my life; a divinity that had morphed from the pieces of intervention all along the way. In one facet or another it had impacted me. Even if I had missed it then, I surely felt it now.

CHAPTER THIRTY-THREE
THE QUIET WHISPER

I jumped off the boat and into the cool water, trusting and subservient to the powerful element that once almost took my life. I had grasped the hand of death only to let it go. Sunlight pierced through the turquoise sea. I saw her, for just a moment; the sunken little girl who had drowned. How far, and yet how close, I was to her now. I let the bubbles float up from my mouth as I pinched bits of bread for the tropical colored fish to feed from. The rainbows moved as an ethereal essence; I reached to touch them, in awe of God's creations. I rose to the surface of the sea and inhaled deeply, savoring sweet oxygen. As I stepped back onto the boat, French dialects echoed from nearby yachts, followed by the clinking of wine glasses and laughter. Traditional French music bounced off of the cliffs of Cassis. I laid on the boat, and I stared into the powder blue sky. I thought to myself, *God, I love my life so very much. I can't believe where I am compared to where I have been.*

I allowed myself to be bathed within the salty sunlight, just the way I had on the boardwalk, and I thought of Jesse and how he taught me that love without judgment comes from the most unexpected places and from the most unexpected people. My mind drifted to the memory of Nathan, and how important it is to dream a dream so big that it's enough to live for; how thankful I was to him for reminding me to see a future. I thought of how much Cynthia would have loved the south of France, and I remembered how fragile life on Earth is.

Cynthia taught me the value of breath and life, but even more importantly, what lingers beyond both, kindness. Alex, Heather, Trisha, Maria, my brothers, my parents, my friends, and so, so many more... I thought of all the gold within the once broken pieces. I was so humbled to have had the hands to mend them; the hands built by the soft whispers all along the way.

"Darling, here." Lachlan interrupted my thoughts and handed me a half-filled glass of rosé from the local vineyard, which wasn't far from where we were docked.

We both had listened to our own quiet whispers. The day after he had waited for me, I called him. Being asked out so respectfully stuck with me for days, as did the way he had wound up at the sauna, and how we met. Plus, I would be lying if I said his mystery and accent hadn't appealed to me. Thirty days later he'd called my mother, my father, and my stepmother to ask for my hand in marriage.

He'd bent down on one knee, under a white stone gazebo laced with twinkling lights and vines, and said, "I'm not sure how, and I'm not sure when, but I know we've been together before, and I knew from the moment I saw you that you were my wife. I was just hoping you would want to do it again. Will you, Holly, marry me? Again?"

And I said, "Absolutely." And from that day forward we never separated. Personally, I think he liked that I paid for my own meal on our first date.

We had found each other.

I ran, and ran, and I kept running until I ran across the world into the lucky country to find my own life.

MY DEAR FRIEND...

Ten years later...

I am 39 now. This is Lachlan's and my tenth year together. My parents have all visited me in the lucky country. On her visit, Mother had told me, "Know you can always come home, but...go and make this the biggest journey of your life. Dream big and prove them all wrong. I believe in you; I always have, and I always will."

When my father and Susan came three years ago, my dad said, "I am so proud of you, my little girl, of this life you have made for yourself... From where you have been, I would have never imagined this. But you've done it and you did it on your own. I love you so very much. I love you, my little girl." My stepmother was in the distance, smiling at us.

Today, I will pick up my son from school. He always runs to me with an ear-to-ear smile, and we hug. As usual, every Friday we stop at the beach to greet the waves, and hand in hand I show him how to feed the pigeons. His eyes sparkle and he giggles as he watches them wobble about.

Tonight, I plan to finish my most recent painting, maybe even work on some music. I try and create something every day. It never mattered that I didn't make it as a big star. I didn't need the approval of the world to validate that I had arrived at some place of success. The success is in the doing. Success is the state within my mind. At the moment, writing happens to be my favorite artistic expression. Communicating through art has become my life. Just the way I dreamed it.

My loving husband is on his way home from his office. It will be time for dinner soon.

I have such big goals for our future. I'm like the five-year-old who got so excited, seeing Tina Turner for the first time.

Big wheel, keep on turning...

If you come down to the river
I bet you gonna find some people who live
And you don't have to worry if you got no money
People on the river are happy to give

Big wheel keep on turning
Proud Mary keep on burning
And we're rolling, tell you rolling, we're rolling on the river

-Tina Turner, "Proud Mary"

If you find yourself in a similar situation to the events in this book, please know that there is a way out; there is the ability to begin again. Continue your search. You do not have to be defined by what you have been through. You must be the master of your reinvention.

If you are medicated and choose to become unmedicated, seek professional assistance in the tapering process.

ACKNOWLEDGEMENTS

To my beautiful mother, I love you, your ferocity, your unbridled force of energy, your ability to reinvent, dream, and salvage, without which I would have ended up lifeless. You are, simply put, The Phoenix.

To my father, my guy, my first Valentine, for your fearless courage to dive into the dark unknown, risking yourself, to help save my life.

To my stepmom, for guiding me to believe the spirit speaks in mysterious ways, and for showing me to visualize my future, for without which, I may not be where I am today.

To Henry, my Cher Ami, for igniting the courage within me to write the story, for being my backbone throughout my doubts, and for validating my writer's voice. Your faith in me will forever remain the wind beneath my pigeon wings.

To Elizabeth, for your understanding, backing, and guidance towards refining my writer's voice, so that I may authentically express myself. You have been the pillar that held the house up. I am so grateful to you.

To Ron, Thank you for being my truest friend.

To my husband, for seeing us and filling all the broken pieces with gold.

I consider myself rich in love and so very lucky.

-Holly xx

ABOUT THE AUTHOR

L.A. born and raised, Leanna Bright has been writing poems and short stories since she was eleven years old, tucking them away in the far corners of drawers, never to be seen—until now. Leanna refers to herself as a self-taught writer, having received her education directly from life. Her focus has always been on unheard voices with a tender authenticity. She is a music producer, artist, songwriter, a loving wife, and a mother to a beautiful boy. *I Once Drowned* is Leanna's first book.

CPSIA information can be obtained
at www.ICGtesting.com
Printed in the USA
FSHW021609271221
87209FS